WIZARD'S WOE

To Emma

WIZARD'S WOE

by

Marion Athorne and Osbert Norman-Walter

Marion Athorne

i4w²
ideas4writers

ISBN 978-0-9550116-3-4

First published in Great Britain in 2009 by

ideas4writers
PO Box 49
Cullompton
Devon
EX15 1WX

Cover illustration by Imogen Hallam

Printed and bound by CPI Antony Rowe, Chippenham

To my father
The greatest weaver of tales I ever knew

Acknowledgements

There are a number of people whose help and encouragement I would like to acknowledge, but especially my sister Sheila, whose unfailing enthusiasm nerved me to take the apparently presumptuous step of rewriting someone else's story. I would also like to thank my Wise Readers: grandson Edward, friends Alan, Peggy and Susan with the initial efforts, and pay tribute to all my family's patience. Also to Jenny Sanders for her encouragement to go ahead, to editor Jo Murray, and, above all I would acknowledge my indebtedness to Dave Haslett of ideas4writers, whose help and unflagging attention to detail has taught me so much. Finally, and not least, my thanks to Imogen Hallam, artist and illustrator, who created such a fantastic cover.

About the Authors

Osbert Norman-Walter, writer, playwright, journalist, and Astrological Consultant *Seginus* of the *News of the World* (1937 – 39) conceived *Wizard's Woe*, in his twenties around 80 years ago but could find no publisher. On his death in 1974, his daughter Marion Athorne inherited an unfinished trilogy.

Married with three children, ten grandchildren and one great grandchild, Marion has only recently had the necessary time to commit to working on a manuscript that comprised more than a million words. She enrolled with the Writers Bureau early in 2004, and studied the new writing techniques. The result? The publication of two articles and a win in a short story competition, which helped with giving her confidence to author the revised, edited, and abridged version of a now complete trilogy that is *Merlyn's Legacy*. She sincerely hopes that Book One, *Wizard's Woe* will achieve the wider readership that her father's inspiration deserved.

Contents

PROLOGUE

Sir Humphrey We'ard had always imagined that sleeping with his bedroom door open would give him a head start on intruders. In the event, it was someone clicking away on his dead father's typewriter at an impossible speed that had the thirty-three-year-old Lord stumbling downstairs at two o'clock in the morning. A soft glimmer of lamp light shone under the study door. Throwing the door open brought an instant stop to the typing, but left the Weir Lord staring in disbelief at the tall, gaunt stranger facing him from behind his late father's desk. His clothing registered first: a sports shirt and the glimpse of trousers – both of which Humphrey had found missing from his wardrobe the previous day – and his sandals.

'Who the hell do you think you are, making yourself at home in my clothes and using my typewriter?' Humphrey spluttered incredulously, raising his eyes again to the intruder's face.

'Myrddin Black,' answered the man, his green eyes reflecting a pleasant smile from beneath the fringed mane of ginger hair. Flecked with red-gold strands, it contrasted sharply with the paleness of his skin. He had half risen and was holding out a hand. 'Delighted to meet you, Sir Humphrey!'

Belatedly, the Weir Lord remembered the note left by his father saying that his old friend Myrddin Black had a key to the back door, and he hoped he wouldn't mind him dropping in at odd intervals to use the typewriter. Acutely embarrassed, Humphrey made his apologies, adding stiffly: '... I expected – well, I don't know what I expected. Father said nothing about your "dropping in" at two o'clock in the morning!' Trying to control his temper, he feigned lightness. 'When in God's name do you sleep?'

'Forgive me.' Myrddin's tone was contrite. 'Your father loaned me the clothes and I forget the mortal need for sleep. My work never seemed to disturb him.'

The young Weir Lord pounced on this. 'I don't mean to sound rude, but knowing my father he would never have dreamed of saying so even if it did.'

'Touché!' Myrddin acknowledged wryly. 'But look, I've more freedom now than when your father and I came to that arrangement. I could limit my visits to when you're not here ...?'

A reluctant curiosity got the better of Humphrey. 'What are you writing?'

'How much do you know of your Wardenship of Weir Forest?' Myrddin asked in response.

'That it's a prize headache I've inherited from the old man.'

'Well you won't have to worry about it for much longer,' Myrddin replied.

'Oh? Why?'

'Because Weir Forest will be gone before the next new moon.'

'Gone?' Humphrey's tone was testy. 'What do you mean, gone? You don't look as if you're from the Ministry. Do you know something I don't?'

'Actually, when I asked what you knew of your Wardenship, I meant in terms of the forest's inhabitants.'

'The legendary little kingdom, you mean? Well, of course I know the myths and legends bit, and that the old man took the whole thing very seriously – he really did believe that a whole race of little people lived there.'

'But you don't?'

The Weir Lord shifted uncomfortably. 'I'm prepared to carry on the old man's fight for the forest. But that doesn't mean I have to believe there really are fairies at the bottom of the garden, does it?'

'Of course not,' Myrddin reassured him gently. 'But wouldn't you agree that under the terms of the charter and your inherited title, the little kingdom has a right to expect help from you, its purported guardian, when it needs it? Provided of course that it can communicate that need to you.'

Humphrey waved a hand in agreement. 'Put like that – and *if*, as you say, there were some communication to that effect – then yes, I suppose so. But damn it, man, how do you prove such a thing?'

His visitor held out his left hand, showing a thumb encircled by a great amethyst ring inscribed with small wedge-shaped characters. Humphrey switched on the main light to observe it more closely, noticing as he did so that his guest's pale flesh appeared to have an almost corpse-like blue tint to it.

'If I take the ring off,' Myrddin was saying, 'I shall disappear. These clothes will be a heap on the floor and the ring will be beside them. You can pick them up, examine them, look at the ring … then, when you put it down again, just say the word and I shall come back into this shape *through* the ring. You will have to excuse me, though, as I will be naked. Merlyn's usual apparel in his human form is in the outhouse – it's rather ancient, which is why your father loaned me your clothes, so I could look more … normal.'

Humphrey stared at him for a moment, and then sighed resignedly. 'All right, I believe you … not that I want to,' he added quickly. 'I've struggled against it all my life, but there comes a time I suppose when one can't go on denying something that's been ingrained in the family for so long. Pity really,' he went on regretfully. 'I quite enjoyed believing it was our particular brand of upper class lunacy!' He moved to the drinks cabinet, opened it, and peered in.

'What's yours?' he asked.

'Brandy?'

'Cognac all right?'

'Thanks!'

Humphrey chose a stiff whisky for himself. 'How do you do it then ... this thing with the ring?' he asked, handing his guest the liqueur. 'Where are you when you're not "in the flesh" so to speak?'

'Invisible and rather small, Sir Humphrey. Just a nine-inch-tall elf magician rejoicing in the title of Merlyn's Heir.'

'And your writing?' prompted Humphrey. 'You still haven't told me.'

'Ah, my writing is a record of the little kingdom of the Forest of Three Weirs, for whom your family has been responsible, keeping it safe from incursion for hundreds of years. I hope to leave the record with your family as a token of what the Weir Lord's guardianship has meant to us while we were there – rather like the *Book of Amaranthus* the Marquis of Rules sent your father.'

'Ah, yes! He left a note telling me I should read that before returning it. He also left a ton of other stuff that I haven't even begun to sort out yet.' He looked at his guest quizzically. 'You say the little people are leaving?'

'Inevitably, Sir Humphrey. The forest is doomed and I have to find a new home for them where they will be safe once again. And not just them; there are others who need rescuing too.'

'So how can I help?'

'Quite frankly, I have no idea as yet,' Myrddin said cheerfully. 'Whole thing's a bit like transplanting a cobweb – make a frame, I suppose, and attach it point by point ...'

'Then let's be practical,' said Humphrey briskly. 'My wife and I live in London and the gardener will be keeping an eye on this place while we're not here. I'll leave instructions that it's an "open house" to you at any time. Then when you need to get in touch with me you can use the phone; I'll leave a number where I can be contacted. Diana and the children will be arriving shortly for the funeral tomorrow. They'll be staying on until Sunday, but I'll have to leave straight after the service.' He was silent for a moment, then nodded towards the manuscript piled up on the desk.

'Is that it? Can I read it?'

'I would be delighted if you did, Sir Humphrey. It's only the first section of the whole story, but complete in itself. And it's all yours ...'

PART I

WITCHETT'S

WEIR FOREST — AS KNOWN TO MORTALS

CHAPTER 1

THE LEGEND

The incessant knocking in Ann Singlewood's dream seemed to go on endlessly before it finally woke her. The clock showed half-past six in the morning. She could hear the light steps of her tiny old Aunt Alicia already halfway down the stairs as the summons on the cottage door became ever more urgent.

She'll need help, Ann thought, hurriedly throwing back the bedclothes and feeling guilty at the length of time it had taken to wake her. She slid her feet into a pair of mules and pulled a white towelling dressing gown around her slim figure. Then she dashed to the top of the stairs in time to see the short, ample shape of Mrs Mye, her aunt's housekeeper, entering the hall wringing her hands.

'Oh, Miss Singlewood, ma'am – it's Mr Gus!' the distressed woman was crying. 'I don't know what's happened to him. He said he was going to disappear – and he has! *Really* disappeared, I mean!'

'Mrs Mye,' said her aunt firmly, 'Mr Autrey told you – just as he also told me – that he was going away –'

'Yes'm, but not like this he didn't! You have to come and see!' The housekeeper was out of the door and hurrying back to the adjoining cottage with Aunt Alicia swiftly following. Ann trailed in their wake, trying to tidy her long, shiny chestnut hair into a smooth roll over her shoulder.

Mr Gus was her aunt's tenant, and Mrs Mye kept house for him, just as she did for her aunt. So she had come to fetch her employer when it seemed that something was wrong. Whatever it could be, Ann had no idea. The last thing she expected when she got there was to see a rumpled white shirt on an armchair in the living room, with its tail ends tucked inside the top of a pair of trousers. The trousers had what appeared to be underpants in them, and they trailed over the seat down to a pair of shoes with a glimpse of sock visible in each, just as if their wearer had evaporated right out of his clothes – though not without a struggle. The top part of the shirt looked as if some small animal had fought hard to escape from it.

Her aunt laughed. 'Mrs Mye,' she chided, 'this is one of Mr Autrey's little jokes. He told you he was going away and this is his way of reminding you! There's nothing at all to worry about. He's paid his rent to the end of the month, which is when he said he would be back. Now please put these things away where they belong, and keep the place aired and dusted until he returns.'

The more Ann got to know her Aunt Alicia, the more her ability to take the oddest things in her stride and explain them away amazed her. Her practical approach seemed to calm the housekeeper, though Ann herself remained unconvinced. There was something too immediate – and a little frightening – about the way those clothes looked. It left no room in her mind for any kind of *artful* arrangement. She had a gift for spotting anything contrived – which stood her in good stead in her job as a teacher at an all-girls' school in London. Out of deference to her aunt, however, she remained silent and kept her eyes open. For someone who was supposed to have gone off for a month, she thought the room surprisingly untidy – even for a writer and journalist. Would the man really have left paper in his typewriter, his desk littered with manuscripts, and his pipe and tobacco unpacked?

'… Ann, be a dear and check that everything's all right upstairs, will you?' her aunt was saying. 'My legs aren't what they used to be.'

But what she saw when she got upstairs only added to her disquiet. Mr Autrey's wash things, toothbrush, shaving kit and hairbrush were still in their proper places in the bathroom. Then the housekeeper appeared at the doorway with the clothes she had folded, looking furtive. She held out the trousers.

'Miss Ann,' she whispered, 'Mr Gus seems to have left his keys and his money.' She shook the trousers gently for Ann to hear the clink of metal. Ann thought quickly. She didn't want to alarm the housekeeper by revealing what else she'd found.

'My aunt's right!' she said with a bright smile. 'He *is* a bit of a joker, this Mr Gus, isn't he? Made the whole thing look as real as he could – just as if he really had vanished right out of his clothes!'

The housekeeper was reproachful. 'Oh Miss, he was such a nice gentleman. Wrote lovely stories for the children, he did – they'll miss him ever so.'

Ann made herself sound cheerful. 'But we know he hasn't *really* disappeared, Mrs Mye. He'll soon be back, laughing at the way you were taken in.'

'No, Miss,' the woman insisted miserably. 'His keys *and* his money? Everyone knows he went walking too much in the wrong part of the forest. He ain't never coming back.' Ann felt an unexpected sense of impatience. She'd been looking forward to meeting her aunt's tenant, and she disliked the despondency in the housekeeper's tone. The idea was too ludicrous for words anyway. To say he was lost in the forest when his last physical appearance was plainly there in the house … well, it made no sense. Only a madman would stage such a charade and then walk naked into the night. No, there had to be an explanation, of course – but not that one. She forced another smile.

'I'm quite sure we haven't seen the last of Mr Gus, Mrs Mye,' she said with more faith than she felt . 'He'll be back, trust me.'

'Well, if you say so, Miss –' Aunt Alicia cut her short, calling up from the bottom of the stairs that she was off back home and would see her niece there. Mrs Mye nodded. 'I'll carry on tidying, Miss.'

Ann followed the housekeeper downstairs to do some 'tidying' herself. Gathering papers and manuscripts into neat piles and covering the typewriter, she noticed a loose photograph half hidden beneath a folder. She pulled it free and looked at it curiously. The image showed a young man in his thirties with thick, wavy black hair and lean features. He was dressed in a white tie and dinner jacket, obviously posed for publicity purposes, with front and overhead lighting against a dark background. His dark eyes, slightly impish expression, and just the ghost of a smile seemed to quiz her as he rested his head on a thumb and two forefingers.

I could fall for you! she thought to herself, laughing. Then she blushed deeply as she saw Mrs Mye watching her.

She tried to speak lightly. 'I take it this is Mr Gus?'

The assurance came quickly. 'Yes, Miss, that's him all right! Ever so good, isn't it?' The woman looked at her hopefully. 'I could let you have some of his stories to read. Mr Gus said I was welcome to any that I thought the grandchildren would like. You being a teacher and that, you'd know what children like. You could put in a good word for him with the publishers, couldn't you? He was ever so disappointed when his last one got returned yesterday.' She bent to pick up a piece of paper that had fallen to the floor, while Ann dismissed the idea with a laugh. 'I hardly think so, Mrs Mye. I have no –'

'Look at this, Miss! It looks like a map; maybe part of the forest! Mr Gus must've drawn it.' Ann took the paper and studied the details with interest. It appeared to be a highly selective diagram of the route to a triangular-shaped island surrounded by three lakes.

'I'd like to make a copy of that,' she murmured, more to herself than anything.

'Why, Miss, you ain't never going there, are you?' Mrs Mye's voice was disapproving. 'It's dangerous!'

Ann was amused. 'What do you mean, dangerous?'

'Well, Adder's safe enough I suppose,' the housekeeper allowed grudgingly. 'No one's ever come to harm there. But Dragon's deadly. People as go wandering around there are likely to go mad … or disappear!'

'Mrs Mye!' Ann laughed in exasperation. 'This is the twentieth century for heaven's sake, not the dark ages!'

*

When she returned home, her aunt had cereal, toast and coffee under way.

'Waste of time going back to bed now,' she said briskly. 'You don't mind breakfasting in your dressing gown, do you?'

'Fine by me, Auntie – I'll just slip to the bathroom first.'

She reappeared with her hair fastened in a bun, face washed and wearing a pair of horn-rimmed spectacles. Her aunt's faded blue eyes regarded her critically.

'Such a shame you have to wear glasses, dear,' she observed. 'They make you look so severe. And you've such a pretty face.' Ann's brown eyes remained tranquil. In fact there was nothing wrong with her eyesight at all, but the glasses gave her the scholarly look she wanted.

Even on holiday when she could afford to relax, she never forgot her profession and the need for propriety. She smiled and changed the subject.

'How long have you been retired here, Auntie?'

'Must be five years or so by now, dear. What makes you ask?'

'I was just wondering,' Ann said slowly. 'Mrs Mye is quite convinced that the forest is somehow responsible for Mr Autrey's disappearance –'

'Superstitious rubbish!' her aunt interrupted shortly.

'So there is something …?'

'My dear girl, if you're interested in folklore, don't ask me – ask the locals!'

'And what would you say if I told you that your tenant not only left his clothes behind but his wash things too. And he left his keys and loose cash in his trousers.'

'The man's a walking theatre!' Aunt Alicia replied irritably. 'He makes this kind of gesture. I can just imagine it now, flinging his arms wide and dramatically informing the poor woman, "Mrs Mye, I am going to disappear!" And then doing it as literally as he could make it appear.'

'And what if he doesn't come back, Auntie?'

'Ann, I hope you haven't been encouraging Mrs Mye in her fantasies?'

'No, of course not. I took my cue entirely from you. But just supposing he doesn't come back. What then?'

'*Then* we'll inform the police.'

*

That afternoon, two girls with a toddler in a pushchair arrived at the back door with a bulky parcel for Ann.

'Please Miss, Nanny Mye asked us to bring this round to you,' said the tallest. Her blue eyes looked curiously at Ann from a thin face framed with straight hair the colour of corn. Ann had to smile as she took the parcel and opened it to find a manuscript. The housekeeper certainly seemed determined to prove her case. She invited the children in with the offer of homemade lemonade and currant buns. The taller girl introduced herself as Stella.

'... And this here is Johnny, my brother – he's nearly two,' she said proudly of the chubby youngster with fair hair and eyes even bluer than his sister's. 'And this is Edie Adams, my cousin – she's ten –'

'We think it's the Witchett as took him,' Edie interrupted boldly, her stocky build reflecting an uncompromising attitude.

Stella gave her cousin a sharp nudge with her elbow. '... And I'm nearly twelve.'

'The Witchett?' asked Ann, setting the drinks before them and reaching for the cake tin.

'He's the Wizard that lives in The Wandle – that's the funny-shaped island in the middle of the Weirs,' Edie got in quickly before Stella could stop her.

'It's just a fairy story, of course,' said Stella, going pink. Ann smiled.

'But the grown-ups say we mustn't ever go there,' said Edie.

'I know,' said Ann. 'Your grandmother wasn't very happy with the idea of me exploring the forest either. But I've got a map of The Wandle and it looks like *just* the kind of place where someone like that might live.' The two girls looked surprised. Outsiders didn't usually take them seriously.

'That's what Mr Gus said, Miss, and that's why we liked his stories,' said Stella. 'He told us one about the Witchett, and he called him Hellbane Harry ...'

'... The Wicked Wizard of Witchery Wood and his Dragon Dreadful! And his servants Fizzlebane and

Fumingwort,' finished Edie, with a giggle. 'It's ever so funny!'

Watching and listening, Ann realised the reason for their missing storyteller's popularity. Their 'Mr Gus' had enabled them to laugh at their fears of the forest's legendary inhabitants. She felt she was beginning to like him even more.

'So how does the *real* legend go?' she asked.

The two girls glanced at each other, then began a chant they appeared to have learnt from early childhood. Little Johnny seemed to be learning it too, for he was waving and beating his little fists to the rhythm.

> The Dragon made the Dragon's Woe
> And Adder made the King's
> The Witchett made the other one
> That from the Adder springs
>
> The Dragon and the Adder strove
> The forest to ensiddle
> But neither won full half of it
> 'Cos Witchett stole the middle!
>
> So Dragon wards the woeful side
> The King the Wale doth hondle
> While Witchett sits atween the two
> A-laughing in The Wandle

Ann listened fascinated, recognising that the words were likely to have had their roots in a long-forgotten piece of folklore. Fetching pen and paper, she made Stella recite the verses again while she wrote them down.

If Stella was delighted at her elevation to chief informant, Edie was not to be outdone. 'And there's another one you can write down too, Miss,' she added excitedly. 'It's about the forest.'

> Never go nigh it at night,
> Never go nigh it alone.
> Never set toe in the Weirs,
> Never set heel in the Woe.

'Well,' said Ann, when she had it all noted down. 'No one can say you children haven't been warned!'

'So you do believe there's something there, Miss?' asked the older girl, earnestly.

Ann regarded her gravely. 'Let's just say there's never smoke without a little bit of fire, Stella,' she said cautiously. 'I think there might perhaps have been something there *once* upon a time. But until the grown-ups find out whether it's gone for good, I would do as I was told and stay away.'

'Ooo!' Edie exclaimed, her eyes wide. 'You think the fairies really are there, Miss? Stella said it was fairies as stole her dolly's tea set – the one Mr Gus gave her for Christmas – *and* the dolly's dress and bonnet he gave her for Easter too! Nanny Mye was *ever* so cross.' Ann wondered if she detected a note of envy, and gave the child a sharp look.

'So who was Nanny Mye cross with?' she asked lightly. 'Stella or the fairies?' They seemed to find the idea of Mrs Mye being cross with the fairies funny, and they both giggled.

'She was cross with me, Miss,' Stella owned up. 'She said I shouldn't have been so careless. But I wasn't careless, Miss, honest I wasn't. I just didn't like to tell her about the fairies.'

'Would you like to tell *me* about them then?' Ann asked. Stella looked at her doubtfully.

'Maybe you could tell me what they looked like?' Ann prompted.

'Well, that's it, Miss,' answered the child. 'You couldn't tell! Their heads and hands and feet were invisible, see. You could only tell they were there because of what they were wearing. And their clothes were ever so peculiar, Miss. A bit like toy jackets and trousers, only they weren't properly made – they were all bitty and untidy like. And there were two of them, and they carried the tea set off in little sacks over their shoulders.'

'How big were they?' Ann asked. Stella held out her hand about nine inches above the floor. Ann felt a sense of shock. Children usually imagined gossamer-winged creatures of three to four inches, not nine-inch-high little manikins! She hid her disquiet with a serious nod, and asked, 'Would you like to tell me where you saw them?'

'Wisher's Mead, Miss,' Stella answered readily. 'We're allowed to go there for picnics.'

'Well, I shall certainly keep my eyes open from now on,' Ann promised. 'And if you see any more, I hope you'll tell me about them?'

'We will, Miss, we will!' they chorused happily, and went off home.

*

Curled up in an armchair that evening, Ann started reading the manuscript she had been given and found the stories a delight. Written from a child's-eye view of an adult world, they bubbled with humour and whimsical fantasy, yet revealed such visions of drama and pathos that she found her eyes stinging with tears. It was nearly midnight before she went to bed.

CHAPTER 2

THE FOREST

'Ann, you're dreaming!' her aunt accused her over breakfast the following morning.

'No, I'm not!' she answered quickly, a blush tinting her cheeks. Ann had always put her career first and never given much thought to the opposite sex. Now that she found herself haunted by a photograph, she wanted to keep it to herself. She told herself she was being silly, but it was no good. She couldn't get Autrey's half smile and impish humour out of her mind – nor the map he had drawn of the forest. If she wanted to know more about the man, then she was going to have to explore the forest.

Her aunt was tut-tutting about something in the newspaper 'I would have thought science had moved on sufficiently to find the cause of death in most circumstances nowadays – especially when two people die in the same place at the same time,' she said impatiently.

'What's that, Auntie?'

'A retired naval commander and his batman, over at Hurstlea last week. Both found dead; one inside the house, the other outside. No sign of foul play, and it says here that the post mortems have found no discernable cause of death.'

'I thought you said this would be a nice quiet holiday for me?' Ann smiled. 'Two deaths and a disappearance within the space of a week seems quite lively!'

'The tragedy drew county-wide attention for that very reason,' said her aunt. 'As for Autrey, he has *not* disappeared! I told you –'

'Auntie, I'm only teasing!' said her niece. 'I was thinking, if you haven't anything else arranged for this morning then I'd like to go for a walk. I'll be back in time to help with lunch. Will that be all right?'

'It's your holiday, dear. If that's what you would like to do, then that's fine. But do be careful. There's a nasty piece of marsh on the west side of the forest. People have been known to get lost there. The east side is safe enough, if that's where you're going. And you might meet Sir Edward We'ard, the Weir Ward,' she added. 'Please remember me to him and give him my regards.'

'Thank you, Auntie, of course I will.'

*

Half an hour later she set off, her trim figure looking smart in a tweed skirt and finely knitted sweater, her feet comfortable in a pair of stout shoes, and a light scarf knotted under her chin to protect her hair. Thinking they might be useful, she had also slung a pair of binoculars on her shoulder. These she steadied with one hand while swinging a walking stick in the other. The map was safe in a pocket.

The layout of the village of Three Weirs was unusual, with all its houses on the north side of the high road. The road connected it to the larger village of Hurstlea in one direction, and the township of Corsham in the other. South of this lay Weir Forest. Ann found Wisher's Lane easily enough, and the River Weir running alongside the large meadow of Wisher's Mead. Remembering Stella's account of the oddly clothed little people, she was almost tempted to stop and look around it herself, but she pushed on. Wisher's Barn turned out not to be a barn at all, but a railed-off circular cluster of stunted spruces. From there the lane entered the forest proper and changed to a sharply rising track. Worn by torrents of rain and melted snow, the track had sunk, exposing the roots of the great overhanging beeches so that they spread across the path like groping talons. It made progress difficult and she was glad of the stick. Further along, the path had a left turn into what was marked on the map as the Ween, where it appeared to peter out to nothing.

She kept to the track she was already on until it turned off to follow a seemingly well-swept path which rose steadily. The beech trees gave way to birch, oak and ash. A glimpse of sky up ahead gave little warning of what she would find when she emerged.

She had come out on the crest of a great cliff. With the trees falling away behind her, she found she was standing at the edge of a vertical drop. Clinging ferns and grasses plunged headlong into two large lakes glimmering in the shadows below. According to the map, the cliff was called Wandleside; below it the water to her right was King's Weir and to the left Witchett's Weir. Through her binoculars she could see no sluice, lock, or outfall of water from one to the other that could justify either of them as weirs. So why? she wondered.

She scanned her binoculars along the low island – marked on the map as The Wandle – that rooted the densely packed spruce on the Weirs' far side, and tried to find a glimpse of Dragon's Woe beyond it. But the firs, which she followed upwards into their serrated canopy of solid green, hid it completely.

Remembering the gulf at her feet, the height of the trees made her catch her breath. Feeling giddy, she lowered the binoculars and the trees receded to a safe distance. Viewed from above, The Wandle looked huge, and so densely packed with trees that it seemed a place of impenetrable gloom; primitive, silent and awe-inspiring. As if it were holding its breath, she thought with a shiver, then laughed at herself for being so fanciful. But a discomfiting sense of presence persisted, making her feel suddenly vulnerable. She tore herself away, but the scene remained in her mind as she retraced her steps. She had never have imagined that such a landscape could exist within the close confines of the Sussex countryside.

When she got back to Wisher's Barn, a tall, elderly man coming towards her caught her attention. He raised his cap.

'Good morning!' he said. 'I trust you enjoyed your walk?'

'You must be Sir Edward,' she answered, remembering her aunt's words and holding out her hand. 'I'm Ann Singlewood. My aunt, Miss Alicia Pettiford, said to give you her regards.'

'And mine to her also, please!' he said, taking her hand. 'A most remarkable, down-to-earth and pleasant woman! I hope she warned you to be careful in the forest?'

Ann smiled. 'She did, and so did our housekeeper.' She felt so at ease with him that she soon found herself telling him about the strange disappearance of her aunt's tenant the previous morning. Her words seemed to rush away from her and she caught herself in surprise. She was usually so reticent with strangers. 'I-I do beg your pardon, Sir Edward! It must be the forest. It does something to you. I've never seen anything so remarkable before. That view above Wandleside …' she stopped. 'My goodness, there I go again!'

'And why not, m'dear?' he said, smiling. 'You are right. It is a wonderful place. But I am intrigued. Not many people speak of that cliff as Wandleside – and certainly not strangers.'

Ann showed him the map. 'The young man I was telling you about – Mr Autrey – we think he must have drawn it. I'm only borrowing it. I shall make a copy and return it before he gets back.'

'So you think he will be coming back?' asked the Weir Ward.

Ann found it hard to judge from his tone of voice whether he was curious for her opinion, or asking for some other reason. 'What do you make of his disappearance, Sir Edward?' she countered.

'I'm grateful you have told me about it,' he admitted. 'I think it a little unfortunate that young Autrey should have apparently staged such an odd departure – it is bound to fuel rumours in the village that he has been spirited away by the little people. Obviously no one outside Three Weirs is going to believe that for a moment, but it will give rise to a missing person's enquiry if anyone comes looking for him and he cannot be accounted for.'

Ann could see that the idea troubled him for some reason. 'But that would be a good thing, wouldn't it?' she prompted. 'If he really has gone missing …?' She left it hanging, and his reaction surprised her.

'No, Miss Singlewood,' he said firmly, 'it would not! And now, if you will excuse me, I have an appointment to keep. Good day to you!' He raised his cap again and was off.

'Good day,' she echoed faintly, watching his retreating form striding away into the forest.

*

'It was so odd,' she said, as she related the incident to her aunt later on. 'At first he was so friendly, and then so abrupt. I mean, if your tenant has gone missing, why wouldn't Sir Edward allow every avenue to be explored?'

'Because young Autrey spent too much time in the forest!' her aunt snapped crossly. 'If the police get involved they could well send in search parties – and that's the last thing Sir Edward wants. Under the provisions of an ancient charter, his family were made wardens of the forest to keep it safe from intrusion. As I understand it, they once held feudal rights to the whole forest – even kings couldn't ride in it without the Weir Ward's sanction. As the current Lord of the Weirs, he wants to protect the forest from modern day incursions, and I'm not surprised he was upset. You young people go trampling around without thought or regard to local feelings or sensible advice.'

Well, thank you, Aunt Alicia! Ann thought rebelliously as she went to prepare lunch. Anyone would think *she* was responsible for the disappearance of a man she had never even met.

Sleep was a long time coming that night. The view from Wandleside, dominated by the dark mysterious Wandle, stayed in Ann's mind. When she did eventually drift off, she dreamt she was on the island, the trees far higher and more widely spaced than she had imagined. Walking through them she came to a circular clearing of intense green. There was an archway of white stone engraved with symbols, and sitting before it was the graceful figure of a woman about the same height as herself. Her hair was the colour of pale gold and fell in waves down to her waist. A circlet of silver, alight with diamonds, bound her brow. She was clothed in a medieval-looking garment of flowing white, girdled with a band of silver – which was also encrusted with diamonds – so that her every movement was scintillated with pricks of fiery light. She was bent in concentration before a tall white loom, engaged in smoothly, yet impossibly, spinning and weaving at the same time. Gossamer filaments drawn from thin air by a silver wand in her left hand twisted fluidly into shining white threads, feeding two silver shuttles that flew back and forth by themselves through the shed of the loom. Her small silver-slippered feet pressed the treadles to raise and lower the warp threads, changing the pattern, while her right hand combed each new thread deftly to the weft with the reed. It all came to a standstill, though, when she lifted her head and turned to smile at her visitor. Her eyes, luminous and unearthly, made Ann draw her breath sharply, for they held neither pupil nor iris.

'Welcome, dreamer!' the woman said softly in a voice that reminded Ann of rippling water and laughter. 'It is woven – see!' She indicated the shimmering material that fell from the loom in gleaming white folds to the grass. 'Your Weird is woven and waits only to be sewn with the pattern of your Destiny …'

Ann was engulfed by terror. The lovely dream had become a nightmare – like finding a huge white spider at the centre of a web that was set to catch her. She tried to scream but nothing came from her throat. When she struggled awake, she found the sheets tangled around her. Heart pounding and in a cold sweat, she freed herself and switched on the bedside lamp. It was a quarter past four in the morning. What had given her such a vision? But of course she knew. 'That blessed forest!' she muttered, still trembling and breathing rapidly as she got up. She needed to wake up properly before daring to go back to sleep.

Deciding that a hot, strong cup of tea might help calm her, she reached for her dressing gown – and stopped. It was white, like her mules, and until then it had been her favourite colour. But now it was the last thing she wanted to wear. With a shiver, she wrapped herself in the pretty blue coverlet that had fallen on the floor, and padded downstairs in her bare feet.

CHAPTER 3

THE LORD OF THE WEIRS

After the nightmare, it surprised Ann that she ever got back to sleep at all. Yet somehow she did, and woke up feeling refreshed. But her mind remained unchanged about her dressing gown.

'Auntie, do you have a sewing machine?' she asked after breakfast.

'It's under the stairs, dear. What do you intend making?'

'I thought I'd go into Corsham this morning and find some lightweight material for a housecoat. It's so warm now, and the robe I've got just isn't suitable for lounging in.'

For a moment she thought her aunt was going to lend something of her own, but she appeared to think better of it, which was a relief. Ann felt that the only way to fend off further nightmares was to keep herself busy. And that was how it seemed … for a while.

By evening the housecoat was complete, and while the machine was still set up, she helped her aunt with her work for the Women's Institute by running up a few items for the village fête. After that there was the never-ending demand for jams, jellies and cakes to keep up with, until finally, a week later, her aunt had to protest that her niece was supposed to be on *holiday*.

'But I'm really enjoying this, Auntie! Honestly! I'm learning so much, and they do say a change is as good as a rest.' She had been sleeping well too. So much so that she felt she could safely undertake some further research into Weir Forest by visiting the local Public Records Office.

'If you really insist that I should rest, Auntie, then perhaps I could go into Corsham and visit the library?'

'I *do* insist! And have lunch out too. Take yourself to the cinema. I shan't expect you back until after tea.'

*

In Corsham, she came face to face with Sir Edward We'ard, who was leaving the library as she was about to enter. He doffed his hat with a 'Good morning, Miss Singlewood' and made to carry on, but Ann stopped him.

'Sir Edward, please,' she begged, 'I would like to apologise for being so insensitive when we last met ... I really had no idea ... I'm here now to see if I can track down any history of the forest.'

'Then perhaps I can be of help?' he offered gravely.

'That would be very kind, but I wouldn't like to be a nuisance –'

'Not at all, m'dear – it would be my pleasure! Are you in town for long?'

'Well, I only came in to see if there were any records. I don't know how long that will take, but Aunt Alicia isn't expecting me home 'til late this afternoon.'

'In that case, perhaps you would like to meet my wife? You might also do us the honour of staying to have lunch with us.'

She hardly knew what to say. 'But surely you wouldn't want –'

'We most certainly would!' he assured her firmly, offering her his arm. 'My car is just down the road.'

*

If an unexpected guest was the last thing she wanted, Lady We'ard's patrician features gave no hint of it. She welcomed Ann warmly.

'I'm Margaret,' she said. 'Edward has told me about your aunt's tenant. Still no word I suppose?'

Ann admitted that there wasn't.

'Ann is interested in the history of the forest, dear,' said Sir Edward significantly. 'I thought we might have time for a coffee in the library before lunch.'

'I'll get Jeremiah to bring it in, dear,' she answered at once. 'You see to Ann. I'll have a word with Cook.'

When he had settled Ann into an armchair in his library, and seated himself in the one opposite her, Sir Edward admitted that he had a confession to make. Ann felt an immediate sense of disappointment and raised an enquiring eyebrow.

'You must forgive me, Ann,' he went on, 'but I'm afraid I've brought you here under false pretences. Please remember that I am the Weir Ward, and rather than encourage your interest in Weir Forest, I'm afraid I have to actively *dis*courage it – for your own sake. There is a very old tradition that people who take too close an interest in its mysteries – and I can't help citing young Autrey as an example – sooner or later meet with tragedy in some form or other.'

'Tragedy?' she exclaimed in astonishment, hiding the frustration she had felt at his words. 'Surely it's a little early to dismiss Mr Autrey as an example of tragedy?'

'I am honestly disturbed about the fellow,' confessed Sir Edward. 'He disregarded the warning about wandering alone in the forest. I understand he did it continually. And now he has disappeared in mysterious circumstances. I'm afraid we'll soon hear that he has been declared a missing person and the police will become involved.'

The butler arrived with the tray of coffee. Ann waited until he had gone before asking, 'And what will the police do?'

'Make a systematic search of the whole forest,' came the grim reply. 'Police and troops, private snoopers and the press trampling over every inch of it – including The Wandle.'

Ann felt a stab of exasperation; was the forest *really* all the man ever worried about? 'But you don't *know* that he's gone there. No one does!' she found herself bursting out incredulously. 'He disappeared from my aunt's house – he could have gone anywhere – Timbuktu even! Why does it have to be the forest? The way his clothes were left, he could just as well have been taken by a flying saucer.' The Weir Ward's indulgent smile nettled her. 'I saw his clothes, Sir Edward. You didn't,' she reminded him. 'Spontaneous human combustion is strange and weird too, but when nothing else in the vicinity of the burnt body is so much as singed, one doesn't ignore the evidence of one's own eyes.'

Sir Edward relaxed back with a laugh. 'My apologies, Ann! You certainly know how to put things into perspective! You are quite right, of course. We *don't* know! He indicated the coffee pots. 'Black or white?'

'White, please. And Sir Edward, you don't have to be worried about *me* disappearing in the forest.'

'Why's that?' he asked with interest, handing her the coffee. 'Sugar?'

'No – thank you.' She took the cup and went on, 'Because I have no intention of ever going near it again. Not after last time. It gave me a nightmare!'

The Weir Ward was immediately attentive. 'Would you care to tell me about it?' he asked.

Ann related her dream, and the Weir Ward was silent. He seemed so deep in thought that she decided his mind must have wandered onto something else while she had been speaking. 'Sir Edward …?' she prompted diffidently.

'Please, you must excuse me,' he answered slowly. 'I was trying to make up my mind whether I ought to tell you something rather remarkable – and yes, I feel that I should. You see, my uncle Studley We'ard had a rather similar experience.'

Ann could hardly believe her ears. 'You don't mean Studley We'ard, the Sussex historian?'

'Yes, why?'

'We have his book in the library at Hillman's College, where I teach,' she answered. 'I wouldn't have thought to look for any connection there – but I certainly shall when I get back!'

'No need!' he said, rising. 'I have a copy here.' From a shelf by the fireplace he pulled out a slim, green leather-bound volume, opened it at a bookmark, and handed it to her. 'He put in an account of the dragon, but you won't find much about the mysteries of Weir Forest. He deliberately played down that aspect.'

Ann took the book and read:

> The Forest of Weir, between Hurstlea and Corsham in Sussex, boasts a long history of habitation by a monster. It is said that in the fifth century a saint came to slay a dragon there, but only succeeded in wounding it. Its blood splashed down and beds of saw-toothed reeds sprang up at an alarming speed. After the fight, the saint bound the dragon in the marshes with his prayers. The local adders, being the dragon's nearest relatives, were also deprived of their stings. To this day it is well known that no one is ever harmed in the part of the forest known as Adder's Wale. Stories of strange

things lurking among the trees linger still, however, and the marsh known as Dragon's Woe, with its 'Dragon's Teeth' reeds, is best avoided. Since that time, the forest has been protected by Royal Charter, held by the Ward family – the name being corrupted to We'ard – whose titled head, Lord of the Weirs, has the responsibility of keeping it safe from the intrusion of men.

'Studley felt he needed to emphasize our Wardenship – and, in particular, our family's ancient obligation to prevent encroachment on the forest,' said the Weir Ward, taking the book back with a sigh. 'It's a task that becomes increasingly onerous every year. There have been several proposals to build housing estates on the Wale.'

'Which you must have successfully bypassed?' she guessed.

'Only by arousing county-wide feeling,' he admitted. 'I am now engaged in promoting a permanent association for the forest's preservation.'

'I'm sure I'd be happy to support you, Sir Edward, if I could be persuaded that it was for ...' She paused, not wanting to say 'for good', instead searching for a word that would convey how she felt without offending him.

'Ah, you're thinking about that dream of yours, aren't you?' he said. 'And I was going to tell you about Studley, wasn't I? Oh dear, this isn't going to sound terribly good ... but I did promise. So be it ... Studley was found dead on the marshes beside Dragon's Woe. That was nearly fifty years ago. And yes, he had probed deeply into the forest's mysteries. When my father died and I inherited the title and all his effects, I found a diary that Studley had been keeping. A few weeks before his death he had actually explored The Wandle. What he wrote about his experience there wasn't a dream, but a kind of subsequent recollection. He wrote that while he was there he had met "*One that dwells in the heart of The Wandle*" and from him had learned a number of secrets. The only one he could even remotely remember was something that concerned "*The Deathless Dragon of the Weirs*". "The rest," he wrote, "has to do with my destiny; a Weird that is waiting for me to wear."'

Ann was stunned. 'But that's a bit like "Your Weird is woven and waits only to be sewn with the pattern of your destiny!"' she said.

'Rather more than a bit, I would say,' said the Weir Ward dryly.

'Only in my case it was a she, and to your uncle a he. Perhaps whatever the Witchett is, it appears as a male to men and a female to women. But you have no need to warn me to stay away from the forest, Sir Edward,' she assured him earnestly. 'Wild horses couldn't drag me there now!'

'Then I was right to tell you,' he said with evident relief and satisfaction. 'I shall now enjoy luncheon with a clear conscience.'

'I can't possibly thank you enough, Sir Edward. There's only one thing that bothers me though: why would you want to preserve a place with such a terrible reputation?'

'For good or for ill, it is our heritage. But who knows? Perhaps seeing that it stays undisturbed is to keep it under control – to prevent whatever it is from escaping.'

'Ah … yes,' she agreed slowly. And seeing him in a completely new light, she added, 'I have to say, it seems an extraordinary coincidence that I should have met you this morning, Sir Edward.'

'Not really, m'dear,' he answered lightly. 'We We'ards have often been prompted and guided by the other-world guardians of the forest.'

Ann felt a sense of gratitude. 'I'm glad to hear that it's not all up to us then!' she said. 'I shall certainly support your efforts to keep it intact.'

'I can't ask more than that, can I?' he returned with a smile. 'And now, if I'm not mistaken, Margaret will have seen that lunch is about ready ...'

Nothing more was said on the subject and Ann enjoyed a pleasant meal with them both. Sir Edward drove her home afterwards, leaving her with the assurance that she could contact either himself or his wife whenever she needed to.

'You make me feel like a marked woman!' she joked.

'Can't forget Studley,' he said briefly. 'Just call me if you have any more of those dreams. Promise?'

She promised.

Ann's heavily edited account of the morning gave nothing away, but satisfied her aunt and impressed the listening Mrs Mye. After describing the lunch and sharing a few details about the We'ard family's interests, she started to tell them about their thirty-year-old son, Humphrey. She had learned that he was now pursuing a career as a barrister after leaving Cambridge with an honours degree in law. But noting the sudden gleam it brought to her aunt's eye, she quickly changed the subject.

'Sir Edward said there's to be an eclipse of the moon tonight, Auntie. Shall we watch it together? It's quite early, really – totality around ten.'

'No, dear. You can if you like, but I'd like an early night. It's the fête tomorrow and we're doing strawberry and cream teas for the WI. We've been preparing it all morning, and I want to feel fresh for the afternoon.'

Ann was reproachful. 'You should have *said*, Auntie. I'd have stayed and helped.'

Her aunt smiled. 'I know, dear – that's precisely why I didn't tell you!'

*

Curled up in a chair with pen and pad that evening, Ann started a letter to her parents while she waited for the eclipse.

But she soon fell asleep and dreamed that she was once again in the forest. She woke at three in the morning, freezing cold and with such a confusion of images in her mind – it felt like clutching at handfuls of water to try and catch even some of them before they were gone.

The writing pad with its half-written letter was still in her lap. Shivering with cold, she tried to note down all that she could remember.

But there was one thing she knew she would never forget: she had looked into the eyes of the man in the photograph, Augustus Autrey. She had recognised him, and his eyes had responded with the same startled recognition of her! It had only been a moment, and then it was lost in a kaleidoscope of brilliant colour and movement; a joyous dance with hundreds of golden-skinned elfin people as tall as herself, all delicately but traditionally dressed in every colour under the sun – or moon. The earth's shadow had passed, and she had felt the full orb of the moon's light shining on her like the warmth of the sun.

Another fragment of memory held the White Lady from her first dream. But this time she had been Autrey's partner, a pillar of iridescent white, countering his scintillating black, standing either side of a golden throne on which had sat the commanding upright form of a King, his crown like a pale gold star.

There was also a teasing memory of the White One impressing Ann with something important; an instruction which Ann had had to repeat back ... but could no longer remember.

Stiff with cold and still shivering, she climbed out of the chair, made herself some hot chocolate, and went to bed, her whole being rapt by the unexpected recognition in Autrey's eyes. It was so tantalising, since, to her knowledge, they had never met. 'It's just a dream!' she reminded herself almost savagely. 'And a dream's nothing more than wishful thinking.' A pang of jealousy flared, however, when she thought of the White One. Who – or what – else could *she* be but the Witchett? Could she have caught Autrey, just as she had tried to catch Ann?

'Oh, for heaven's sake, Ann!' she exploded crossly. 'Grow up!'

But still she cried herself to sleep.

CHAPTER 4

DEAR MR WITCHETT

Ann was in turmoil the next day, torn between jealousy and anger over her dream. She knew it was irrational, but she knew she had seen Autrey. She would never forget the shock she had felt when the unearthly brilliance of his wide eyes had met her gaze.

She remembered how alien his eyes had become; almost as alien as the White One's, except that the coal-dark iris and pupil remained. He was still human. Perhaps it wasn't too late – maybe it was still possible to rescue him.

She thought about all the folklore she had read of people – usually simple country folk – being taken by fairies to be their servants. In 1691 the Reverend Robert Kirk had written in *The Secret Commonwealth of Elves, Fauns and Fairies* of how they lived much like humans. Another writer, William Bottrell, had observed that they had little sense or feeling. What served them as such was merely the remembrance of what had pleased them when they had lived as mortals. There was also a stern warning for people who tried to rescue anyone trapped in their realm to avoid eating or drinking anything that was offered or pressed on them.

That reminded Ann of another part of her dream. A jolly little red-nosed, round-faced gnome had been plying everyone with wine from what appeared to be a bottom-less jug. When he saw her he held out a golden goblet full of a rich ruby liquid – and someone had stopped him. She tried to bring the scene to mind but, like the rest of the dream, it was only a fragment. Yet if someone *had* known she was human and *had* saved her, that person could only have been … Augustus Autrey!

Oh, what an impossible name, she thought, with both amusement and irritation. Surely 'August' would have been more believable –?

'… Ann!' Aunt Alicia's sharp voice broke her train of thought. They were at breakfast and her aunt was looking at her suspiciously, teapot in one hand, coffee pot in the other.

'Oh! Er, coffee, please,' she said, passing her cup.

'So, what is it today, dear?' her aunt asked, filling it. 'Another trip into Corsham?'

'I thought I was helping you at the fête this afternoon?' Ann answered, looking blank.

'That's right, dear. But I was wondering if your mind was really on it.'

'I'll be there, Auntie, I promise. I've just got something I need to do this morning.'

She wanted to contact Sir Edward, but she needed privacy. The telephone in the cottage was out of the question, so she went in search of a public call box. She got through to his wife, who told her that her husband was on his morning walk in the forest.

*

The Weir Lord gave no sign of being surprised when he saw her coming up the sunken track to meet him on his way down.

'I won't ask the obvious, Ann, m'dear,' he said after they had greeted one another. 'You wouldn't be here if it wasn't to keep that promise.'

'Can we sit somewhere?'

Sir Edward indicated a curious bench that she had missed seeing before, formed from the tangled beech roots.

They sat, Sir Edward resting his polished walking stick against his knee. His eyes closed for a moment, as though enjoying the peace and comfort of the summer morning.

She had told him yesterday that wild horses couldn't drag her back here. He must be curious about what had made her return. But he seemed to be hiding it well.

'I've seen Mr Autrey!' she said, then stopped. It sounded so incongruous.

'You have?' Sir Edward sounded relieved and delighted. 'Where was he?'

'No,' she said quickly, 'not like that. It was last night – I dreamt that I was here again in the forest ... on The Wandle ...' She told him all that she could remember. '... So I was wondering if it was possible that he could be rescued?' she concluded. 'Whether there might be anything in your records ...?' She tailed off, watching him hopefully.

The Weir Lord was silent for a moment then got to his feet, offering her his hand to help her rise. She stared at him in surprise. 'I thought –' she began.

'I really think it would be better if nothing more was said on the subject here,' he interrupted quietly. 'Let us return to the village.'

Ann was stunned. 'But you said –'

'And you kept your word,' he reminded her gently. 'Now please, it is time to go – trust me.'

She could tell from his tone that there was no point in arguing.

Fighting her intense disappointment, she accepted his proffered hand and allowed him to guide her back down the track. Nothing more was said until they had crossed the road and the Weir Lord indicated a picturesque pub. 'I do believe our Green Dragon is open,' he said cheerfully. 'A cup of coffee, m'dear, or something stronger?'

She was tempted to refuse. How could she make small talk when there were more important things that needed discussing. It seemed churlish if he was trying to make amends.

'That would be lovely, thank you,' she said.

After ordering a pot of coffee, Sir Edward steered her towards some French windows at the back. 'There's a rather pleasant garden through here,' he said. 'Somewhere quiet where we can talk.'

She looked at him in surprise. 'I thought there was nothing more to be said?'

'My dear Ann, there is a *great deal* more to be said,' he answered. 'But nothing that could be discussed where we were.'

The walled garden was trellised with pale pink and yellow tea roses, and he ushered her towards some wrought iron tables and chairs that were scattered on the small lawn. He chose a table where they were unlikely to be overheard and drew out a chair for her.

'You see, Ann,' he said, taking a seat opposite, 'you are quite right to think that our family has records – after the hundreds of years that we've been here, it would be more surprising if we did not. Of course, I made no mention of them at our last meeting. It hardly seemed necessary. But I have to tell you something else: yes, your dream was true. I now know that you have seen and met the real powers of the forest – the King and his two greatest councillors, White Wand and Black Wand. They guard his realm in balance with each other against a terrible power – something far worse than a mere dragon.'

'But Autrey ... August ...?'

'I'm sorry, Ann, there is no calling him back. He cannot be "rescued" as you put it. I doubt he would want to be anyway – indeed it would be catastrophic if he was.' He stopped speaking while their coffee was served, then continued. 'That is why we couldn't discuss it in the forest. Nothing happens there that is not known by the little people. Their happiness and well-being depends on their guardians. Can't you imagine how your talk of "rescue" could have sounded like an abduction? You must understand, these little ones are elemental; they no longer reason as they did when they lived as mortals.'

'I had no idea you knew so much about them, Sir Edward,' Ann said somewhat sharply. These little people appeared to be getting more than their fair share of consideration and attention – and at poor Autrey's expense.

The Weir Ward caught the tone of her voice and sighed. 'I'm sorry you feel that way, m'dear,' he said, 'but they are my responsibility.'

'I can't believe we're actually having this conversation,' she said, shaking her head. 'This is the twentieth century, for heaven's sake. And here you are, a Peer of the Realm, talking about the happiness and welfare of phantom fairies being more important than a man's life!' She sat back, suddenly appalled at her impertinence and near to tears at the thought of poor Autrey drifting further and further away from her. 'I do beg your pardon, Sir Edward,' she apologised. 'That was unbelievably rude of me.'

Sir Edward seemed quite unruffled. 'My dear girl,' he said, 'I have been accused of far worse by the borough council – and without the justification that you have!'

'I *am* sorry –'

He cut her short. 'Don't be. Take an old man's advice instead and believe in your love for young Autrey. It will bring you together.'

'H-how did you know?' she asked in astonishment.

'From the way you've spoken about him – it wasn't hard to guess.'

'But you said he can't be rescued,' she pointed out, 'so how can it bring us together?'

'How tall would you say Autrey was when you dreamt of him? Was he shorter than you, or taller?'

'Why, taller,' she answered with a puzzled frown.

'Yet if I were to tell you that the little people are no more than nine inches high, what would that say to you?'

She thought back to her dream – everyone had been her own height. 'I must have shrunk!'

'Quite,' he agreed. 'And if Autrey no longer has a mortal form …?'

'Then he can't be rescued,' she answered sadly.

'But if you love him, he *can* be reached.'

'In my dreams!' she said. 'Where the White One has him!'

The Weir Lord smiled. 'Do you know what *I* would do, m'dear?'

'What's that, Sir Edward?'

'Just follow my heart, Ann,' he answered. 'Just follow my heart …'

*

That afternoon, Stella Mye and Edie Adams sought out Ann at the fête. The stall was busy, but there were enough helpers to allow her a short break to hear what the children wanted.

'Miss, we've written a letter to the Witchett!' Edie announced proudly.

On the pretext of watching Johnny's father helping his son to lasso a rubber duck for a prize, she moved them out of immediate earshot.

'It was my idea, but Stella did the writing,' Edie explained.

'But now we need to think how to post it,' said Stella. 'So I thought you might have an idea, Miss?'

'Would you mind if I read it?' she asked, stalling for time while she thought of a convincing answer.

'It's not sealed down,' said Edie, producing it from behind her back and handing it over.

Dear Mr Wichit

Please will you help find Mr Gus what went away last month? We love Mr Gus ever so much and so does Nanna Mye. Johnny calls for Uncle Wug, too. And everone is upset becos we lost at cricket against hurstlea last Saturday as he wasn't there to bat for us and they say you must have wanddeled him. Well if you have will you be so awful kind dear mr wichit and send him back home as soon as you can becos he never finished the story abot crisobel what made all the cakes becos her father was so pore.

Please send Mr Gus home and we will ransum him with our Saturday penys, mine and Stellas and Johnys sweets as well.

Yours respectfull, Edie Adams, and Stella and Johnny Mye.

P.S. Was it you what took Stellas dollys tea set and dress and bonnet on wishers meed?

Ann smiled. 'It's a lovely idea,' she said, secretly amused at what Autrey would have made of it. She decided that she would wait a couple of days then write a reply for the children herself. She would also go into Corsham and see if she could find a tea set similar to the missing one.

Thinking of a credible way to 'post' the letter, however, was difficult – until Johnny's delighted cry at catching a duck gave her the idea she was looking for.

'How about making it into a paper boat?' she suggested when she had their attention again. 'You could float it down the river; that will take it to the Weirs.' Then, remembering that she had been banned from going within fifty feet of any river or pond when she was a child, she added, 'We'll do it tomorrow, and I'll come with you to make sure you don't fall in.'

They couldn't wait to put the idea into action. But the next morning only Stella and Johnny turned up to go to the river, as Edie had to stay at home for misbehaving.

Without Edie around, Stella was far more chatty and open. She confided that she had often dreamed of the fairies – but last night it had been different.

'The Witchett was telling the fairies one of the stories Mr Gus wrote,' she said. 'The one about Hellbane Harry that he never finished. I dreamt that he told them ...'

Ann listened in wonder when she realised that Stella was continuing the story from where the author had left off – and doing so in the same whimsical manner that Autrey wrote in. It would have been beyond the child's ability to invent it.

She set the small paper boat afloat with a silent but fervent prayer: *'Oh, August, if you really are in the forest, please find a way of telling me so.'*

CHAPTER 5

'IT'S FOR YOU, MISS ANN!'

Three days later the whole village seemed to know that Mrs Mye's grandchildren had written to The Witchett and that Stella's doll's tea set, bonnet and frock had turned up in their back garden.

To Ann it seemed like a direct and personal answer to her prayer, and she was in turmoil. It had been impossible to find a tea set with a pattern anything like the one Stella had described, let alone replace the bonnet and dress. Mrs Mye was adamant that what had turned up were the originals, and pointed out parts of the floral design that had worn off the china, just as she remembered. She also knew that 'Mr Gus' had ordered the bonnet and dress specially from London, and the maker's name was sewn into them.

When Ann met up with the Lord of the Weirs that afternoon, he seemed to think that she had instigated the letter, and questioned the wisdom of her actions.

'There is much talk in the village, and the press have been making enquiries,' he told her with a frown. 'The last thing we need is publicity.'

'Sir Edward, the letter was entirely the children's idea,' she answered. 'They wanted me to think of a way of posting it for them. I suggested floating a paper boat down the river and went along to see that they came to no harm.'

They were in the forest, resting on the same bench-like tangle of roots that they had occupied previously.

'I never expected the tea set to turn up! I've been trying to find one to match it. Look ...' she rummaged in her pocket and brought out a crumpled note. 'I even wrote a letter to the children to go with it.'

Sir Edward took the note and read it.

Dear Stella, Edie and Johnny,

Do not be sad about Mr Gus. He is safe and well. I am sure you will not blame me for wandling him away so suddenly when I tell you that we little people are very fond of stories too. And so we intend to keep him as our guest for a while until he has told us all his tales – although I am afraid this might take a long time. So you see there is no need for you to pay any ransom money, because he is not a prisoner but a very honoured guest.

I am sorry about Stella's dolly's tea set. Some very naughty fairies took it away because they wanted to play at being mortals and drink out of cups like humans do. So I have waved my magic wand over it and made it brand new again. Please forgive the naughty fairies. And don't be sad about Mr Gus any more, because we love him too, and he is having a simply wonderful time.

Yours magically
Mr Witchett of The Wandle

When he finished, the Weir Ward looked at her with respect. 'Ann, my dear, I have gravely underestimated you. I can only hope that you can forgive me for doubting your intention. This is a fantastic letter – I wish the

46

children could have seen it. May I hold on to it? It could be extremely useful if the press come back. I can show them this, tell them how you were involved, why you wrote it – with your permission of course. Hopefully it will see an end to their interest.'

'By all means, Sir Edward, please do.' She sighed. 'I only wish I could find a way of dreaming myself back into the forest. It hasn't happened since that time I told you about. But, do you know?' she turned to him with sudden excitement, 'I've discovered that Stella dreams about being in the forest too, and she's told me some incredible things!'

'Go on …'

'She usually just dreams about the fairies themselves, but in her last dream The Witchett was telling them the story of Hellbane Harry – the story August was working on when he vanished. I've read that one – she was continuing it in the same way that he began it. It has a whimsical style that she couldn't possibly have replicated by herself.' And she told him exactly what Stella had said.

'Difficult to see how she could have invented *that*,' Sir Edward agreed when she had finished. 'And I am astounded that you should also have discovered that there is a Witch as well as a Wizard on The Wandle. We We'ards have always been aware of it, of course, but not the villagers living in Three Weirs. To them it has always been a single person – "*The Witchett*" – and we have never contradicted them. But the differences in spelling in the ancient writings leave no doubt that there are two personalities indicated –'

'Shush, listen!' Ann cut him short, putting a finger to her lips. 'I heard sounds.'

'Probably other people in the Wale,' he suggested in a low voice. 'Sounds carry a surprising distance when one is at a height.'

Ann shook her head. 'No, these are *tiny* voices, not distant ones.'

He nodded. 'I thought I heard them too,' he admitted reluctantly, 'but I didn't want to give you any ideas.'

'Have you heard them before?' she asked, still looking around her.

'I believe I might have done,' he confessed, 'but I've never seen anything. Yet now you hear them too … why, bless my soul – look! What are those?' He pointed to the roots opposite them.

'Where…? Oh!' She stared in disbelief. 'Those queer little bundles bobbing around …?'

The Weir Ward nodded. 'Yes. Good heavens, they *are* moving. They're going up the bank just as if … Oh, no, it's impossible!'

'Like little bundles of clothes!' Ann squeaked in her excitement. 'They *are* clothes! Look, there's a pair of little trousers climbing over that root near the top there! You know, Sir Edward,' she turned to him, 'it's exactly the way Stella described the little people who took her tea set!'

'Well, they seem to have gone now,' he said rubbing his eyes, and peering hard at the roots. 'Extraordinary! Most extraordinary! I knew they were here, but I've never seen *anything* like that before.'

'According to Stella their bodies are invisible,' she reminded him. 'Perhaps they meant us to see them. Maybe they were trying to get our attention but we frightened them off …'

*

Ann never knew if the press ever got back to Sir Edward, nor did she ask. And she was thankful that no one came asking for her side of the story.

She went out exploring the forest nearly every day now, and Aunt Alicia seemed relieved that she was relaxed enough to start enjoying her holiday. But Ann was lovesick. She wandered Wale and Woe hoping against hope that she might find some clue, some little indication, of where August Autrey was. Then one night, she dreamed of the White One.

Relating it to Sir Edward the following day, she told him: 'I found her sitting in The Wandle embroidering the magnificent white cloak she had woven; only now it gleamed so brilliantly that I could scarcely look at it. I watched her for a while, and then she looked up and smiled at me. But it wasn't like the smile I'd seen before; it was terribly, terribly sad, as if something awful was weighing her down. I thought she was my enemy, but now I wanted to run in and comfort her – which was strange. But I couldn't move. And then she asked me, "Have you learnt the lesson I set for you, dreamer?" I said yes I had, and she told me to repeat it …' Ann dug the toe of her shoe into the track, reluctant to continue.

'And what did you repeat?' the Weir Ward prompted.

'I can't remember,' she confessed. 'That's the awful part of it. I know I repeated something – something wonderful and logical that made sense of everything. But whatever it was, it's gone now. And that's what's awful – because it was so important.'

'Remember what I told you about Studley,' he said. 'He *knew* he had learned secrets, but he couldn't remember what they were.'

'There's something else I haven't told you.'

'You mean there's more of your dream?'

Ann nodded. 'The White One seemed very pleased with what I repeated to her, and then she said something that I remember very clearly. She said: "*And now my Weird is well nigh worn, Little Sister. But dire is the woe that must whelm ere that which is woven be worn*." I have no idea what she meant but she was very, very unhappy about it. I can't help feeling that some dreadful calamity is about to befall the forest, and that it's all my fault.'

'What on earth makes you say that?'

'I don't know,' she answered sadly. 'It's the way the White One looked at me – as if I was somehow responsible. I haven't told you this before, but I know that August Autrey is protecting me, so I don't feel afraid of her any more. I know it's silly to think that I might matter to him, but I can't help wondering if it's caused a rift between them.'

'If that were true then it *would* be a calamity,' the Weir Ward admitted. 'But we don't know that it is true, so you are not to worry about it.'

*

In the early evening a few days later, Charlie Beale, the village policeman, spotted little Johnny Mye's sister and cousin returning from the Wale with an empty pushchair.

'Good evening, young ladies! So what have you done with the baby, then?' he joked.

The girls broke off from their animated chatter and looked at him blankly. Then they looked down at the empty seat and their expressions turned to horror. Their frightened, tearful answers made little sense, and the constable soon realised that they were unable to account for the missing toddler. He raised the alarm at once.

An hour or so later, in the growing dusk, it seemed that the whole village had assembled. Some people were allocated areas to search in different directions, just to give them something to do, while the Weir Lord took charge of the main search party, which also included Ann, Mrs Mye and Johnny's parents. Carrying torches, lanterns and blankets, and committed to a long and strenuous search, the group set off to search the forest where the children had said they had been. Ann held Stella's hand and let the tearful child lead the way as far as she could remember.

Tensions were running high. One of the older men shook a finger at the policeman. 'It's not afore time we made a proper search for Mr Gus too!'

'It's like I always said,' panted another, arriving late and flourishing a knobbly walking stick at the unfortunate constable. 'He's been wandled! Mark my words. You can laugh at me, Charlie Beale, but the old Witchett baint dead. He be alive as much as you and me. He's mazed Mr Gus and no amount of looking will bring him back.'

'If you don't stop waving that stick in front of my nose, Joe Harmer,' the constable said severely, 'I'll book you for common assault.'

Sir Edward did his best to calm things down and reassure everyone. 'The child will be perfectly safe. We are in the Wale. It is quite impossible for anyone to come to harm here.'

One or two younger people in the group might have thought 'Silly old duffer, what does he know?' but none dared say it aloud. Instead, they prodded the undergrowth sharply with their sticks, and got told off for not thinking about how much they would hurt the baby if he had crawled in amongst it.

Everyone trod carefully, feeling their way through the bracken, their plaintive cries floating up on the evening air: 'John-ee! John-ee…!'

Suddenly, Sir Edward turned to Ann and pointed. 'Your eyes are younger than mine – what's that bundle at the foot of the tree there…?'

It was Johnny, sleeping peacefully.

Ann picked him up gently so as not to wake him, though that became a fond hope when his mother came running up screaming, 'It's him! It's Johnny!' She burst into tears as she took him in her arms.

'Pass up a blanket somebody!' the Weir Lord called. 'And pass word back that all's well. The baby's been found safe and well.'

'Here, give him some barley sugar,' said someone, offering a stick. But instead of grabbing it, the child twisted urgently in his mother's arms and looked around making gurgling noises.

'What is it, my love?' she asked anxiously.

'Uncoo Wug!' he exclaimed, and took the barley sugar.

'That's his name for August!' Ann breathed in astonishment, her heart leaping. 'He was here, Sir Edward! Johnny would never have said his name otherwise. August must have found him and left him where we would find him!'

*

In the middle of the night, Ann was woken by the incessant chatter of a typewriter. After listening for a while, she found it so comforting that she drifted back to sleep without even wondering who the typist was.

To her surprise, when she woke the next morning the typing was still going at a tremendous pace. Curiosity getting the better of her, she leaned out of her bedroom window and could just see a window open on the ground floor of the cottage next door. Her first thought was that there had been a break-in. But burglars didn't usually spend the whole night typing. So it could only mean one thing – August must have returned! She sat back down on the bed in a welter of emotion, unable to work out whether she wanted to laugh or cry. She was disappointed that he wasn't The Witchett after all, but on the other hand she *was* at last going to meet the man whose photograph she had fallen in love with. Her happy excitement was tinged with shyness and uncertainty though – it could all end in terrible disappointment, she admitted.

Mrs Mye came as soon as she could to tell Aunt Alicia the wonderful news that 'Mr Gus' had indeed returned. Ann listened from the top of the stairs.

'Nigh gave me a heart attack, it did, ma'am!' Mrs Mye was saying. 'I nearly fainted, but he jumped up like a flash and caught me. And then, would you believe it, ma'am, he kissed me and said, "Why, you sentimental old thing – I do believe you've been worrying about me!" Then he insisted on making me sit down while he put the kettle on. Really, he were like my own son, the way he fussed …' Her voiced faded as she followed Aunt Alicia into the kitchen. Ann could hear an animated murmur from behind the closed door as Mrs Mye continued telling her exciting news.

Ann dressed carefully in a cream summer dress with a delicate pattern of blush rose blossoms – just in case, she told herself. Then she went down for breakfast.

'… There were piles of sheets he had done. And he said he had –' Mrs Mye broke off as Ann appeared. 'Morning, Miss, I was just telling –'

'I heard,' said Ann, reaching for the coffee pot. 'Did he say where he'd been? What he'd been doing?'

'Not a word, Miss! He made me tell him everything that's been going on here though. And you wouldn't believe how much he's changed.'

'Changed?' Ann tried to keep her voice from sounding too curious.

'He looks older, Miss – and ever so much thinner. And his eyes –'

Aunt Alicia interrupted her impatiently. 'Mrs Mye is trying to say that young Autrey is not quite the same as he was when he went away. But I'm sure *I* shall still recognise him when I see him!' She turned back to the waiting woman and said with cheerful firmness: 'So thank you Mrs Mye for letting me know of Mr Autrey's return. I'm sure you'll want to spread the good news around the village and, as it *is* your day off, I won't keep you any longer. Off you go now!'

Mrs Mye appeared not to mind her employer's abruptness. She was probably used to it, thought Ann. But she challenged it herself.

'That was a bit rude, wasn't it, Auntie?'

'Ann, she'd be like that all morning if I let her. She'd drive me crazy. I'll be having a strong word with Mr Autrey myself later on. And letting him know the undesirable effects his theatricals can have on susceptible old ladies.'

*

Aunt Alicia's sense of decency, however, held her back from distracting him from his work. No one else intruded apart from Mrs Mye who took care of his immediate shopping needs. She called in to see her employer again at the end of the day with an update.

'He's still typing, ma'am, Miss Ann,' she said when Ann joined them in the kitchen. 'And he's not eaten a thing all day. I've left him some sandwiches so's he can have them later on.'

'I shouldn't worry too much,' Ann advised her. 'Some writers are like that. They'll keep going 'til they drop. I'm told Handel didn't eat for a week when he was composing *The Messiah*. You'll probably find him asleep over his typewriter in the morning!'

He was still working when Ann went to bed. She stood at the open window listening, wondering how he could go on like that for hour after hour, without even a pause for a mistake or revision. She tried turning her attention to the dark silhouette of the forest, but the continuous and monotonous sound of the typewriter made it impossible to concentrate on anything. She closed the window and went to bed, plugging her ears with cotton wool.

Mrs Mye arrived next morning with a worried look. 'He ain't been to bed all night,' she said, as Ann and her Aunt sat down to breakfast. 'And he ain't touched the sandwiches I left for him, either. He's as bright as a cricket though, and he said he ain't got much more to do, so perhaps he'll eat something then. I noticed one thing, though ...' she added with a sudden smile, '... it's for you, Miss Ann!'

Ann's heart skipped a beat.

'What *do* you mean, Mrs Mye?' demanded Aunt Alicia.

'Nothing really, ma'am. It was just this big envelope I saw – like the ones he uses when he sends his stories to magazines and such. It were addressed to "Miss Ann Singlewood", ma'am.'

*

Ann was busy in the kitchen making raspberry jam when Mrs Mye opened the back door later that afternoon and peered around.

'Is the mistress in?' she asked quietly.

'No,' Ann answered, 'she's in the village. We needed some more sugar.'

Mrs Mye's air of secrecy vanished at once, and she entered carrying the mysterious envelope she had mentioned earlier. It was large and bulky. 'He's just given me this to bring to you, Miss!' she said excitedly. 'And he says would you please read it as soon as you can.'

'Really!' Ann exclaimed, her hands suddenly shaking. Then she turned back to the preserving pan, feigning indifference. 'Could you just leave it over there on the table ...?'

Mrs Mye hesitated. 'But the mistress ...'

'My dear good woman!' Ann snapped, wishing she would leave her alone. 'If you're suggesting that my aunt would interfere with something addressed to me ...'

'No, Miss! Of course not! It's just that she seemed a bit annoyed this morning. I thought she might get upset if she saw it lying around.'

Privately Ann thought the same. There would be no peace if her aunt knew she had the manuscript. Ann would either have to read it to her, or her aunt would insist on reading it for herself before letting her see it. That was the last thing she wanted. It was silly to have lost her temper with the housekeeper though.

'I'm sorry I spoke to you like that, Mrs Mye. It was wrong of me. I'd be grateful if you would take the envelope up to my room, please. Thank you.'

'Of course, Miss.' Ann was sure she detected a smug smile on Mrs Mye's face as she left the room.

*

The rest of the day dragged on so long that in the end Ann invented a non-existent headache and retired to bed early. Curled up on her divan, she pulled the manuscript from its envelope and began to read ...

PART II

WYCHY

THE LITTLE KINGDOM — AS THE FAE KNOW IT.

CHAPTER 6

'HAEL AND WYN, WICCA'

Dear Ann,

This is for you, because you were there at this tale's beginning and you are the reason for its end.

You know who I am, my name and occupation, and perhaps my age of thirty-three. What I urgently need to tell you is what happened to me the day I vanished, and how and why I have come back.

It began the very day you arrived to stay with your aunt. I was supposed to be going away the following day to research another angle on Weir Forest. By late afternoon, however, I thought I was having an attack of the 'collywobbles' from something I'd either eaten or drunk. I had come in from writing in the garden for a scotch and soda – only I'd run out of soda so I had it with water instead. I sat in the chair wondering where I was going with my story of Hellbane Harry and the Wicked Wizard of Witchery Wood – which seemed to be nowhere because I was too jaded to think creatively. But I felt distinctly odd, as though there was something weird going on inside me. I wondered if I should call a doctor because my eyes seemed to be losing focus as well.

Then the most extraordinary thing happened. A three-inch-long gold and ebony stick started writing on the wall in golden letters the words that I had spoken to my house-keeper that morning: *'Mrs Mye, I'm going to disappear!'*

I must have lost consciousness then, for the next thing I remember is opening my eyes to find myself enveloped in some kind of white material. Mystified and alarmed, I fought to escape. It was like struggling inside the folds of a deflated barrage balloon. It billowed, heaved and twisted about me as I strove to break out of it. When I finally managed to free myself, I faced another shock: I was standing in the middle of my armchair – naked and no more than nine inches tall! I must have been unconscious for some time because moonlight was streaming in through the windows. And now I could see the white stuff I had been fighting – it was the collapsed folds of my own shirt!

My first thought was for poor Mrs Mye. What would she make of it when she came in the morning? What had happened to me? I pinched myself hard, but the pain was all too real for a dream. I looked down at myself and saw that my tiny form was almost golden in colour, and my hands and feet were tapered and slender. I tentatively patted around on my head and discovered a widow's peak and pointed ears. I decided that I *was* dreaming after all, only it must be a nightmare. I needed to try and wake up. But how?

I climbed up onto the arm of the chair where there was a shaft of moonlight falling through the open window. I was amazed to find that it warmed my skin, just like the sun. I shaded my eyes and squinted up at it in awe; its warm, brilliant light filled me with the most intense happiness I had ever experienced. Fear and panic forgotten, I leapt from the arm of the chair to the window-sill to bask in the warmth. The jump was effortless – almost as if I could fly. I looked out of the window. The half circle of the moon an object of indescribable beauty that filled me with joy. Inky black shadows on the stone wall at the bottom of my garden appeared to be solid, as if they had been carved by knives. Slanting shafts of moonlight shone through the branches of the solitary apple tree and fell on flowerbeds, which glowed with vibrant colour – white, gold, mauve, blue, yellow and red. At the base of the wall, young plants shot up in streams of living colour, and the lawn was greener than I had ever seen it by day. I felt drunk with ecstasy. It was *moon-day* – and it was mine!

I barely realised I had jumped before I was racing across the lawn. Though my feet barely seemed to touch the ground, I experienced inconceivable delight every time they made contact. Hidden waves of energy surged up from secret springs below, and honeysuckle perfume coiled around my flying body and caressed it. In another enormous bound I reached the far wall. At that very same moment I heard a sound and looked back. At an open window next door I saw a girl – it was *you*, Ann. But I stared at you without understanding – it was as if you were alien. I seemed robbed of all ties with humanity. Your hands were resting on the windowsill as you leaned forward, staring in my direction. I noted your every feature – the thick brown curls framing your oval face, a perfect button nose, half-parted lips showing white, even teeth … and all the while I gazed into the deep wells of two beautiful brown eyes that gazed back into mine. Even though I didn't know whose face it was, in the instant before I flung myself from the wall, a name rang through my hypersensitive mind: *Ann Singlewood*. And the next moment I was racing down the lane behind our cottages with the hysterical exhilaration of a prisoner unexpectedly freed from a life sentence.

I had put nearly a mile between myself and the village before I stopped running, and by then I was well within the precincts of the forest. Some elemental instinct was sending me joyfully into Adder's Wale by way of Wisher's

Barn where the forest lay in dense shadow. The whole place was breathing new meaning into me, and I longed to rush headlong and embrace it. But I suddenly sensed something dark and disapproving that put a halt to my joyous abandon.

Abruptly, I turned aside and sped into Wisher's Barn, dived under its lowest iron rail, and stared up at the dwarf conifers that now stood immense and commanding. I was in shadow and my mood began to readjust. My exuberance had disappeared and my usual rational self had returned. So I stood there chewing my lip, filled with doubt and wrestling with resentment. Here I was, nine inches of nothing, completely naked and receptive to all kinds of rubbish. The elemental state that I had been in was pulling at me, drawing me in, begging to be accepted. But I was instinctively repelling it, unwilling to surrender to anything I couldn't understand. I realised then that I had become two distinct personalities: one artless and instinctive, the other reasoning, critical and sophisticated. Wild happiness tore at my heart on the one hand, while on the other a grim determination held me fast.

My emotions began to slip from side to side. Trying to retain any mood was as difficult as keeping my balance on a rubber ball. 'Hang it all,' I argued inwardly, 'the whole thing is absurd!' This sort of thing just didn't happen. It was irrational, unreasonable – and quite, quite impossible. I suddenly shouted aloud, 'What's happening to me?' And as I shouted, ripples of movement radiated out from me, splashing like pebbles falling into a pool, rattling against the trees, clattering through the railings and quivering the tips of every blade of grass in the meadow beyond.

'Extraordinary,' I said quietly. Then, because I was so intrigued, 'Ha!' and 'Hum!' and 'I'll be blowed!'

Suddenly I heard a voice right next to me: 'Hael and wyn, wicca! Hael and wyn!'

I swung around in alarm. The speaker was a fellow of my own proportions, with large elliptical eyes and a pleasant but concerned expression. I felt self-conscious as I noticed that he was clothed and I was not. But what clothes! A jerkin of russet, held with an amber encrusted belt, hose of marigold yellow, and soft shoes of the same shade as his jerkin. In his hand, a high-pointed cap, doffed for the moment with his greeting.

'Who the devil do you think you are?' I demanded.

'We are the little people, brother,' he replied.

His dignified response struck right to the heart of all I was trying to fight. He cocked his head on one side and said sympathetically: 'Haven't found your sea legs yet, old man, eh? That's what it is, isn't it?'

'You what?' I exclaimed.

'Tell you what,' he said, 'suppose I start by telling you what happened to me?'

That sounded more reassuring, so I nodded. 'Go on.'

'I've only been here a week, so I can remember more than most of the half born – that's what we call the new arrivals. It began with Simmonds watering down my whisky. The fool thought I wouldn't notice! And I didn't until I'd taken a couple of sips. Too late then, of course; the damage was done. Simple as that, you see. Though how the stuff got in, I don't know.'

'Hang on! What stuff?'

'Wizard's Woe. You wouldn't know about that, of course, but it got into my whisky, same as it must have got into something you ate or drank recently –'

'What does it –?'

'No, just a minute, old boy, please don't interrupt. I'm explaining it, aren't I? Now, Wizard's a tiny plant – so small that botanists haven't even discovered it yet. Trouble is, it has a fatal effect on certain human constitutions, with the result that these people not only pass *out*, they also pass *on* ... to this sort of extra-dimensional existence. You follow me?'

'Sort of,' I said, remembering the water I had put with my own whisky. I tried to remember where it had come from. Not the tap, no ... there had been a jug of it on the sideboard ... put there by Mrs Mye when she saw that I was short on soda.

'Good. Well, after an hour or so, I began to notice that things were no longer under my control. Felt queasy – kind of drying up sensation in the tummy, if you know what I mean. Rang for Simmonds to phone the MO. Simmonds didn't arrive of course, because he'd already had a nip out of the bottle himself and was unconscious in the pantry. Tried to ring the doc myself. Couldn't – blacked out. Swish! Just like that!' He made an extravagant gesture with one arm, and then looked at me speculatively. 'Next thing I knew, I was crawling out of the bod like a butterfly out of a chrysalis. Gruesome experience – last thing I wanted to see! After that, every-thing seemed to come crashing down on me. Had to get away. Suppose you felt much the same, eh?'

'Y-e-s,' I said slowly. There appeared to be an elusive something that didn't quite match up in our experiences. Curiosity compelled me to ask what had happened to Simmonds.

'Oh, found him as soon as I got outside. Streaking across the lawn – starkers – broad daylight too! Of course, he'd no more understanding of what had happened than I had. Just knew we had to get to the forest. Disappointed in Simmonds, though. Ex-CPO ought to be able to adjust himself to any surroundings. But the fool won't even admit he's a half born. Well, that's the story. Can't substantiate it, of course.'

'You don't have to,' I said quickly, as things suddenly clicked into place. 'For the past week the whole county has been discussing the inexplicable deaths of Commander Cochrane Laudley, Royal Navy Retired, and his man, ex-Chief Petty Office Simmonds – both of Hurstlea. Their post-mortems found no discernable cause of death, and both were presumed to have died at the same time.'

'Well there you are, old man!' He spread his hands and beamed with delight. 'Exit Cocky Laudley – enter Loy! That's what I'm called here by the way. What's your name?'

'August Autrey,' I said distractedly, my mind busy with the implications of what he had told me. 'What about getting back?' I asked.

'Getting back? Who'd want to?' he answered in surprise. '*I've* no worries here. I've got a whole new, and very enjoyable, way of life – and I'm young again! I've no bod to go back to anyway.'

'Ha!' I said, suddenly recognising the difference in our experiences. Laudley had 'crawled out of his bod' – he'd seen it from the outside and run away from it. But it hadn't been like that for me. I'd crawled out of my shirt – there was no 'bod' left behind. So it still had to be somewhere … which meant there must also be a way of getting back.

'Someone did mention something called Wych's Bane,' Loy answered when I pointed this out. 'Seems it's another weed – a sort of opposite number to Wizard's Woe. I understand it's one of the ways out of the little kingdom – if you *really* wanted to go …'

'Where is it?' I asked eagerly. 'Lead me to it!'

'Sorry old man, wouldn't know it if I saw it. Besides, there's some kind of snag with it. Unpleasant subject – you'll have to ask the Wands.'

'And what the devil are they?'

'Who – not what, old man!' I was corrected. 'Darned if I can say, really, now you come to ask. It's what they say round here. Anyone asks you a question you can't answer, you pass the buck by referring them to the Wands. As far as I can gather, there are two of them; a pair of VIPs who're responsible for our wellbeing. But actually *asking* them anything – now that's another matter entirely. I wouldn't even know *how* to find them. All I know is that they live in a place called The Wandle – if you know where that is …?'

'I do!' I said. 'According to local tradition in Three Weirs, it's where some kind of prehistoric magician called the Witchett lives.'

Loy stared for a moment, then burst out laughing. 'Well that's a new one on me, August! Shows how much rural memory gets addled over the centuries, doesn't it? Your *Witchetts* must mean our *Wychies*.'

I shrugged the distinction aside. 'Witchett is also the name they give to the lower of the two Weirs this side of The Wandle – Witchett's Weir.'

'*Wychies!*' he broke in emphatically. 'And it isn't Weir, it's Weird – *Wychies' Weird*! See what I mean?'

'It's weird, all right,' I grumbled. 'Probably why I can't see the difference.'

'A Wychy or a Wych,' said Loy, as carefully as his irresponsible nature allowed, 'is the equivalent of a wizard or a witch. And a Weird – well, that's a number of things. It's one of the three Weirds round The Wandle, as you said. It's also one's fate or destiny. And it's a kind of cloak as well – something the Wychies always wear, or so they tell me. And now we've got that out of the way, how about joining some of the lads and lasses – or wiccas and wiccies, I should say?'

'Hang on!' I stopped him. 'Am I really expected to make social calls in the altogether? Or is there a nudist colony I can join?'

'Clothing is sure to be provided, August,' he said lightly, bounding out of the trees, turning a somersault, then standing erect, his arms raised to the moon, while I joined him in a more sedate manner.

'Isn't she wonderful!' he exulted. 'Can't you feel her goodness pouring into you?'

Of course I could. Flooded again by the rays, the same wild surge of delight filled me. It took a tremendous effort to fight it.

'Remarkable thing, y'know,' Loy went on, 'We're only awake when the sun or moon is above the horizon. You'll understand what I mean when Mona sets in about an hour's time. Between then and sunrise you'll simply pass out, so it's important to be under cover by then.' He led the way along the track, then laughed and shouted, 'Look – a reception committee!'

I had seen them too; three colourful figures sitting on a low bank. They sprang up immediately and ran to meet us.

'Meet Ringo, Honeyball and Winzey!' Loy shouted joyfully. Then he added proudly, as if I was someone special, 'Wiccas, this is August!'

The three were so excited they could hardly keep still. Their arms fluttered for a second or two as if they wanted to embrace me, but then, when their clear honey-coloured eyes met mine, they wavered and looked hesitantly back at Loy.

'What is it, dear fellows?' asked the wicca anxiously. 'What's wrong?'

'Nothing *wrong*, dear Loy,' answered Ringo after a pause. ''Tis only that … but have you not already noticed?'

'His eyes, Loy,' said Honeyball. 'They are not like ours.'

Winzey nodded in agreement. 'They are not the eyes of a wicca, Loy. Ours are clear – amber, hazel or gold – eyes that are open and easy to read …'

'Well, I'm blessed!' said Loy staring at my eyes. 'Thought there was something, but couldn't quite put my finger on it. August, your eyes are *grey – deep grey!*'

'So what?' I said brusquely, 'Some people call them black!'

'They are wyché eyes!' said Honeyball quietly, as if this accounted for everything.

'Meaning?' I challenged, feeling nettled by this strange discussion.

'Wyché means ... *wise*, August,' he said. 'It's all things which are unclear to us – things we don't understand. That's the only way I can explain it.'

'All right then,' I said, mollified by the apparent compliment. But the other three had disappeared. Before I could ask where they'd gone, they were back, scampering over the bank with a selection of clothes that made my eyes widen and my jaw drop. Passing the garments swiftly from hand to hand, they laid them out for my inspection and began discussing the most suitable.

'The wild cherry,' voted Winzey, shaking out a gossamer doublet. 'And here's a cap to go with it, banded with the breast feathers of a bullfinch –'

'No,' said Ringo, 'this wandle-side green is better –'

'Or the May-sky blue?' suggested Honeyball.

'Okay,' I said, 'if I've really got to wear this clobber ...' I leant down and selected a set that had attracted me from the start. '... then I suppose this is as good as any.'

'Knew you'd fall for that one!' cried Loy in triumph. 'The grey-blue of the woodpigeon. And here are the shoes and cap to match.'

When I was dressed they hustled me over to a puddle of rainwater to see my reflection by moonlight. I didn't look too bad, I thought, and I smiled. I thought about how ungracious and boorish I had been, so I thanked them for all they had done. 'It was kind of you to go to so much trouble.'

'No trouble!' said Honeyball happily. 'The clothes were right there!'

'Weren't you all sent to meet me?'

They shook their heads.

'Doubtless we were wandled!' said Winzey with a smile.

Remembering the conversation about The Wandle and the two omniscient beings said to live there, I made no effort to ask what he meant.

'Let us tarry here no longer, wiccas!' called Honeyball suddenly, his head on one side as if listening. 'Mona is nearly to her couch as we must be to ours.'

'What did I tell you?' Loy reminded me as we hurried up the track. 'Got to get under cover before moonset.'

'Why?' I asked. 'You said that as soon as the moon set we'd pass out until sunrise. Why can't we sleep in the open?'

'Oh, no, no!' Ringo stopped and turned to me anxiously. 'You must *never* do that, August! The Scathe will find you ... and you'll be wannioned!'

I felt a bitter chill run through me, and shook it off with some effort. 'All these Anglo-Saxon words sound very romantic,' I grumbled, 'but what the blazes to they mean?'

Winzey shuddered apprehensively and whispered, 'The Scathe is the breath of Dragga which lures the little people to their doom. He breathes it out from his Weird whenever Sunné and Mona are not above to protect us. So we must hide until daybreak ...'

''Tis said,' cut in Ringo in an even lower voice, 'that when Mona disappears into Sunné's embrace – as happens once between each High Moon – it becomes the Wreak – which is terrible!'

'You mean at new moon?' I said, a distant memory returning. 'I've heard about that. They say there's a gas that rises out of Dragon's Woe – some kind of miasma. That must be what you call the Scathe.'

'You must mean Dragga's Weird,' Honeyball corrected me. 'There's no Dragon's Woe here.'

'Okay,' I waved it aside. 'But what is wannioning?'

'Too dreadful to think about!' said Honeyball. 'Please, August, don't talk about it or we shall catch The Mortal Sickness.'

But I was too engrossed in thought to pay much attention. 'Wannion ...' I mused aloud. 'That must come from the Anglo-Saxon word "wane" – to diminish, to fade away –'

'*August!*' they implored me, covering their ears and looking at me with pain in their eyes. '*Please!*'

'But I'm only explaining the meaning of a word,' I protested. 'Everything wanes sooner or later. The moon wanes every month ...'

Before I could say any more, Loy and I were alone. He was hopping from foot to foot, clearly torn between going after the others or staying with me. 'I promise you, August, we *do* need to move,' he pleaded.

'All right,' I said, humouring him and thinking what a strange mixture he was – one moment remembering his life as royal naval officer and the next in fear of his life over some silly superstition. Still, when in Rome ...

He said nothing more until we came to a huge tree at the centre of a clearing. 'Ah, Great Oak!' he exclaimed with relief. 'We call it the Trysting Tree, the meeting of the ways, because every path in the forest leads to it – which is jolly useful for me because my hideout's just there.' He pointed to a decaying oak near the large one.

Jumping lightly to a hole three feet up from the ground, he waved and disappeared. I followed him and found steps inside leading down to a bed of bark dust. It gave off a pleasant, wholesome and reassuring fragrance when I sank into it, and I was soon in a dreamless oblivion ... where I remained for the next few hours.

CHAPTER 7

HYLLIS

I woke with the dawn, feeling more than simply content – I was wholly happy. The colours of my costume delighted me; their subtle iridescence changing from shining blue to grey and grey to blue with every movement I made. I fingered the silken thongs at my neck and wrists, tightened the sapphire-studded belt, donned my cap at a jaunty angle, and bounded up the steps.

A wonderland met my eyes. Inquisitive sunbeams lit up dew-laden blades of grass in a sea of flashing jewels. Spiders' webs stretching between them spread breathtaking patterns of light: ruby, emerald, topaz, sapphire, carnelian, opal and amethyst, each radiating starry auras. A sprinkled carpeting of bluebells caught my eye, and my enchanted senses heard tiny ripples of bells, echoing and bounding from bloom to bloom, making me gasp in wonder. Every direction glowed with colour; yellow archangel and pimpernel, the soft mauve petals and yellow spikes of woody nightshade, spires of pink spotted foxgloves, and arching branches of delicate wild rose.

The approaching sound of Loy and four companions brought me back to myself – and I goggled at the sight. Loy was wearing brown and gold, with one of the males in rose and green, and the other in crimson and blue. They were accompanied by two visions in robes that were almost transparent; one in the pink and white of apple blossom, the other in love-in-the-mist blue. I leapt from the tree to meet them.

Loy clapped me on the shoulder. 'Jean, Lettice, meet August, the new half born. You've met Winzey, old man ... and this is Fizzy – short for Fitz-something or other, he's forgotten the rest of it.'

We wiccas smiled, bowing to each other and to the wiccies, who curtsied in response. I could hardly take my eyes off the golden-haired Lettice in her blue gown. I had never seen anyone so exquisitely beautiful.

'Well, is it not tasteful?' asked Winzey, drawing attention to my costume.

'Possibly ...' Fizzy cocked his head to one side, one eye half closed, '... a shade more mellow in the hose ...?'

'Of course,' said Loy. 'I had intended blue and gold but was persuaded otherwise. I think he could do with a touch of embellishment though, here and there –'

'No, Loy!' interrupted the dark-haired wiccy called Jean. 'The pigeon-grey and blue is perfection for August – 'tis nearest the hue of his eyes.'

Lettice stood behind me and rested a soft hand on my shoulder – a delicious contact that sent electric waves through my body. I turned to look into hazel eyes that searched mine, and my heart turned over.

'They are the hue of water-worn stones shining in the summer rain,' she said. 'And are wondrous wyché.'

Since my eyes seemed destined to become a permanent source of comment, I opened them a little wider, but she looked startled and turned her head away. Her reaction surprised me, and I was not a little disappointed.

Loy and the others were strolling away from the oak, and I slid an arm around my new admirer's waist to go after them. She accepted it and, to my delight, slipped hers around mine. In that moment this bright new world became a thousand times more wonderful. I bent my head close to hers and whispered, 'Are all wiccies as beautiful as you, Lettice?'

She smiled back warmly. 'None is *un*-beautiful, August. But some are more beautiful.'

'I don't believe it,' I said, and continued with unaccustomed ardour, 'Your golden skin is truly wonderful. There are no blemishes in it anywhere … at least, as far as I can see!'

'You speak as one who has the Mood upon him, August,' she said doubtfully.

'The Mood?' I asked. 'Well, if it's the feeling I'm getting at the moment then it's a good thing.'

She looked at me, her lovely eyes wide as she again searched mine. Then she sighed. 'No, August; what you are feeling is not an elfin mood. You look at me like Barney does, and he does not understand the Mood.'

'Who's Barney?'

'Barney is a half born who cannot forget his mortality,' she said sadly. 'His eyes are all over a wiccy's body – he doesn't see the essential being within. *Please*,' she entreated, shrinking against my arm, 'don't *you* look at me like that, August.'

'But you are so beautiful, Lettice – I can't *help* looking at you. I've never seen anyone as stunningly beautiful as you before. Surely there's no harm in telling you how lovely you are? Your shape is so perfect and –'

'August, *please*! No!' She began to tremble and her arm fell away from my waist. 'I am not in the Mood! It is not good that you should draw me like this. Your words are like sharp thorns tearing my heart. Dear August, I beg you to stop, you are wiling me to your weird with such sweet pain; it is like a dark fire that has no flame.'

'I was only being honest and saying how much I admire you,' I said, feeling like the injured party. 'I meant no harm. I wouldn't hurt you for worlds. Don't be angry with me.'

She shuddered violently and drew away. 'Harm? Hurt? Angry? These are *awful* words, August. They fall from your lips like the droplets of blood a sparrow sheds beneath the talons of a hawk. And your eyes are as hard as granite. Go away! Go away!' She cast me one last look of horror, then fled.

Dismay overwhelmed me. What had I done to deserve such awful words? I was too surprised to follow her immediately. When I did, she had disappeared – along with the rest of the party – leaving me to wallow in anger and remorse that I could neither understand nor control.

When I calmed down sufficiently to see the truth, I realised that I had committed a crime. I had given pain to one of the gentlest beings this world could ever know. Of course she couldn't be angry – the very sound of the word had made her distraught. Whereas, fired by her delicate beauty, and excited by the touch of her hand, I had desired her with all the greediness of human passion.

Lost in this perplexing whirlpool of emotion, I wandered unseeingly towards the sunken track leading to the heights. Leaping down onto it, I surprised a couple of ethereally clad wiccas wandering by, chattering and laughing. They stopped, stared at me for a second, and were gone – I had no time to even hail them. I realised now that something was very wrong – that it was the deadly, mortal part of me, still at the surface, that had scared them. I felt even more desperately alone. Something newly found was gone; something impossible to miss until I had lost it. The towering trees I passed appeared aloof, silent and critical.

I arrived at the crest of the sheer cliff overhanging the two Weirs – or Weirds as Loy had called them – and threw myself down on the grass, staring across at The Wandle. If

I hadn't been so upset I would have been ecstatic at the sight. But instead I felt disconsolate as I wondered what to make of this unbelievable existence. It was, I decided, anything but a dream. It was too rational. Everything I had experienced so far, everything I had learned, made sense. It locked together like a well-devised structure that definitely wasn't dreamlike. And what about the people, whose thoughts and emotions were all so perfect? They were all so … Arcadian.

I looked down at the waters. Compared with my human memory, they were vast; King's Weir and Witchett's Weir – or, as I now knew them, King's Weird and Wychies' Weird. Dragga's Weird was out of sight.

Dragga, I thought, was an Anglo-Saxon word meaning *to draw*. It was a simple misinterpretation on the locals' part, calling it Dragon's Woe. But what a difference in the meaning! What had Loy said? 'Dragga's breath *draws* us to our doom.' I shivered. Fairyland had its dark side too, it seemed. But who were these two Wychies that the country folk insisted were the Witchett? I gazed across at the enigmatic Wandle and suddenly grinned as I remembered my own creation: Hellbane Harry, the Wicked Wizard of Witchery Wood! I had based him on the mysterious Witchett and his woody Wandle.

A squirrel scuttling between the pines made me look round. The little grey robber froze for an instant, his graceful tail a furry plume over his back. He examined me and decided I was no threat, then returned to his work with an urgency. He needs food, I thought. But *I* didn't! I felt neither hunger nor thirst, only an intense desire for Lettice's love. I thought enviously of Loy. He seemed to have no difficulty with Jean; I had seen them wander off happily with their arms around each other. Why couldn't I be like him and simply succumb to this carefree existence? But something in me stuck fast. I was a prisoner. I had *not* died – I had been *hijacked*! Show me the way out and August the immortal would scarper back to mortality so fast the little people wouldn't see his heels for dust!

'Hael and wyn, wicca!' A brown-haired vision in forget-me-not blue sank gracefully down by my side. I must have been very deep in thought not to have sensed her approach. A bandlet of turquoise around her hair caught my attention almost as soon as her golden eyes did.

'I think you are too beautiful for sadness, August,' she said, with surprising frankness and an inviting smile.

I lifted myself onto an elbow. 'I am too sad to feel beautiful, wiccy,' I said. Her refreshing presence was calming me.

'You *are* a disturbing person, August,' she said, her head on one side studying me, as if confirming something she had been told.

'Seems to be a habit of mine,' I said. 'Someone else said much the same thing this morning.'

She nodded. 'I know. Lettice is fully born and easily hurt. I have sent her to the Wands for comfort.'

'Everyone speaks to me in riddles,' I complained. 'And I'm getting tired of asking questions. There are things I want to know and all anyone ever says is "Ask the Wands".' I turned to her. 'So what's your name?'

'Hyllis.'

'Hyllis …' I savoured the sound for a while, then said earnestly, 'Hyllis, I am riddled with woes. Things are going around in my head – I don't suppose you'll understand, but I'm different from you people. I am a *man*, not a fay. My name is Augustus Autrey; a mortal born, immortally undead. My age is thirty-three. I come from sturdy Sussex stock. I live in a house. I have travelled in aeroplanes, ships and trains. I eat and drink. I think all the time. I work. I'm used to solid things. I … I …'

The touch of her hand stroking my hair brought me to a halt. It was soothing – and enormously stimulating.

'I thought I had forgotten, August … but now I remember …' she spoke softly and dreamily. '*All* half borns feel like this. It is not easy. We have to learn how to live all over again. Some are never reconciled – like poor Sinjohn, who believes he is still human, and tries to live and speak and act like one.'

'He sounds like a job for the Wands,' I said dryly. 'But I *am* human, I am *not* dead!'

'Then, by your own words, you too sound like a job for the Wychy!' She laughed, drawing tendrils of hair aside from her face. She was so lovely that I was content to watch her graceful gestures, the movement of her lips, and the changing shades of colour in her smiling eyes as she spoke.

'Aren't you going to run away from me – like Lettice?' I asked.

'How can I when you draw me to you, August?' She smiled, her fingers caressing my cheek. 'If we wiccies admire a wicca, we tell him so. If we need him to love us, we leave him in no doubt.'

'Hang on!' I said. 'That's all I did to Lettice – and look what happened! I told her I admired her, and she said I was behaving like some big bad wolf called Barney!'

'And weren't you?' A twinkle in her eye belied her demure tone. 'Poor August! You don't understand. And how can you? It was many moons before I understood the real nature of the Mood. Perhaps if Lettice had been in the Mood she might not have become so alarmed.'

'So what about you?' I asked. 'You don't seem scared of me.'

'Then perhaps I should be!' she said, glancing at me mischievously. 'I'm afraid you're going to upset a good many wiccies before very long, dear August. It's your eyes. They're like black pearls, and very, very inviting. They can be like a storm, yet they are kind. These matters are hard to know. White Wand could explain. She would guide you.'

'And who is White Wand?' I asked.

Hyllis sighed with contentment. 'She is the loveliest of all the fae, August. She is very, very wise. All the little people worship her, but only the Wychy may love her – and live! The wiccas sing to her when the Mood is upon them – as the wiccies do to Black Wand. When he hears their song, he sends love into the heart of a wicca that he may consummate her love. 'Tis a very sad song,' she assured me dreamily, and began to sing with yearning and earnestness:

> Black Wand! Black Wand!
> Be thou my wizard, Wand!
> Wyn me my wicca, Wand
> Anguish is on me.
>
> Woe's in my heart, Wand
> Dread's in the depth of me!
> Sped is my happiness
> Joy is gone from me!
>
> Come with thy wealing, Wand!
> Love has bewrayed me!
> Bless with thy healing, Wand
> Wyn me, my Wand!

The simple words filled my heart with my own despair – and longing for her.

'You *are* still thinking like a man, August,' she chided softly. 'Your heart is in anguish, and I cannot understand it, but it draws me to comfort you. You draw me with your eyes, like Barney. He *speaks* to a wiccy like a man, but he *stares* at her like a satyr …'

I caught the hand stroking my cheek and kissed it, unable to resist revelling in the symmetry of her face, the majestic arches of eyebrows no mortal hand could pencil, the lashes that lay in perfect fringes on her golden cheeks, and the lips that smiled and moved with tacit invitation.

'And do *I* stare at you like an insatiable satyr?' I asked. She was certainly making me feel like one.

She laughed. 'No, August, you are too wyché; the distress is in other ways.'

I kissed her palms and murmured, 'Explain more of the meaning of the Mood, enchantress.'

Her hands joined mine and our fingers entwined.

''Tis the commencement of the Sickness, August. 'Tis an illness that cries in pain for succour. *Lo, I drown in the dark waters of despair. Help me for I languish –*'

'But *I* don't say any of these things,' I said breathlessly, pressing her weaving hands even closer.

'Dearest August, you don't need to – there's mortality behind your every look. 'Tis in the timbre of your voice. What wiccy can resist such poignant appeal?'

I opened my eyes and saw a new Hyllis – a languid, yearning being, consumed with elemental desire. A moment later she framed my face with hands as delicate as the petals of a rose, and drew it down to hers. Eyes of clearest amber looked into my own, and breath sweeter than honeysuckle fanned my cheeks. Then a pair of exquisitely melting lips merged trembling with mine …

CHAPTER 8

HELLBANE HARRY

The sun had descended behind The Wandle and the moon well risen before we left Wandleside and meandered, arms entwined, speaking in low loving tones, our words besprinkled with endearments and caresses.

'And this is the Immortal Mood, dear heart?' I asked.

She leaned her head back on my shoulder and kissed my chin. 'Not altogether *Im*-mortal, beloved!' she laughed happily and nestled in my neck. 'Your kisses burn like a flame into a wiccy's soul! The Mood should bear one up to transcendent bliss – but *your* love is like a storm. It is irresistible; frightening – yet compelling. Your eyes rend my heart as lightning the oak. Oh, August, you are both misery and joy! Be sparing of your love, dearest one – lest you send all your lovers hurtling back into Mortality.'

We sauntered on in silence while I thought about this paradox. Then:

'I must find Lettice and apologise for this morning. Where shall I find her, dear heart?'

She gave a merry laugh and squeezed my fondling hand. 'Foolish August! Did I not tell you that White Wych has comforted her?'

'You said,' I recalled, 'that you had "sent her" to White Wand. So how do you know that she got there? How did she cross the Weirds? And if she did, how could she know where the Wych lived in The Wandle?'

Hyllis greeted all this with another little laugh. 'Oh, August, how I love you! You are just like a baby bird teetering on the edge of his nest – so eager to fly – so fearful of the empty air. Do not worry for Lettice, my love, she is content again.'

She sighed. 'I wish I knew whether *I* were happy or sad, beloved. I am unsettled, I know, and I think I too shall need to find the Wands.'

'But –' I began, and fell silent, frustrated by her earlier assurance that the matter was unexplainable.

As if she read my thoughts, she said: 'The Wychies are very wise, August. They know us all, love us all, and feel every pang we suffer. Please, be patient.'

To my utter surprise, she then gently released herself from me, clasped my hands for a second, kissing them, and with a valedictory 'Hael and wyn, beloved one!' she was gone!

The suddenness of her departure left me stunned. I rushed off in the direction I thought she had taken, imploring her name. But after dashing this way and that through a forest of bracken I realised that she was simply nowhere to be found.

I felt like an abandoned child. There was a terrible ache in my breast and tears in my eyes as I wound my way forlornly through the bracken stems.

Then my sterner side resumed control and I castigated myself for giving way to such infantile sorrow.

'You snivelling idiot!' I sneered. 'There's your answer. "Cry for succour," says she. And what happens? You howl like a banshee with a belly ache. And get what? Nothing – except knowing you've made a complete fool of yourself!' I turned and ran in a contrary direction and came upon Loy tripping down a forest path without a care in the world. He waved a hand.

'Hael and wyn, August! Settling down?'

'Not in the least,' I was happy to assure him grimly. 'Know where Hyllis is?'

He looked at me curiously. 'Not pulling my leg are you? According to the bush telegraph you and she – well, not my business of course – but still, if *you* don't know …'

'I've lost her, Loy! She went off about half an hour ago …'

He made noises intimating sympathy. 'Too bad! Twice in one day, old man! You'll be getting a bad name, you know!' He fingered his chin reflectively. 'Shows you though, doesn't it? I thought the Forest Telegraph Service was infallible.'

'What *are* you burbling about?'

'Not come across it yet? Well, there's a sort of communal intelligence that runs through the Forest. I don't know how it works yet, but everyone – except me – seems to know what's happening just as it happens, if you get what I mean. Sometime this afternoon a little bird whispered in my ear that you and Hyllis were up above Wandleside. And – well – I expect the details were a bit exaggerated, but the general impression was that you and she …' He made a comprehensive gesture. 'Still, if you *weren't* …' he added disappointedly, '… then that's that. Pity, all the same –'

I laughed and sat down at the side of the path with my back against a sapling.'This is a mad hole, Loy! I can't make head nor tail of it. One minute you're in unutterable misery, the next in overwhelming joy. One girl screams with fright because you make observations on her vital statistics, the next one – well, we won't go into that! Apparently the *News of the Pixie World* has already distributed a pretty lurid account, from what you say – or don't say.'

Loy's brow creased with perplexity. 'Poor old Aug. You do seem to be in a bad way. You talk like poor old Sin. *He's* always worrying about how to put things right –'

'Sin? I've heard of him. Who is he?'

'Name's St John – shortened to Sin. He's one of the rebels – one of the fellows who won't give in, you know. Good old die-hard. Won't admit he's not alive as a mortal. Won't wear our clothing, won't mix, won't do anything we do. Those are his principles and he's sticking to them. But at least he keeps himself to himself. Doesn't go round scaring the wiccies like that bounder Barney –'

'That's another name I keep hearing,' I interrupted.

'Short for Barnsley,' he said. 'Fellow with a roving eye. Fancies he's the answer to every wiccy's prayer. Always chasing them and frightening them – they mostly keep out of his ways these days. I suppose he's really as harmless as a puppy that hasn't been house-trained.' He sat up with a startled expression. 'Good wiccy! You have me moralising, old man. Here, I'm off before I start looking for the beams in my own eyes!'

I pressed him back with a laugh. 'Loy, you're tonic for an ailing man! Don't leave me – my sanity depends on you, you lazy, lounging elf! How dare you sprawl at your ease without a care in the world? How I envy you; life's good to you, and you enjoy it.'

Loy sighed. 'What a strange fellow you are, August. Can't understand you at all. You're one of the intelligent types; they tell me you wrote stories. I'd have thought you'd have settled down in this sort of land-of-dreams-come-true without a qualm –'

'Oh, should I?' I snarled back, annoyed. 'Let me tell you, Loy. The infantile figments of my imagination at least made sense. Fairies were fairies – and nothing else! And my Wizard was an out and out brigand – you knew where you were with him...' I proceeded to relate some of the history of Hellbane Harry of Witchery Wood. To my discomfort, Loy began to shriek with mirth. 'What's wrong now?' I demanded.

But he only laughed louder. I left him to it and stalked off, wondering whether my fortunes would have been better if my editors had been afflicted with the same sense of humour.

I met Fizzy and a wiccy in lilac and lemon hurrying up the path. 'August!' cried the former. 'What have you done to Loy?'

'Surely he's unwell to make such a commotion?' said his pretty companion in concern.

'He probably will be if he doesn't stop soon,' I judged morosely.

Then Loy's voice came rippling down the path: 'Hellbane Harry the Wicked Witch of Witchery Wood! Oh – oh! I shall burst! Hellbane Harry – ! Oh, no – *can't bear it!* August, it's positively killing me –'

Fizzy and the wiccy sped off towards the sound.

Later, when the moon sank, I returned desolately to Loy's oak, scrambled up and went dejectedly into its depth. I somehow knew he wouldn't be there, and within seconds had drifted away into velvety unconsciousness.

*

I woke at sunrise, turned a somersault for pure joy in the confines of the tree, then remembered Hyllis and became sad. I desperately wanted her. With Hyllis at my side, I believed I could learn to reconcile myself with my surroundings. I walked sombrely up the steps to the opening and jumped lightly to the ground. I was just wondering which way I should go that day when a chorus of voices acclaimed me:

'Hael and wyn, August! Hael and wyn!' About twenty laughing, dancing figures closed in. Hands pulled, patted, caressed and teased me. The babble of voices was almost deafening. I recognised Fizzy and plunged towards him.

'Fizzy! What's to do? Why this alarming popularity?'

"Tis Loy,' he said, then began to laugh immoderately. 'He told us – ha, ha, ha – !' He held his sides, hilarious with glee.

'Hellbane Harry!' someone shouted.

'The Wicked Wizard of Witchery Wood!' continued another.

'Fizzlebane and Fumingwort –'

'Fizzy!' I shook him by the shoulder.

'They want you to tell them your stories, August. They are so, *so* funny!' he explained. 'And we *love* stories –'

'Oh, do you?' I firmly removed a pair of lovely arms from around my neck and another pair from my waist. 'Then go and ask the Wands to oblige!'

'Oh, August! Unkind! Unkind!' came a chorus of reproach. The cry was so sincere, it came to me that they were not laughing at me for being the author of such absurdities, but that they really found the characters irresistible and genuinely wanted to hear more.

'Very well, then,' I agreed graciously. 'Gather round, children, and I will tell you a short one – a *very* short one because I have some business appointments to keep.'

This evoked shrieks of delight at the ridiculous suggestion that a wicca could ever have serious appointments to keep, and they scrambled to find seats around me. I found one on a slightly elevated root of Great Oak, and a flurry of wiccies descended at my feet. The attention was flattering and I gathered two of them in my arms and made them sit on either side of me. A third, unbidden, in speedwell-blue and silver, knelt with forearms crossed on my knees and gazed up out of clear shining eyes. I acknowledged all this with a confidential wink, and began:

'Once upon a time there was a very wicked Wizard. His name was Hellbane Harry and he lived in a dark and dreadful wood –'

'Witchery Wood,' sounded a silvery voice in my ear.

'Like The Wandle?' asked a wicca further out in the crowd.

'Oh, *no*!' he was contradicted by a chorus. 'The Wandle is *dark*, but not *dreadful.*'

I ignored this and continued: 'He lived in a large and dismal castle upon which the sun never shone, and –'

'What was the name of the castle?' demanded someone.

'What did he look like, August?' another enquired.

At this rate, I reasoned, the story was not going to be as short as I had intended.

'His castle was named Castle Dreary, and Hellbane Harry was very tall and very thin. He had a long hooked nose, and very fierce dark eyes –'

'O-o-oh!' The arms round my waist squeezed with delicious anticipation.

'– and thick, bushy, black eyebrows …' I began to enter into the spirit of the tale, giving my voice the necessary emphasis. After all, I reflected, it was because my wood and my wizard were *un*real caricatures of their *real* Wandle and Wychy that they found the images so intriguing. I leaned my cheek against that of the rose and grey clad nymph on my right and continued with an air of cross-my-heart confidence:

'Now the wicked wizard had two familiars –'

The nymph turned wondering eyes on me, asking softly, 'Familiars?'

'Er – imps, my darling,' I said.

'And what are imps, August?' asked the speedwell fay at my knees.

'An imp, delicious…' I began, and hesitated how to describe the chimerical thing. I made an attempt: '… is a very naughty, disobedient spirit. Like … a half born who hasn't yet learned how to be good and kind and loving and beautiful, like you!'

My audience dissolved in merriment.

'Like Sin and Barney!' laughed the wiccy in thrift pink on my left.

'And August?' asked the fay in speedwell softly – but not quietly enough to avoid reaching the ears of the remainder of the circle. Their laughter rang loudly at the quip.

I held up an admonitory hand for silence while I looked down at her archly smiling features and said sotto voce:

'I'll remember that, angel's eyes!'

'My name is Leila,' she whispered intimately.

'I'll remember that too!' I promised.

I had no memory of Hyllis just then. In that hour, I had become as near elemental in my companions' joy as had yet been possible.

'Now these two familiars were named –'

'Fi-zzle-bane and Fu-ming-wort' everyone chanted together.

I bowed to the inevitable and repeated the intonation, 'Fi-zzle-bane and Fu-ming-wort! Fizzlebane was a very long, thin, black fellow with a sad and sorry countenance, whereas Fumingwort was short and round and very fat –'

'What colour are Fizzlebane's eyes?' asked a very solemn look wicca in a rich plum-coloured jerkin and hose.

'Green!' voted someone.

'Yellow!' guessed another. 'Is that not so, August?'

'You are both wrong,' I announced. 'They are green with a yellow iris, and sprinkled with little red spots!'

'I know nothing of eyes like that,' said he of the plum-coloured suiting solemnly. 'Can he see in the dark, August?'

'Of course he can see in the dark, Smye!' a voice answered for me. 'Like foxes and hedgehogs and owls. Else he'd not be black –'

I took advantage of the argument to ask the thrift pink fay on my left, 'Where is Loy?'

'In the brambles with Jean,' she replied as if that accounted for everything – which it did. 'We will see neither of them until sundown.'

'And where …' I suddenly remembered, '… is Hyllis?'

'In The Wandle,' murmured the one on my right. 'Her heart is very sad, August. 'Tis said you were not kind.'

'Not kind –?' I began to retort heatedly, but realising the general argument had suddenly stilled at the words, I stopped. Expectant faces turned towards me, waiting, wondering – and I hastened to fill the gap.

'So, Dreadful the Dragon was sent by his master in search of the maiden Chysobel –'

They pulled me up promptly, reminding me that I must have 'turned over two pages', then led me firmly back to Fizzlebane and Fumingwort and politely requested that I carry on from there.

For another hour or so I continued, improvising and editing, until I declared that the rest of the story must wait until the morrow.

The decision was received with a wail of reproach, for a number of newcomers had not even heard the beginning. There were by then at least a hundred, standing, sitting, and reclining, looking like a variegated bed of richly flowering plants. But I was adamant – and a little anxious not to wear out this popularity too quickly.

So they rose and wandered off in little groups, declaiming the villainies of the characters, imitating my expressions and intonations, and laughing and gesticulating with unconcealed delight.

It was not so easy to dismiss my handmaidens though. When I released them, rose to my feet and kissed their fingers gallantly, they wailed in dismay.

'But why are you leaving us, August?' asked Leila.

'A business trip, my dears –'

'Business? What is business?'

'Well … just now, it means a serious discussion –' I began.

'But, darling August, there *is* nothing serious to discuss!'

They were gently manoeuvring me away from the direction I wanted.

'There is only one serious subject,' Leila insisted. 'And that is the Sickness. You haven't got the Sickness, have you, August?'

'I don't think so –'

'Then how can you be so unkind as to leave us like this?'

With my arms, shoulders and neck encircled by three pairs of some of the loveliest arms in the Little Kingdom, I nearly began to wonder the same thing.

'I really, really do want to make some enquiries,' I said firmly.

'What about?'

'About – well, about myself. Why I'm here, and –'

'The Wands will explain all those things to you in their own good hour, dear August!' said Leila sweetly, holding on to me.

'So I've heard,' I replied, trying as kindly as I could to disengage myself. 'But until they do, I am thrown on my own resources –'

'August!' she wailed. 'You are hurting my hand!'

'Sweet child – if you will only let go of mine …!'

'Who are you going to see?' asked the wiccy in thrift pink.

'Actually, a fellow called Sin,' I said doggedly.

'*Sin!*' Their undisguised dismay should have melted my heart. 'Please, August, please! Don't go to him! If you talk with Sin, he'll steal your heart and harden it against us. You'll stay forever in his horrid house – and we shall never see you again!'

Their hands plucked at me urgently; their faces begged with looks that tore at my heart.

'August, we have just begun to know and love you! Please, please, dear August …'

They suddenly smiled invitingly.

'Stay with us, dear one! We will show you un-imaginable things – beautiful things, things of which your mortality has never dreamed.'

I shook my head sadly, tremendously puzzled even then that I should be able to resist such lovely supplicants.

'Don't fear for me, dear hearts! I have some strange doom to follow. It will not let me rest. I will not desert you. Have I not promised to continue my tale at tomorrow's day-spring?' I drew my hands from theirs and stood back while they gazed at me wistfully.

Leila whispered suddenly, 'Come away, wiccies. August is not to be stayed. We will go and cry our woe to the Wands. They will protect him. They will not let us weep.' The others nodded, then turned together. Leila held their hands and they disappeared between the trees.

And I started walking resolutely towards … nowhere at all.

CHAPTER 9

THE DIE-HARDS

The moment he came into view, I recognised him from the expression on his pasty face, which not even his elfin characteristics could disguise. He leered at me from beneath an imitation Tyrolean hat complete with over-sized jay's feather. He was wearing a belted tweed jacket with uneven patch pockets, a poorly knitted sweater and badly fitting trousers. The neatest part of him was a trim looking pair of moccasins gracing his feet.

'You're Barney,' I said.

'S'right!' He grinned cunningly. 'Barney for short. Jeremiah Barnsley for full measure. And you'll be the new boy – the one they call August, eh? Short for Augustus, I suppose? Well Gus or Gussy's good enough for little ol' Barney. Okay?'

'No.'

'Okay, then. Let's settle for Aug. Anything for a quiet life. Got a fag?'

'No.'

I had never imagined the encounter would be so difficult. His speech grated and his eyes peered with a knowing smirk that nauseated me. No wonder the wiccies avoided him.

He shrugged. 'No harm in asking. No one's ever got any anyway. Want one?' He produced a couple of roughly rolled miniatures from his pocket and grinned.

I shook my head.

'Genuine tobacco, y'know. Found some stubs and re-rolled 'em.' He extracted a non-safety match from another pocket and waved it. It was nearly as big as his arm. 'Stand well back, chum!' he cried.

I already had.

He scraped the thing violently against a piece of sandstone, and threw it on the ground the moment it flared. Then he flopped onto his belly and crawled cautiously towards it, holding a cigarette at arm's length. Then he rose again, flourishing the now smoking weed triumphantly.

'How's that, Aug! Nothing you can't do with a little ingenuity, eh?'

'You can say that again!' I shouted angrily, grabbing the largest fallen branch I could manage and beating at the flames. 'Get something and help me put this out before the whole forest catches fire, you gormless lunatic!'

'Blimey! Sorry, Aug – didn't think.'

It took all our energy to prevent the fire from spreading among the dry oak leaves around us. And I discovered a curious fact: when I stamped on an errant spark, nothing happened; it continued to glow as before. Only the weight of the wood in my hand proved effective.

'S'matter of fact I've been told to look out for you,' Barnsley said when the danger was over and we walked on.

'Oh, by whom?'

'Fellow called Sinjun – though why he spells his name Saint John and calls himself Sinjun, I don't know. I just call him Sinjy.' He changed the subject abruptly. 'I'm supposed to missionise among the new arrivals and get them to join us in St John's Wood.'

'How many of you are there, then?'

'Well, Sinjy got hold of Baddenham – he's a card! Sin and Bad, see? Then they press-ganged a naval type called

Simmonds, which made it Sin, Bad and the Sailor! After that, it was me, then Skinney.'

'Skinney?'

'Miss Kinney. She insists on the "Miss", so all the gremlins call her Skinney. She's vegetarian, anti-vivisection, anti-blood sports, anti-games on Sundays – and anti-fun and games at any time. You'll loath the sight of her,' he promised. 'But she's a good sort in some ways,' he added with belated generosity. 'She spins and knits – after a fashion. Made all these togs for me.' He indicated his clothes without enthusiasm.

Our route took us through a small clearing. Before us the Wale fell sharply away in the direction of Three Weirs, but I stopped short in surprise. I could clearly see the tops of trees marking Wisher's Barn, and Wisher's Mead beyond them. But after that was … nothing! No highway. No village. The landscape just ended, as if a curtain of sky had encircled the forest.

'Funny that, isn't it?' Barnsley said. 'You'd swear there was nothing further, wouldn't you? And a lot of the goblins believe that. Only a few of us new ones can remember there's a village with cottages, and a very good pub, and a road that hums all day long with cars and lorries and the good ol' stink of petrol fumes and dust an' all that. But it's there all right, and it's something I don't ever let myself forget – 'cause one day I'm going back!'

'Oh, did you live in Three Weirs?'

'No.' He jerked a thumb over his shoulder. 'My place is down by the sea. Pretty little shanty – bungalow. Can't remember its name though. Lilac'll be out in the front garden now. Got to get back. Got a wife and kiddies, see? Can't think how they'll be managing without me.'

He didn't seem terribly disturbed about it to me – just nostalgic.

'Why not take a trip?'

'Like this?' he asked indignantly. 'They'd laugh at me! Dog'd chew me up on the lawn. Besides ...' he said, treating me to a sidelong leer, '... a pint-sized husband wouldn't be much use to a life-sized wife, would he? No, I'll go back when this lark comes to an end.'

'And when do you think that'll be?'

'Creepin' catfish! You don't think this is *real* do you, Aug?' He stood back and faced me. 'I mean, take a butcher's – do I *look* like a bloomin' fairy?'

'More like a bad hangover,' I said truthfully. 'Look, if this is all a dream then why don't you enter into the spirit of it and forget about the past until you wake up?'

He stared at me and looked deeply offended. 'What, and let the gobs get me? They're only a blasted illusion too!'

He paused as two little figures crossed a patch of grass below us and caught his eye. 'Phee-ew!' I heard him breathe. 'Are they peaches or are they peaches? Hey, Aug, take a gander at that one in the transparent mauve! Now is that a fig-u-ar or what?' He gave a loud and enthusiastic wolf whistle.

The wiccies looked up, saw me, and waved gaily, then wandered on out of sight.

Barnsley nudged me in the ribs. 'See that, Aug? Come on, boy – we've got a date! Bags I the mauve one!'

I yanked him back by the collar. 'You don't want to waste your time chasing illusions, do you?'

He freed himself and haughtily rearranged his jacket. 'I mistook you for a gentleman, Aug,' he complained.

'And that's what I am – but maybe not the kind *you* mean. Look, I really need to find Sin.'

He leered at me and winked. 'Plenty of sin here, Aug! 'Specially that mauve one!'

I said nothing but looked at him solemnly. '*Okay*, I suppose you mean Sinjun,' he said, sounding somewhat deflated. I nodded curtly and he pointed straight ahead. 'He's up there at the house – *Mens Sana* they call it.'

It wasn't far, and there was no mistaking the solid, neatly thatched single-storey dolls' house, complete with veranda. 'Someone's put in a lot of work here,' I said, looking round in astonishment. There was a spacious lawn of miniature grass, surrounded by a herbaceous border containing equally diminutive cowslips, primroses and violets.

'All we do is weed the place,' Barnsley explained. 'The flowers aren't real, nor's the grass.'

I read the name printed unevenly over the door, and chuckled.

'What's the joke?' he asked.

'The missing bit from *Mens Sana*.'

'I don't get it. Latin innit?'

'Yes. The phrase in full is *Mens sana in corpore sano* – "a sound mind in a sound body". The omission of the "sound body" is ... interesting.'

'That's Sinjy all over,' Barnsley agreed. 'Always talking about our minds being the only sound ones in these parts – oh, look out here it comes, the face that wrecked a thousand ships!'

A figure had just come round the side of the house and now stood looking at us. She was recognisably female, but when I saw the frilled organdie frock and shady bonnet she was wearing, it gave me quite a shock.

'That's Stella Mye's doll's outfit!' I exclaimed. 'I gave it to her last Christmas. I'll swear it's the same one.'

The severe and frigid face beneath the bonnet drooped dispiritedly. Between her fingers, an equally dispirited worm also drooped.

'Not exactly a pin-up, is she?' muttered Barnsley before stepping forward and announcing: 'This is Aug, old dear. Aug, meet Miss Kinney.'

She withdrew a slimy hand from the worm and held it out to me. 'Welcome to St John's Wood, Mr Aug,' she said, her face creasing into a polite smile.

I accepted the hand, and released it quickly.

'How d'you do, Miss Kinney? By the way, the name is August and the surname is Autrey.'

'I'm so sorry.' She looked round for Barnsley but he was out of sight. 'You will be staying for lunch, of course. Please tell Edmund I shall be back as soon as I have fed my chicks.'

Barnsley reappeared. 'Bet she was mad when you recognised the dress and titfer,' he said as we moved on to the house. 'I got 'em, see? Some kids were having a picnic in the meadow one day, so I nipped in and lifted 'em off one of their dolls.'

A stocky figure appeared on the veranda.

'Sinjy – Aug. Aug – Sinjy,' Barnsley proclaimed, bounding in through the door.

St John greeted me with a genial smile, seizing my hand and shaking it warmly.

'Delighted to make your acquaintance, dear boy. Welcome to *Mens Sana*. You *will* stay to lunch, won't you?'

'Miss Kinney apparently expects me to,' I answered, noting the fellow's blotchy and pimpled complexion. A pair of blue and white pyjamas hung round his paunchy figure. His feet, like Barnsley's, were in moccasins. 'She said to tell you that she'll be back when she's fed her chicks.'

He looked peeved. 'Confound the woman!' he muttered. 'It's bad enough having to remind her to feed *us*, without her wasting time on those blasted tits.'

A lean looking fellow in home-made shorts came into view, talking to a shorter, stolid looking type, who I assumed was Simmonds.

'Baddenham!' called St John, 'Come and meet our guest.'

Moving jerkily, the thin figure came forward. He wore a permanent frown and gesticulated nervously. 'How d'you do? Been hearing about you from Barnsley.' He turned to St John and said in a low voice: 'Edmund, you really must exert your authority. This fellow Simmonds is getting above himself.' He turned back to include me. 'It's a rule of our little community that everyone pulls his weight. We've worked like Trojans, Edmund and I, to keep our end up against the goblins.' He waved an arm erratically. 'We've only the most primitive instruments and it really *is* vital, Autrey – our very existence depends on our labours.'

'Why?' I asked.

'Why? *Why*? You mean, you can't *see*? Oh, for heaven's sake – Edmund, explain it to him. I'm devastated, utterly devastated.' And he rushed away with his hands over his ears.

'Oh dear,' said St John. 'I'm afraid this isn't one of his best days, poor fellow.' Then he turned briskly to the ex-CPO who was standing with his arms crossed and feet wide apart, glowering at us.

'We'll have the cocktails on the lawn before lunch, Simmonds.'

'Not from me, you won't,' he said. 'I'm getting out. Had a bellyful, and that's a fact. Been here a week working my backside off and not a blind word about wages.' He cocked a thumb in the direction of the vanished Baddenham. 'He's as batty as a coot. And as for Skinney … well you know what *she* can do, don't you, the interfering cow.' He turned his back and marched off.

I turned to St John with interest to see how he would handle the situation, but instead he led me over to a rustic table surrounded by deckchairs and invited me to sit.

'Please pay no attention to these foolish scenes, Autrey. We are a terribly devoted bunch really. Although, of course, there are bound to be *some* slight differences of opinion. In normal life, by the way, Baddenham is a psychologist. He has some interesting ideas too. He's convinced that this is an ephemeral existence entirely due to a schizophrenic condition in each of us – a condition which will yield to treatment provided we do not resist it. You follow the idea?'

'One half of a split personality getting out of hand, so to speak,' I said, nodding. 'Yes, I can see that, but –'

'Well, *there* you are!' he interrupted triumphantly.

'I don't think so,' I objected. 'Because if that's the case then all of us – and certainly all of *you* – are destined for the loony bin. And that being so,' I continued, waving his splutters aside, 'then how could one lunatic *possibly* cure another?'

St John looked at me rather acidly. 'I happen to know that *I* am completely sane – though I can't speak for the others. All I've done is give you Baddenham's views. That doesn't commit me to them, does it?'

He cheered up at the sight of Barnsley coming out of the house balancing a tray. 'This place is an absolute riot!' Barnsley said on reaching us. 'Baddy's gone berserk and Sailor Simmo's on strike. Lucky you've got me, Sinjy old man, or you'd be sunk.'

He placed the tray gingerly on the table. It had on it the cap of a thermos flask, a small uncorked scent bottle, and some nutshells, each with one end hacked off.

'Now,' Barnsley gestured hospitably and looked at me, 'what's it to be, Aug? Cherry brandy, sloe gin, straight gin or Plymouth?'

'Forgive our primitive tableware,' said St John. 'We are rather handicapped. Appropriate vessels are somewhat hard to come by.'

'But the stuff's all right – most of it,' Barnsley assured me. 'The brandy's home-made and so's some of the gin. Not the Plymouth though. I lifted that from an old geezer who'd nipped into the forest for a quiet soak. Strange what some people get up to, isn't it?'

'Very,' I agreed.

'Isn't there anything to go with the gin?' asked St John.

'Blimey, yes!' Barnsley answered, and sped away gleefully.

'He's a good soul,' said St John. 'A lazy devil, but very resourceful on his foraging expeditions. Makes such a contrast to Baddenham and Gwendolyn. I suppose Simmonds will desert to the goblins now – and much good they'll do him.'

'Ta-da!' Barnsley reappeared with an old earthenware ink bottle filled with cider, his arms barely reaching around it. He part-filled a nutshell with gin from the scent bottle, slopped in an unequal proportion of cider, and passed it to me before filling a second for St John and a third for himself. They raised their drinks solemnly. I followed suit, sipped my drink – and suddenly felt very ill.

'I expect you've been told you need no sustenance in this state?' asked St John.

'I gather we draw our energy from the moon …' I began.

'Stuff and nonsense!' he said. 'You must hold on to the old standards of practical thinking and commonsense. Otherwise you'll degenerate into the same amorphous mass as the creatures around you.'

'Those *ghastly* goblins!' Skinney's voice creaked as she returned to the garden. I stood up but she waved me back down and sank into another chair.

'They *won't* work,' she complained, accepting a nutful of cider from Barnsley. 'And if one doesn't work, how can one eat?'

'They seem to survive,' I said mildly.

'I don't believe they go without food,' said St John. 'Every living thing needs nourishment. They're probably secret eaters – or perhaps they've some formula for concocting juices and so forth.'

'Wouldn't that entail work?' I asked. 'And if they do have some secret method of eating, it must be remarkably efficient.' I looked meaningfully from St John's blotchy features to Barnsley's sallow complexion and Skinney's red nose. 'They manage to imitate the bloom of youth and beauty remarkably well, don't you think?'

'A *man* wouldn't know how a woman can possibly imitate nature, of course,' said Miss Kinney venomously. 'And their conduct is perfectly shameless. There's only one word to describe them – hussies!'

'Whores and harlots!' agreed Barnsley, giving me a salacious wink.

'Quiet, Jeremiah! It's scandalous, Mr Autrey. From what I am given to understand, they don't even know the meaning of the word *marriage*!'

'Well,' I replied, 'the Wale is rather like heaven where there is neither marriage nor giving in marriage.'

Skinney put down her nutshell and exploded to her feet in a fine display of hauteur.

'Mr Autrey, I'll have you know my father was a Canon!'

'You could describe "Barney" as a bit of warfare too,' I said callously. Miss Kinney promptly flounced off in a huff and Barnsley almost rolled out of his chair with laughter. Even St John appeared amused against his will. I thought I'd better change the subject. 'Tell me what happens to us when the moon sets,' I said.

'Why, er, we go to sleep –' said St John, looking bemused.

'Blackout!' interrupted Simmonds as he strolled up to join us, looking as dour as ever. He examined the tray of drinks, poured himself a gin and gulped it down.

'It must be a strange hallucination if it works with such astronomical precision,' I said.

'Well that brings us back to Baddenham's theory,' said St John. 'He maintains that the moon's influence on the mentally unbalanced –'

'But you said you were completely sane,' I reminded him.

'Sane?' Simmonds laughed derisively, and then looked at me earnestly. 'D'you happen to know what's happened to my guv'nor – Commander Laudley that was?'

'I do – in fact I'm staying with him.'

'*Are* you? So he really *has* gone to the gobs?'

'If you mean is he making the most of his new life, then yes, I can assure you he is.'

'I suppose he told you we had a bit of a misunder-standing about the scotch?' he asked.

'I don't think he harbours any ill-feeling.'

Simmonds brightened. 'He's a good man, is my guv'nor. I suppose he's got a new man by now?'

'I don't think so.'

'Well if he hasn't, will you let him know that I'm willing to let bygones be bygones? After all, what's a noggin of whisky after twenty-two years' service?' He made to top up my nutshell, but I shook my head. He poured himself another tot.

'Do the gobs get any decent drinks?' he asked.

'Not to my knowledge,' I said cautiously.

This made Barnsley sit up and grin, and he gestured us all to lean closer. 'I'll tell you something; I've had a spot of their stuff and – oh boy! – I nearly signed on as a gob straight away!'

'When was this?' St John asked suspiciously.

'Shut up Sinjy, and listen. It was like this: I was out on one of my searches one day and I ran into this strange fellow sitting behind a small keg surrounded by goblets –

the real stuff, solid silver! Well, I stops and looks at him, and he looks at me. And I licks my lips, and he grins. Then he puts a goblet under the tap, turns it on, and says "Hael and wyn, half born!" and gives it to me.' Barnsley closed his eyes and continued dreamily, 'It sparkled like sunlight on the sea and tasted like all the best drinks you've ever had, but a hundred times better.'

'So?' urged Simmonds. 'What happened then?'

'Dunno, Sailor. I passed out. When I came round, he'd gone, and – oh my Gawd!' Skinney was approaching with a tray. 'Here she is with another witch's brew!'

'I am very sorry, Mr Autrey, but lunch will be delayed.' She glared daggers at Simmonds. 'None of the vegetables have been prepared. Until they are, I simply cannot cook.'

Simmonds flung down his nutshell and crossed his arms again. 'I've quit,' he declared.

Skinney ignored him. 'So I've brought out some little cakes and some tea for you.' She honoured me with an approach to a smile. 'Don't you just love the china?'

I stared in amazement at the china tea set I had given Stella Mye the previous Easter. I didn't know she had lost both my presents. Mrs Mye must have been too upset to tell me. And she would have blamed Stella for being careless.

'Another one of Barnsley's "finds",' St John whispered to me.

'Mr Autrey,' Skinney said before he could tell me the details, 'perhaps *you* can give us a reasonable explanation of our unhappy predicament here?'

'From all the data that has come my way, Miss Kinney, I have reason to believe that our mortal bodies are dead, and we are now alive as wraiths.'

She looked shocked.

'That's *his* theory,' said St John quickly. 'It *could* all be an hallucination. We might still be dreaming in our beds –'

'Or bashing our nuts against the walls of a padded cell!' chuckled Barnsley.

'I can't answer for you, Barnsley,' I said, 'but I know for a fact that Simmonds here isn't going to wake up in bed, or in a cell. He and his employer were both found dead a week ago. And their physical bodies have been well and truly taken apart to try and find out why!'

'Edmund!' wailed Skinney. 'If this is true ...' She burst into tears and rushed back into the house.

'Now look what you've done – you and your theories!' said St John angrily. 'We shan't get any lunch now. She'll mope for hours.'

'Well at least you won't die of starvation,' I assured him unsympathetically, and I rose from my seat. 'Well, I'm off. Thanks for the talk.'

'You're not leaving us?' St John sounded incredulous. 'You can't go back *there*!'

'Just watch me!' I told him. 'And any time *you* want to join us, Simmo, you'll be very welcome.'

CHAPTER 10

MASTER OF GNOMES

I made for Great Oak, still feeling ill and promising myself I would never again forsake my true companions of the forest. All further questing after truth would be with them.

'Hael and wyn, August!'

I looked up. Jean and Loy were sitting on a fragile branch above me, smiling happily. I returned the greeting.

'Running away from Sin, old man?' Loy asked mischievously.

'News gets around pretty quickly,' I answered.

'You'd be surprised,' he said. 'We've heard all about this morning, too –'

'Fi-zzle-bane and Fu-ming-wort!' Jean interrupted delightedly.

'Jean was afraid you wouldn't come back. But I knew you'd have too much common sense to be fooled by those idiots at *Mens Sana*. How's Simmonds getting on?'

'In a state of mutiny, actually. He wants his old job back. I promised him I'd let you know.'

'What?' Loy nearly fell off his perch laughing. 'Does he really believe he needs a job now?'

'You ought to do something for him, Loy,' I said seriously. 'He doesn't stand a chance with that bunch of morons.'

'Not my responsibility any more. Death cancels all contracts, doesn't it?'

'I think you've got a *moral* responsibility. He still thinks very highly of you.'

'But what on earth could *I* do? Set up house just for his benefit?' He turned to Jean. 'What do you think, my love? Shall we set up house together and take him on as a manservant?'

'A *house*, Loy? A house is nothing but a place to sleep when Mona has gone to rest and Sunné has not yet risen. What would a manservant do?'

'See what I mean, August?' Loy spread his hands with a smug expression. 'No beds to make, no silver to polish, no door to answer. He'd be at a dead loss.'

'I appreciate that,' I said, 'but I'm appealing to your …' I was going to say 'humanity' but stopped short. 'What I mean is, the fellow's one of the little people now. If we could get him away from *Mens Sana*, he'd soon discover the truth – and you're the one to do it. Maybe a little quarter-deck treatment …?'

Loy shifted uncomfortably. He was drifting very agreeably into the carefree attitude of our kind. Serious considerations were unwelcome. 'Yes, but … these things aren't our pigeon, old man,' he said, looking confused. 'We don't have to worry about them – it's the Wands' job.'

'And what are *they* doing about it?' I asked angrily. '*Mens Sana* is a madhouse. Baddenham's off his rocker, Barnsley's a raving sex-maniac and Miss Kinney's poisoning everyone with indigestible food. What right have the Wands to allow it?'

'But if that's the way they *want* to live, dear August,' said Jean quietly, 'then isn't it up to them? *You* don't need to think about it. Why not just ignore them like we do?'

'Because they're anachronisms! They're not happy. I thought the fae couldn't bear to see others unhappy. But *you* don't seem to care. Well, *I* do – and I'm going to do something about it.' I waved a hand and moved off.

'Wait!' cried Loy. 'Where are you off to now?'

I stopped and looked back. 'To Wandleside … by a roundabout route.'

'Why do you need to go to Wandleside?' asked Jean

'To try and find one of the Wychies, my dear.'

Jean looked alarmed. 'Oh, but you won't find them that way, August!'

'Then which way shall I find them?'

'Not by trying to get to The Wandle, dear August. Please, Loy, do make him understand.'

Loy jumped down and Jean followed gracefully into his arms.

'It's like this, old man,' he said. 'There are certain things that just aren't done, and intruding on the Wands' retreat is a definite no-no.'

'That's *their* problem!' I answered stubbornly. 'They won't come to me, so I'm going to them.'

'But no one's ever done such a thing,' said Jean, looking seriously troubled.

'Then it's about time someone did – and if you can't help me, I'll find my own way!'

I had gone only a few steps before they caught up with me.

'Jean's agreed to show you a way,' said Loy. 'Since you won't listen to reason, I've persuaded her that it's best if we come with you and try to keep you out of trouble.'

I thanked them and we walked in silence until we reached the top of Wandleside. Once we had arrived, Jean touched my arm and whispered, 'There's a little path down from here. 'Tis called Windaway. It leads to the narrow waters between the Weirds.'

Loy and I followed her down a tiny track that would have been invisible to the human eye. It zig-zagged down the cliff face from one end to the other, making it a long trail, and we sped back and forth as twilight came and deepened. The darkening conifers rose higher and higher in a solidifying mass above the mirror-like Weirds as we went ever lower. Everything seemed cloaked in a silence that was oppressive.

When we reached the foot of the cliff at the point where the Weirds met, it was so still and silent that it numbed our senses. We stood and gazed across the glassy surface of the lakes, and up at the towering phalanx of trees on The Wandle with the moon just appearing above them.

I found myself wishing that I had been less headstrong, and I was conscious of some intangible presence closing in around us. And still, despite the overwhelming sense of dread that filled me, I knew I had to go on. I realised then what it must have meant to my companions – especially Jean – to stay with me.

There was only a narrow neck of water between me and The Wandle. With the first step, however, I knew the enormity of my impertinence. With every further step, I was pushing a boundary beyond all possible acceptance. Then, as I reached the water and made to force my foot down into it, I fell into blackness.

*

I opened my eyes in the knowledge that it was past sunrise and that I lay on my back in the usual corner of my oak tree apartment. Filled with the same unthinking elemental joy as usual, I flung my arms and legs to either side in abandon – and one hand smacked into someone sitting beside me.

'Hael and wyn, August,' came Loy's voice, full of relief.

I returned the greeting, apologising for the thump, and asked, 'What happened? How did I get here?'

'You passed out, old man. Sort of fell backwards and went to sleep peacefully at our feet. We waited for you to wake up, but you didn't. So I picked you up, slung you over my shoulder, and carried you home.'

I stared at him contritely. 'That was decent of you, Loy. I don't deserve friends like you and Jean. I suppose the saga's gone the rounds by now. I can just imagine the morning's headlines: *Adventurous elemental attempts the impossible! August the Awkward out for the count!*'

Loy shook his head. 'You've still got an awful lot to learn, old man. Come and see for yourself.'

He sprang up the steps and reached the opening. I hesitated for a moment, then followed and we looked out together. The glade was crowded with fae dressed in every colour of the rainbow. There seemed to be hundreds of them, like a variegated carpet of colours woven into the brilliant green of the grass. They broke into a united shout of joy at the sight of us:

'Hael and wyn, dear August! Hael and wyn!' The pageant moved, the carpet rolled with figures leaping and dancing, while waving hands invited me down.

Loy gave me a look that said, 'What did I tell you?' before jumping down.

'Hael and wyn, beloved friends!' I cried, and jumped after him. They caught me before I landed and kissed and manoeuvred me from one side of the glade to the other. Then the crowd parted and I stood facing Great Oak.

A magnificent blue and silver rug now decorated the root I had sat on the previous morning. I gaped in astonishment at two huge effigies flanking the throne. On the left, the tall willowy form of Fizzlebane, with two enormous deep green eyes encircling yellow irises from which peeped small red flower buds. On the right grinned the short round form of Fumingwort, showing a large yellow belly of corn marigolds entwined with sweet woodruff.

Between tears and laughter, I tried to thank them all. The lovely speedwell blue and silver clad Leila, who was nearest, kissed the tears away. 'The Wands are kind!' she whispered. 'They heard our prayer, dear August and they protected you.'

I returned her kisses, and those of the two other eager lips on either side of my shoulders, who I found to be Sylvie and Dina, my attendants from the previous day.

No one seemed to mind my three handmaidens' self-appointment as they sat me down and took their places, one on either side, with Leila preferring to kneel as before, resting her arms on my knees.

'Now … Dragon Dreadful –' I began, and should have known I wouldn't get far.

'Please, August!' appealed Smye – an inveterate gossip with an imagination almost as vivid as my own. 'Is it true that because a dragon is so fiery inside he lays molten eggs?'

This started an involved discussion about supernatural zoology, supplemented with endless questions. Where did the fire come from? How can he breathe out fire if he didn't breathe it in first? How many toes? Does he have more than two eyes – and of what colour? At this rate, one story would last me at least three months.

When the origin, habits, habitat and temperament of Dragon Dreadful had been settled and I was allowed back to Hellbane Harry, Leila gently rubbed my knee with her elbow. 'Did the wizard have a wych, August?' she asked.

I looked into her apparently innocent eyes with misgiving. There seemed to be a personal nuance behind the question. 'Hellbane had no wych, dearest Leila. But you have to realise that he was not a very attractive kind of wizard. Nice wiccies – like you – wouldn't want to know him. That is why he had to send forth Dreadful and Fizzlebane and Fumingwort –'

'Fi-zzle-bane and Fu-ming-wort!' chanted my audience.

'... to capture the Maiden Chrysobel.'

'Was he in the Mood?' asked Dina.

'I expect he was,' I answered cautiously, not certain how far I could answer that one. 'He certainly wanted her for his wife –'

'In that case, August,' said Smye, 'the Maiden Chrysobel *must* have been a wych.'

This was greeted with such a hush that I realised I could be on the edge of disaster. I had already been told that only a wizard could love a wych and live. I had to presume that it was the same the other way round too.

'She was *not*,' I said firmly, smiling at the universal consternation. 'But, as you will hear – and it's a pity you have forced the dénouement so early – Hellbane Harry did *not*, in the end, marry the Maiden Chrysobel.' I smiled again, this time in triumph.

A stunned silence ensued, during which I caught sight of Loy. He held up his thumb to signal a victory – or so I thought. But I had reckoned without Smye. He sent over such a fast one that I couldn't even stonewall it.

'What is a maiden, please, August? I can't remember.'

That stumped me. Even if I tried to explain what a virgin was, who could I quote as an example amongst these endearing people to whom morals had no meaning?

Loy rushed gallantly but foolishly into the breach. 'A maiden, old man, is a wiccy who's never been loved.'

I groaned, and met Leila's laughing eyes. 'Poor, poor, darling Loy!' she giggled. Loy soon needed all the sympathy he could get. Scandalised members of both sexes either hotly repudiated the notion that *any* wiccy could *ever* go unloved, or challenged him to quote an example of such a travesty of nature.

Smye listened blissfully to the storm he had unleashed while – I am certain – he cast around for the next spanner to throw in the works.

Loy hedged desperately. *Wiccy*, he said, had been a slip of the tongue. He had really meant a mortal female not old enough for the joys of love.

'Like Skinney?' suggested an over-bright wicca, quoting the very example I had been dreading.

'Skinney is no longer mortal.'

'Nor is she truly a wiccy …'

'But how can she not be old enough?'

'August, is Skinney old enough?'

I replied evasively, and truthfully, that I had no idea how old she had been when she left her mortal life.

'But is she a maiden *now*, August?'

I made a non-committal gesture.

'But, *August!*' Fizzy's mildy astonished voice floated down from an airy perch. 'You've *seen* her – you *must* know.'

Leila's inventive wit rescued me. 'Fizzy, dear, would *you* like to make love to Skinney?'

He stared down, nonplussed, and after a spirited cross-examination was compelled to admit that he, a wicca of wiccas, recognised the existence of a wiccy with whom he would hesitate to share the exaltations of the Mood.

'Bless you, angel,' I said, before returning to the story.

'So … Dreadful set off through the howling storm, flying high above the tops of the trees, with the two familiars clinging perilously to the spikes on his spine. The thunder rolled in volleys of sound that rocked the valleys below –'

'But August, you said he was flying over trees …'

We were off again.

When the session was over, I confided in Leila that I was still feeling queasy.

'You shouldn't drink gin with Sin,' she murmured, looking at me through her lashes. 'Mortal gin is not good for wiccas. Be happy you did not eat their awful food as well.'

'So is there nothing I can do about feeling sick, then?' I asked.

'You can come and drink with us at the Wealspring,' she invited. 'Come, we'll show you.'

Taking my hand, she led the way with Dina and Sylvie down one of the countless faerie tracks that criss-crossed the forest beneath the bracken. We soon arrived at a tiny glade. Something about its appearance seemed familiar, and I realised it was the one that the two wiccies had passed through yesterday and which I now also recognised as being part of the forest known as the Wynn. I looked up, suddenly remembering one of Barnsley's remarks that he came this way every morning to look out over the Weal.

And he was there, in the same position, gazing nostalgically over the landscape. He looked down at almost the same instant as I saw him – and his gape of astonishment spoke volumes. Fortunately we passed out of the glade without his harassing wolf whistle, for which I silently thanked him.

No human eye could have found the tiny two-foot-high Lilliputian grotto hidden under arching brambles where the Wealspring had its source. Light filtered in, despite a lip of overhanging rock and dense greenery, illuminating a welling fount of sparkling water. Leila knelt and took a small golden goblet, which she filled. Then she rose again, her fingers brilliant with tiny gems of reflected gold and green. She sipped a little before handing it to me without a word. There was a pledge in her eyes as I accepted the cup silently and drank.

It was cold, as all spring waters are, but this was different. It penetrated every part of me. The queasiness vanished, ice-cold fire lit my brain, and I felt for one wonderful moment that I knew all the secrets of the universe. Then the vision faded and I found myself looking into the amber pools of Leila's smiling eyes once again.

'Did you wish?' asked Sylvie anxiously as I lowered the goblet.

'No,' I said. 'Should I have?'

'Of course! You should always make a wish when you take your first drink from the Wealspring.'

I gave Leila a reproachful look. 'You never said.'

'Perhaps another time,' she answered with an unrepentant shrug that told me she had never intended to. 'You know, August, your expressions are all in the lines of your face. Your eyes do not speak clearly. They are not faerie eyes – yet neither are they the eyes of a half born.'

I was mystified by these repeated references to my eyes. 'Do they frighten you?' I asked uneasily.

'No, beloved – they are never unkind.' Her head moved closer to my cheek with an exquisitely endearing caress. 'And yet they tear woefully at my heart,' she confessed. 'But it is a sweet, sweet pain. I am forever lost in your magic, August.' She sighed, and added in a tone that affected me deeply, *'Thou art my weird, wicca, thee will I wear.'*

I had already realised that Leila was a lover who could not be avoided. From the moment we had met, she had singled me out with quiet assurance.

'Isn't a weird a fate?' I asked nervously. 'A kind of doom? A destiny?'

'Yes, beloved. Therefore it is worn like a mantle – as the Wychies do. Their Weirds are woven and sewn with mysterious symbols that only they can read. And that is their fate. Poor August!' her voice caressed me. 'You, who are so wyché, do not understand so small a thing as a faerie doom!'

There was no time to ask what she meant because Sylvie and Dina were reminding Leila of their promise to show me other wonders. Taking my hands, they led me from the Wealspring grotto back along the path towards the Wynn and then up a boulder-strewn hill pitted with crevices. From one of these there suddenly bounded the round form of a happy looking fellow whose skin-tight clothes appeared filled to bursting point. He seized Sylvie by the waist, kissed her soundly, and beamed at us over her shoulder.

'Hael and wyn, August, Leila, Dina! The Master is waiting for you!' He vanished back into the crevice with the laughing wiccy on his arm.

With Leila and Dina on either side of me, I found myself pulled headlong into a faintly lit tunnel which we raced along at breakneck speed. Unlike their cousins the fae, it seemed that gnomes preferred to live, work and love at high pressure.

The tunnel suddenly opened into a large, irregularly shaped cavern where excited figures were milling around a denser mass at its centre – which seemed to be Sylvie. A shouting, laughing knot detached itself and swarmed around us. Dina and Leila were welcomed and roundly kissed, then our hosts hurled themselves on me, slapping my shoulders, pummelling my ribs, and asking with admiring winks and shameless curiosity how I enjoyed making love with Leila.

Then we were hurtled away through a labyrinth of tunnels and chambers until we came to a breathless stand-still before a large, bearded gnome in scarlet and gold. We were in a great hall, with walls covered in what appeared to be scintillating tapestries. One that particularly caught my eye showed a cascading mountain stream. The light sparking from the water was depicted in diamonds, and its shadows were aquamarines, making it seem to be actually flowing. Brown rocks of cairngorm overlaid with a lichen of turquoise, garnet and kunzite gleamed blue, dark green and lavender. Topaz and chrysobel formed the banks, and in the background were jade, emerald and malachite trees, and bushes with trunks of cairngorm and amber, all quivering somehow in sunlight.

The Master, covered with jewels himself and seated in a golden chair at a silver table, raised his eyes from a heap of precious stones he had been examining, flicked an enormous ruby ring to an attendant, and welcomed us with a huge grin and loud cry: 'Hael and wyn, wiccies! Hael and wyn, August!' He peered at me closely. 'So this is the teller of tales, the master of musings! Come, sit beside me and tell us your marvels, brother. We are lonely fellows, we gnomes, so we *love* long tales!'

He waved a hand and jewelled chairs appeared, one for each of the wiccies, and one for me that was placed at his side. I asked what kind of a story he would like.

He plunged a hand into his great beard, giving me a mischievous wink. 'We like tales of love – of flashing eyes and ruby lips and heroic achievements,' he replied.

My existing repertoire held nothing like that. So I racked my brain and improvised …

CHAPTER 11

LEILA

'Once upon a time there was a great King called Hammerfast who lived in a haunted castle in the Holdfast Mountains,' I began. 'King Hammerfast had a daughter, Princess Celestia – a princess whose hair was like molten gold as it pours from a crucible, and whose eyes could be mistaken for sapphires shining in a sea of pearls ...'

I saw at once that I had struck the right note as the gnomes stole soulful glances towards the three wiccies. So I added five hundred ladies-in-waiting to the princess's entourage. It won a general smile of appreciation, and a number of gnomes clapped their fellows on the back with the assurance that there would be plenty of female company for everyone. And then I added a secret race of little men who also lived deep in the mountains – strong, cheerful, industrious fellows who worked in stones and minerals the whole day long.

'But alas, these five hundred ... and one ...' I added on the spur of the moment with a sly glance at the master, '... gallant fellows had no pretty ladies, let alone a princess, amongst their company.'

The atmosphere was now tense. From this point I laid on sentiment with a trowel, and in no time had the lovely princess and her friends listed as missing, captured by a wicked troll with three heads and six arms. With the King of the gnomes and his merry men in hot pursuit, I filled out the action with descriptions of palaces and people that left my listeners in no doubt that their master was the energetic King who led the search.

It was hard work, with neither help nor hindrance from the gnomes. No questions. No interruptions. Just approving grunts, despondent sighs and excited waving of fists when I brought on the five hundred ladies of the chorus at regular intervals – for the most trivial of reasons.

At last I decided enough was enough, and ended the story with Hammerfast welcoming the King of the Gnomes as his son-in-law and distributing his daughter's five hundred ladies-in-waiting as a reward to the five hundred brave warriors who had rescued the princess from the troll.

The audience went wild with delight. They sprang to their feet, cheered, laughed, shouted, flung their caps in the air, capered, jumped and wrestled together. And Leila, Sylvie and Dina disappeared beneath a wave of admirers.

The Master beamed and turned to an attendant. 'Say, Feldspar, what shall we give August that will mark our esteem?'

The gnome dived into the heap on the table and drew out a glittering diamond necklace. The Master laughed. 'For a wiccy, yes! For Princess Leila! Come, Princess ...' Leila reappeared from the crowd and he placed the necklace around her neck, kissed her rapturously, and clapped a hand on my shoulder. 'Now you shall choose something for *him*, Leila. What present is fit for a princess's lover?'

Eager hands again dived into the pile and held up a bewildering array for her selection, as The Master listed them: 'A thumb ring of jade? Amethyst? Garnet? Ha! Here we have it – a belt of blue diamonds and fire opals! Remove that tawdry thing he wears.'

In a flash my belt was gone and a glowing strip of stones was placed in Leila's hands.

'How say you, princess of the sapphire eyes? Such a girdle is worthy of a Wychy, is it not?'

She laughed and nodded happily, but I held up my hands in amazement. 'Master, I do not deserve such generosity! The value is inestimable –'

'Strange if it were not!' he retorted with amusement. 'No mortal eyes have ever feasted on such treasure! No, August, 'tis no more than your due. Fasten it upon him, Leila, that all the forest may see that we of the magic fingers know how to honour our guests.'

By the time Leila and I had been given a boisterous send-off by our jubilant friends, I wasn't surprised to find that the moon, now intermittently visible through scudding clouds, had taken the place of the sun.

I looked around for Sylvie and Dina, but Leila only chuckled. 'The gnomes are always lonely,' she said. 'They are seldom seen between High Moons when we meet them on The Wandle. They work so hard and pine so much; we wiccies can never resist their appeal.' She fingered the flashing stones of her necklace. 'They are a very generous people.'

'They are indeed!' I looked down at the glittering brilliance around my waist. 'I expect those two will be literally staggering under their generosity by the time they show up again,' I added dryly.

Leila shook my arm admonishingly. 'Naughty, naughty, August! That is *not* the reason they have stayed behind. They have stayed because ...' She pressed closer to my side and asked, 'Do I really need to tell you why they've stayed?'

'Perhaps not. But I wouldn't mind hearing it all the same!'

We both laughed together and stopped to kiss. Suddenly she giggled with delight and told me that Honeyball, Winzey and a number of others were at that very moment constructing a Dragon Dreadful.

'How can you know this?' I asked.

'You will grow into it, dearest August. One morning you will wake up and just … hear everyone. Oh!' she added. 'Loy has journeyed to St John's Wood! He is talking to his friend Simmo.'

'Is he now!' I answered, feeling pleased. 'What are they saying?'

'Loy is trying to persuade him to leave Sin and come away to the forest. But Simmo can't make up his mind. He says he would like to come, but only if Barney and Baddy come too.'

'So what's stopping them?' I asked.

'It's something to do with Baddy. They say he is unwell. I do not think it has anything to do with the Sickness. Barney says Baddy is "nuts" and they've had to "clap him in the cooler" for his own good. What does he mean by that, August?'

'I can't explain very easily, Leila. Baddenham doesn't believe he's really here. He thinks he's in some kind of dream and that he'll wake up soon and find himself back in the otherworld.'

She nodded. 'That must be it, because they're saying he has threatened to prove it by committing suicide. What is suicide?'

'Something that doesn't make sense, Leila,' I assured her quickly. 'Where are we going?'

'There is a little stream not far away,' she said. 'We call it the Brook of Wynn. Beneath the moon 'tis a silver ribbon winding between the birches and the willows. It sings all night long with a rhythm like no other stream, and there are arbours and bowers all along its banks.'

*

I woke at day-spring with Leila by my side. The memory of Hyllis returned suddenly and powerfully, and I realised that she had been out of my mind for more than twenty-four hours. Now I had to ask Leila what had happened to her.

'She has withered her weird, August,' she answered gently.

My heart went cold. 'I ... I don't understand.'

'It means she has left us, dear heart. She took the Sickness so she went to the Wychies. She has not returned, and this can only mean that White Wand has given her the Bane. Now she enters a new cycle of mortality.'

I was dumbfounded.

'Poor August, you don't understand, do you? You are neither faerie nor half born, but something much, much stranger – too wyché for us to understand. But the word has gone round: "August is mortal". Every wiccy knows it now. We know the Sickness is with you, beloved – it is in your ghostly black eyes, and it is your weird that you give to all your lovers.'

I seized her by the shoulders, horrified. 'No! No! Please, not you, Leila!'

Her hands covered mine as she leaned closer, her beauty invading me afresh.

'Did I not tell you yesterday, *Thou art my weird, wicca, thee will I wear*? I took on your destiny gladly, beloved. I welcomed it, as I welcomed you into my arms last night. What is in you is now in me also.' Her arms were around me, her face close to mine. 'Dearest August, never grieve,' she said. 'Your weird is wondrously compelling. There is magic in your touch and in the music of your voice. My heart is in the hollow of your hand, and such sweet pain flows into it that I have no more need for peace ... only a dark, dark yearning for long-forgotten things ... excitement ... thrilling fears and awesome dreads ...

perilous desires … a love that clings with piercing talons to its own …'

Her face, still close to mine, became withdrawn, as if part of her was preoccupied with another matter. Then she looked at me with a happy smile. 'Listen, dear heart, they are all waiting for us at the trysting tree. Honeyball, Winzey and the others, they have made a most wondrous Dragon Dreadful!'

I remembered the plexus, like gossamer wires of communication that spread from fay to fay throughout the forest. That must have told her. But not August, I reflected a little bitterly – for I was mortal and all I could do was infect my lovers with a death wish.

We arrived at the tree with our arms entwined, in accordance with what was expected – for everyone would know how we had spent the night together. I wasn't as embarrassed as I had been the first time I had learned that there were no secrets in the forest. We smiled happily in response to the noisy greetings, but I wondered how much they knew of our other concerns.

We laughed in admiration at the fearsome Dreadful behind the throne. Squatting on powerful haunches and magnificent tail, with forelegs raised protectively, it reared its crested head. From its wide-open jaws, a long red tongue declared its defiance to the world. I took my seat and squeezed the waists of Dina and Sylvie on either side of me. Leila, at my knee as usual, laid her cheek on crossed hands and did not look up.

The morning session began and I did my best to fulfil the little people's expectations – even Smye's 'Why don't we have babies like mortals do?' which I legitimately sidetracked to the Wands.

When it was over, Leila rose and kissed me impulsively. 'Goodbye, beloved mortal,' she whispered, and vanished from sight amongst the departing throng. 'Shades of Hyllis,' I thought, knowing that it would be useless to go after her.

I wandered off miserably, deep in jumbled thoughts of Hyllis, Leila and the 'mortal' label. Something crawling along the branch of a sapling overhanging the path caught my attention. The sallow, elongated object turned out to be Baddenham, as naked as I had been four days ago. He appeared to be nervously engaged in tying a piece of twine around his perch. Once secure, he stood up, pulled in the free end of the thread, held it level with the top of his head, and muttered, 'Six feet. Let me see ... I'm five foot ten and a half ... so that's ... near enough ... yes.' Holding the measured point firmly in one hand, he began to fashion a noose.

I was alarmed. Could a fay hang himself? I had to do something. 'Nice morning, Mr Baddenham!' I called out.

He looked down and frowned. 'Go away! Can't you see I'm busy?' He slipped the noose over his head, then, seeing I was still there, he sat down, crossing his hands between his legs and glaring. 'D'you mind? You may be a figment of my imagination but I *am* unclothed.'

I seized a possible lifeline. 'Yes, I see that, Mr Baddenham. Rather a bad show though, don't you think? I mean, what if Gwendolyn were to pass this way ...?'

He looked around uncertainly, before confiding in a loud whisper, 'That's just the trouble. One never knows where she might wander.' Then a possible solution came to mind. 'I say – be a good fellow and keep a lookout 'til the job's done, will you?'

I shook my head. 'No go, old man. The old dear's too crafty. And just imagine her embarrassment if she did come along. Bad enough to come across a naked man while he's alive – but to see his lifeless body dangling in the breeze ...' I broke off with a shudder.

He rubbed his forehead, apparently perplexed. 'I'm at my rope's end, Mr Autrey. And it's all because of those two interfering morons Barnsley and Simmonds. They imprisoned me in my room and went off with my clothes. I overheard Barnsley assuring Edmund that I would never venture out in the nude. Well I soon fooled them, because I managed to secure a sycamore leaf around myself with a thorn ... only it split and fell off when I was climbing up here.'

I was only half listening because a possible approach to preventing his suicide had suddenly struck me. 'You mean this is a scientific *experiment*, Mr Baddenham?' I asked quickly. 'How profoundly interesting! Do explain it to me. I might even be able to help.'

He stared down with sudden liveliness. 'My dear fellow, I had the whole thing worked out as soon as I arrived here. It boils down to this: we are entangled in a completely schizoid existence. Don't you agree?'

'Of course!' I moved closer as if to hear him better.

'Good! Then you might also be aware that a person with a schizophrenic mind is the unfortunate victim of two absolutely contrasting existences ...'

'Like Dr Jekyll and Mr Hyde?' I offered.

'Precisely! Although, of course, you must realise that not every schizophrenic is homicidal, Mr Autrey. But the fact is undisputed that there are two, sometimes more, coexistent personalities operating within the same individual.'

'So I understand,' I nodded encouragingly.

'Therefore if, as I believe, one is temporarily confined to one aspect of one's dual personality, then one should act rationally, sensibly and in harmony with that apparent delusion.'

'Absolutely!'

'So, since all other attempts to break out of this dreamlike state have failed, the logical thing is to terminate it by a logical exit. Hence the rope.' He regarded me benignly. 'I'm so glad you see the point, Mr Autrey. You have been most encouraging. Now, if you will keep a lookout for me, like a good fellow …?'

He made to stand up, but I stopped him, pointing a finger. 'I feel sure, Mr Baddenham, that your noose won't fit you. You'll merely slip right through it and ruin a great experiment, which would be a terrible shame.'

He fingered the noose around his neck doubtfully. 'Do you think so? Of course, you understand I am operating under *tremendous* difficulties.'

'Then let me give you a hand,' I coaxed. 'Come down here for a moment and let me help you with a really snug fit.'

Baddenham beamed. 'Would you? How kind. Stand aside then … here I come.'

'Whoa!' I yelled, holding up a hand to stop him as he teetered on the edge of the branch. 'Untie it from the tree first! It won't reach the ground and I can't stretch all the way up there.'

'Oh, how thoughtless of me!' exclaimed the idiot happily. He undid the knot, then leapt, trailing the cord behind him.

'I'm so glad you pointed that out,' he said. 'I might have hanged myself!'

I yanked off the noose, examined it closely and shook my head. 'Just as I thought. This is useless, Baddenham. It's twine – far too light.' I looked back into his anxious eyes. 'What's your weight?'

'Eleven and a half stone,' he replied at once.

I dangled the twine in front of him. 'And could this *really* bear eleven and a half stone?'

'I see what you mean, Autrey. I have been unforgivably dim-witted, haven't I? What would you advise me to do?'

To my relief, at that moment Winzey and Honeyball strolled into view.

'The very lads!' I exclaimed, beckoning them over urgently. 'You two, this gentleman has been caught in a most embarrassing predicament. Do you think you could find him some decent clothing? And when you've fitted him out,' I added, 'you might hand him over to Loy until I get back, there's good fellows.'

They nodded their agreement, took Baddenham companionably by an arm each, and departed, chatting amiably. I watched them disappear around a bend in the track, and felt thankful that I had at last done something constructive. All Baddenham needed now was a draught of Wealspring water and he should be well on the way to recovery.

'Well done, August!' said a voice behind me.

I swung round, wondering who could have stolen up on me so quietly – and gaped in astonishment.

CHAPTER 12

BLACK WAND

Even if the black cloak covered with glittering silver hieroglyphs, and the tall crown with its alternate points of opals and jet, had not given me a clue, the black and gold insignia of office in his hand would have been enough.

'Black Wand!' I gasped. Then, collecting my senses and remembering my manners, I doffed my cap with a bow and greeted him more properly, 'Hael and wyn, Black Wand.'

'Hael and wyn, August,' he answered, and looked up at the branch where Baddenham had been sitting. 'Touch and go, eh?'

'I was scared stiff,' I admitted, relaxing a little. 'The poor fellow's as mad as a hatter! Could he have broken his neck?'

'No one ever dies on the Weal,' he replied enigmatically. 'Nor is he mad – merely … maladjusted. Come!' He walked off in the direction I had been heading.

I went with him, wondering how long he might have been there observing the little comedy. I presumed he had come himself to prevent a tragedy but, finding me more or less in control of the situation, had decided not to interfere. From the direction he was taking, I realised that we would pass Great Oak, and I felt a little embarrassed at the effigies there.

'I expect you know about my morning story sessions?' I asked tentatively.

'I enjoy them immensely, August,' he replied. 'I am delighted that you have brought our people so much happiness.'

I was astonished. 'B-but ...' I began to stammer, 'I thought ...' What *did* I think? I had not seen him in the throng; nor, I was certain, had any of my listeners.

Although the little people might not know where their Wychies lived, they always knew when they were in the Weal, and they would certainly know that Black Wand was with me at that moment. That would account for our not meeting any of them as we walked. The Wychy turned, making for a curiously worn piece of sandstone jutting from the bank. He settled himself into its seat-like depression with a flare of his black and silver mantle and indicated a similar one opposite with his Wand. I sat down.

'You were thinking ...?' he reminded me softly.

'I never saw you,' I replied lamely.

'What? *You* – to whom the wiles of wizards are an open book?' he chided. 'You do not remember that they can transport themselves in the blink of an eye over forest and mountain, into the depths of the sea, and through the uppermost realms of the sky?'

His tone baffled me. I could not tell if he spoke mockingly or factually. But I did suddenly realise one thing: here was Black Wand, the one person I had striven so hard to find, the resolver of all problems, sitting here in front of me. What was I waiting for?

'Please,' I begged urgently before he could vanish, 'is this existence real?' How stupid can you get? I wondered, and added quickly, 'Sorry! Silly question. After all, if it is a dream then any answer you give will be just as unreal.'

'That is the logical premise,' he said gravely. 'But tell me, what would you regard as incontrovertible proof one way or the other?'

'Why, to become mortal again!' I answered at once. 'To be back as I was in the cottage in Three Weirs, writing my stories, playing cricket … all the usual things.'

He inclined his head, acknowledging his understanding. 'Very well, August. If that alone will remove your doubts then it shall surely be so.'

I was staggered. 'You mean I can go? I can *leave* all this?'

'In the twinkling of an eye. In fact you can forget all of this as if it had never been. It is for you to choose freely. I need touch you but once with my Wand and you will suffer a transformation as complete as any effected by the wizards of your imagination.' He lifted the gold and ebony stick.

I shrank back from it, appalled. Despite my mortality, the experience of elemental life was too profound to part with so easily. And yet he had promised '… *Forget all of this as if it had never been.*'

With my eyes fixed on the poised Wand, I realised his meaning. Forgetting everything would mean no regrets. Augustus Autrey would resume his interrupted life, settle down to writing again, and to the dubious comfort of artificialities; being content with the image and foregoing the real.

Foregoing the *real*! Had I answered my own question? Did I believe that *this*, after all, was reality?

I looked desperately from the Wand to the eyes beyond it for a clue, but the long lashes and partly lowered lids veiled them. I could not even see their colour. In one instant I thought them grey, the next blue, or violet or even green. No help there then. But of one thing I was certain: Black Wand was not bluffing – he could and would do exactly as he had promised. But I also knew that mortality no longer bore any comparison to this present existence.

He lowered his wand and toyed with it, saying, 'And the Fairy Prince was sauntering through the magic wood and he chanced upon a Fairy Wizard. And the prince said, "Alas, O puissant wizard, you see in me an eager changeling, a victim of kindly circumstances, a homeless wanderer blissfully content to be far from the land of my fathers. I pray thee, grant me release from this wonderful servitude." And the wizard answered, "Willingly, fair prince! I will grant thee the traditional three wishes that every weaver of magic must yield to his captives. Take then thy first, and be gone!" But the Fairy Prince wavered and the moment passed. The fulfilment of the wish died on his breath …' The Wychy paused, holding the Wand between the long forefingers of each slender hand. 'Only two more wishes may now be granted, August. You are fortunate that The Wychies may grant three wishes, for the little people seldom require more than one. And that, as a rule, is the last of all desires – the granting of the Bane.'

'Wych's Bane – the one that takes us back to mortality? Is it true that Hyllis has taken it?'

He nodded slowly. 'Such is White Wand's privilege, and hers alone – to supply the Bane to any who are beyond our help. Even we cannot wholly defeat the Sickness.'

'So whoever takes the Bane is reborn as a human baby?' I asked.

'That is the law.'

'And eating Wizard's Woe makes one come back again into … this state?'

Again he nodded, and waited while I thought this through.

'I don't understand,' I said at last. 'If every human being who dies becomes a wiccy or wicca we would be crowded out – there would be millions of us here!'

'The number is limited, August. The vast majority of the human race are not of *our* race. Their wraiths are from the mortal strain, not the elemental.'

'So in due time I shall eat the Bane and go back to mortality. Yet you said just now that you could send me back …'

'The Bane of the Wych is *one* of the means by which it is most easily accomplished.'

'Then I have been a little person before?'

'Many times! This is your immortal heritage. If it weren't for the Sickness – our pathological desire for mortality – we would live in its tranquillity forever.'

'So what happened?' I asked. 'What caused it?' It was a critical question, raising what I considered to be a fundamental issue.

'There's a pleasant jingle they sing to human infants hereabouts,' he murmured. 'How goes it …?

> 'The Dragon made the Dragon's Woe
> And Adder made the King's …'

He looked at me expectantly so I continued the rhyme to its end, while he nodded his head to the rhythm. When I had finished, his voice glided in without a pause:

> 'Once Alder and the Dragga slept
> In amity and clover
> 'Til evil came and Mona wept
> And golden days were over
>
> One Weird made twain and ne'er again
> Might King or Dragga falter
> But weave and wage eternal war
> Each other's Weird to alter
>
> Then Dragga dree'd a mortal weird
> And Alder dree'd another
> To separate the Weal from Woe
> The Wychies made another

And that our people be not wiled
The foreign weird to fondle
'Tween Dragga's Woe and Alder's Weal
The Wychies made The Wandle

'Dragga, which we also call *Drawer*,' he explained, 'is the principle that draws immortals into mortal existence – by reason of their curiosity. Once upon a time mankind and the fae were distinct and separate races. Man was mortal and roamed the earth taking no notice of the immortal fae: "*Alder and the Dragga lay in Amity and clover*".

'But there came a time when curiosity drove the fae to consort with mortals – and the mortals then wanted immortality. They drank unbidden from the secret Wealspring of life. But whereas the essence of the fount could only operate for good in immortals, it worked only for evil in men. The stolen essence inflamed their egos and they believed themselves to be lords of all creation. When these new *inhuman* beings stalked the earth the wisest among us grew alarmed, for the lands writhed in torment. Soon the veil between the two races became so tenuous that one could scarcely be told from the other.

'So it was that the two greatest Wychies of our kind secured a royal babe named Alder, who was both mortal *and* immortal, to rule between the two. But a catastrophe engulfed our ancient land, the Fount of Immortality ran dry, and the faerie races were scattered – bereft of kings, bereft of wychies, bereft of wisdom.

'Alder and his two counsellors gathered what remnant they could find of our people and made what peace they could with the forces of mortality.

'The Weird of Dragga was undefeated, but the Immortal Weird is also indestructible. So our people live in both existences, alternating between the two to keep a balance. Such is our tribute to Dragga's Weird – the price of our independence.'

While he was speaking, he idly made a series of intricate movements with the Wand, performing astonishing little tricks that held me mesmerised while I listened.

The sound of nearby voices roused me from my blissful state.

'Well, blimey – if it ain't Gussy! He ought to know. Hi there, Aug!'

Barnsley and St John were standing close by. I waved them away, frowning distractedly and looking around for Black Wand.

'Good morning Mr Autrey,' said St John briskly. 'Do you happen to have seen Mr Baddenham anywhere?'

'In the buff, too!' said Barnsley. 'Not that it matters a fig. But the perishing dope's liable to hang himself.'

'Baddenham's fine,' I said. 'Please go away, I'm talking to someone.'

Barnsley whispered in awestruck tones, 'He's had it, Sinjy ... he's off *his* trolley too!'

'Good heavens!' St John whispered back. 'What are we going to do? He's one of *us* you know. We can't let him drift. It's those blasted goblins again – we never should have let him leave *Mens Sana*.'

Barnsley sounded dubious. 'I don't know, Sinjy. Gussy's a tricky beggar. If he don't want to come, I don't fancy trying ...' They had turned away from me to discuss the situation, so I rose and walked quietly away.

Barnsley's cry of 'Gawd a'mighty, Sinjy! If he hasn't disappeared into thin air!' hardly registered. I was too annoyed that Black Wand had vanished just when I seemed to be getting some answers.

CHAPTER 13

WHITE WAND

There were radical changes in the company that gathered at Great Oak the following morning. Leila was missing, and Loy was sitting between Baddenham and Simmonds – both now dressed in conventional elfin garb and each plainly in a state of wonder.

When I saw that Dina's artless smile had become an expression of ardent longing as she came to my side, I was terror-stricken. How could I avoid sending her the way of Hyllis and Leila? I was safe for the moment, however, so I centred my thoughts firmly on describing the cottage in which the Maiden Chrysobel lived. She was, I said, the only daughter of a poor woodcutter and she supplemented their meagre income by baking delicious cakes and selling them to their neighbours.

There must have been a lilt in my voice or an unconscious rhythm in the sentences I used, for Loy, Jean, Fizzy and Honeyball began leading a chant at every mention of Chrysobel's name:

> Who cuts the wood
> That feeds the fire
> That heats the oven
> That bakes the cakes
> That Chrysobel makes
> To save them from star-vay-shun!

Smye was in his element. What were the ingredients of the cakes? How many cakes to a batch? How big was the village? How many cakes did each villager eat?

But Smye now found himself tackled by a rival, who joined in with great authority. 'My friend, you cannot base such computations upon a hundred percent of any commodity in any community, for the simple reason that not every individual likes every variety of food ...' It was Baddenham and he was achieving instant success, with cheers and laughter after every point of his detailed argument. Only Simmonds remained silent, still with his arms crossed, watching, listening and wondering.

Sylvie nestled closer. 'Isn't Baddy delightful, August? He has such an earnest face, yet he looks so, so sad.'

'Then you could try cheering him up,' I said, taking the opportunity to evade yet another possible disaster. The tender-hearted wiccy must have taken my advice, for when I ended that morning's instalment only Dina clung to my arm.

'Now listen, my sweet,' I said firmly. 'You are a delicious, wonderfully delightful pet, and I love you very much indeed, but you know I am a sick man and I want to be left alone.'

'But you were alone all yesterday,' she pouted sweetly. 'It isn't good that you should pine like this.' She snuggled into my arms and turned up a pair of eyes brimming with love and sympathy. 'There is such promise in your eyes, dear, dear, August,' she sighed.

'Oh, no!' I held her off at arms length in alarm. 'When wiccies start talking about my eyes ...'

'Then you should veil them, as Black Wand does,' she replied unashamedly. 'It is very naughty that you should captivate wiccies with your melancholy glances and then decline the love you encourage.'

This was really becoming very difficult. Fortunately

Simmonds came to my rescue.

'I say ...' he began, striding forward from the dispersing crowd.

'Just the person!' I exclaimed. 'Please look after Dina for me until I get back. I have a most urgent appointment.' I cart-wheeled away from the surprised wiccy, dived into the undergrowth and sped off to Wandleside, for I really did have an urgent appointment. Black Wand hadn't been much use, so I had decided I would find White Wand and see if I could get some assistance from her.

I was so fired up that I was halfway down Windaway before the first doubt struck me. Here I was, about to attempt the same crossing I had so dismally failed at three days earlier ... and with no one to rescue me this time. I looked again at the Weirds, rippling under a light breeze and reflecting the trees from The Wandle and a cloudy sky. There was no hint of the concealed magical resistance that had been my downfall before. All the same, I resorted to cunning.

Arriving at the junction of the lakes, I turned idly southwards and walked slowly along Wychies' Weird, nonchalantly picking up flat stones and making them skip across the water with reassuring results. I wandered on until I found a place where the water was almost level with the path. Then I sauntered close to the edge and let my right foot sink into the boggy margin. So far, so good – either the water was just water and nothing else, or the magical field did not extend this far from the narrows. Perhaps I could swim across. I found a tussock and sat on it with my feet entirely in the water. Then I began to intone a kind of introductory incantation:

'White Wand! White Wand!
Wyn me my wiccy, Wand ...!'

As I sang over and over, I realised the truth of something Leila had told me.

'The sound of "W" is the very essence of wisdom,' she had said. 'There's wicca and wiccy, and Wychy and Wych, and there's Weal and Woe, and Wynning and Wreak, waxing and waning, wither and wend. Then there's Wandle and wandling, and wayward and wile, wyché and woery, Weird, and wondrous and wraith ... the sound of "W" is wholly magical, beloved.'

And it *was* magical. I was beginning to merge with my surroundings. I was becoming one with the water. And then I realised that the trees from The Wandle were no longer reflections but physically around me. So I began to walk. I didn't choose any particular direction, but I found that I was following a maze of faerie tracks. Nothing guided me, yet I walked without faltering. I felt no elation at finding myself on The Wandle, and nothing reminded me that The Wandle was wiled.

I came suddenly into a circular clearing carpeted with grass and flowers, and blinked in the strong sunlight that poured in overhead. And there she was, sitting before a white stone archway engraved with curious markings, on a chair made of the same white stone. On her lap lay a shimmering white garment over which her fingers flew deftly with glittering needle and thread. And on the embroidery rested a Wand – white inlaid with gold – the fellow of the one I had seen yesterday. Her robe was a flowing film of white, sprinkled with a starry motif and girdled with a silver cincture blazing with diamonds. Her figure, rosy and gleaming through the almost transparent garment, took my breath away.

Looking at her, I knew no other and desired no other. I could only stand and gaze in thrilled absorption at her flawless perfection. The curve of her neck as she bent over her work; the slope of her half-revealed shoulders; the delicate bloom of skin wherever it could be seen; and the hair that cascaded from beneath her silver crown and rolled in waves to the level of her waist – she captivated my whole attention. Hyllis had called her 'the loveliest of all the fae'. And it was true.

She looked up casually and stared straight through me as if I wasn't there, and it occurred to me that I should bow my head or make some other kind of formal obeisance. But at that precise moment she lowered her head and returned to her sewing.

On a tripod at her side was a large crystal ball made of beryl. Light and shade played constantly in its depths, and at times a splash of colour, although I could see nothing to account for the reflections. Aware that I could stand still no longer, I walked slowly forwards. My heart thumped in apprehension as I stood before her, hypnotised by the dexterity of her fingers and feeling like a gawky schoolboy summoning the courage to speak.

'White Wand …' I began, while at the same moment wishing that I had never found her.

'Be seated, August.'

The breathtaking sweetness of her voice made my heart pound with delight. With nowhere to sit but the grass, I sank down and wrapped my arms around my drawn up knees. At least from there I could watch her expression. More than anything though, I longed to see her eyes. As if she guessed, she turned them on me for a moment – and I was bewildered. They were not faerie eyes! Their shining clarity hid their depths, but I knew their expression was not altogether friendly.

'I've wanted most urgently to talk to you,' I said reproachfully.

'Do Mortals answer every call, August? Or is their privacy respected?' she answered with shattering sweetness, her hands continuing their work.

I stared back blankly. She continued in her dulcet tones, 'Have our people not treated you with every kindness? And have you not repaid them with rudeness –?'

'Rudeness?' I interrupted. 'Well I like that! Don't I give them long instalments of my story every morning –?'

An almost imperceptible shake of her head silenced me. 'You demand answers to questions they cannot understand. You disturb their peace of mind and cloud their joyous freedom. In short, you behave as you have no right to behave – like a selfish, unmannerly mortal.'

I had no answer, but I felt the need to defend myself. 'I didn't ask to come here, you know. I didn't ask to be changed. I was born mortal and I was quite content to stay that way. But someone put a spell on me and changed me into a … a …'

'And does that justify such ill treatment of our innocents?'

'You mean Hyllis and Leila?'

'Not only those …'

'Where is Leila? I was told she had come to you.'

'She came. And now she has gone.'

'You mean you've already given her the Bane? Why?'

'I cannot refuse the Bane to any who asks for it, August.' She moved the garment under her fingers. 'If you were to ask for it at this moment, I would have to give it you. Do you so desire?' I thought she looked at me quite hopefully.

'No, thank you,' I said quickly. 'And anyway I was asking about Leila.'

'It is profitless to speak of the departed,' she answered. 'But you remain, August, and that is a grave problem for my wiccies. That so many of them ask to be made mortal becomes alarming.'

'It's not my fault. And Black Wand doesn't seem to blame me. He says it's in my weird.'

'August, I cannot presume to question the dictums of my brother Wand –' She broke off and glanced at the ball of beryl, which was suddenly full of movement. Complicated shades and colours ebbed and flowed, creating points of light and dark as they met and crossed. I do not know how I knew, but I realised I was looking at a master plan of the forest communication system that had so intrigued me.

The Wych continued. 'Those unable to mingle with our people set themselves apart – as have those at St John's Wood. They surround themselves with walls of their own devising that do not mar the pattern of our Weal. Yet you not only reject the society of these self-condemned outlaws but destroy what little unity they strive so hard to maintain.'

While she had been speaking, it seemed as if the crystal ball had changed to reflect her thoughts. Its kaleidoscopic background now held a number of darkly opalescent centres. The big one, I reasoned, must be *Mens Sana*; and the three smaller ones that seemed to be moving irregularly around it would be its three remaining inmates. Two others moving away from it must be Baddenham and Simmonds assimilating with their new surroundings. And that other dark blob with stars at its centre … well, that one seemed to represent *me*!

The Wych saw my gaze and looked surprised. 'You can read the Wych ball?' she demanded.

'I think so,' I said. 'I realised the significance of the blobs while you were blaming me for setting the two little dark ones free from the big black hole of *Mens Sana*. And I can't actually see what's wrong with that. Look at those two over there on the left – they're beginning to tone in with their background quite nicely.'

With a dazzling flash of white and silver she flung her work over the ball, completely covering it. 'I might have worked the whole thing out if you hadn't have done that,' I grumbled, rubbing my eyes.

'So I feared,' she answered. 'But these things are secret. No other faerie eyes are capable of even seeing them. There is mystery in you, August. How came you here?' Her eyes, though still largely unreadable, betrayed such obvious interest that I almost laughed for joy. I had begun to mean something to her!

'I think I was wandled,' I replied. 'I am a changeling, spirited away from his world and plunged into a realm that never ought to exist outside romantic fict–' I broke off and changed tack '… White Wand, do you know that you are the most beautiful being in all the little kingd–?'

'Yes, August.' So cool and casual, and spoken before I had even finished saying it; I was flabbergasted.

'Why should you believe one of us has wandled you?' she went on evenly. 'What said my brother Wand?'

I tugged idly at a blade of grass while I considered her question. Her foot moved fractionally and my hand tingled as if from an electric shock. I pulled it away sharply.

'Ow! What was that for?' I asked.

'Destroy no life, August. Only mortals do that.'

Not only was this delectable Wych the possessor of incomparable beauty, she also had a profoundly practical side that missed none of my thoughts and actions. I apologised sincerely. 'Black Wand talked of everything else but wandling,' I continued ruefully. 'In fact now that I think of it, he very cleverly explained absolutely nothing. They say you and he are the wisest of all the little people. And if you can't explain it, how can I?'

'You inhabit a faerie wraith, so you must have eaten Wizard's Woe,' the Wych replied. 'But never have I known so mortal a fay!'

Her eyes fixed me with a look that seemed to examine me to the bone. 'You are both mortal *and* fay,' she said slowly. 'And that is an anomaly. You also read the Wych ball like a book.' She rested her chin on one hand and watched me from between half-closed lids, reminding me of the other Wand.

'There is terrible mortality in you, August – and all mingled with the sweet seeds of immortality that you will not permit to grow. Small wonder no wiccy can resist you.' She paused and then said, 'August, I did not Wandle you. But you no longer wish to go back?'

'No, not while I can sit here and look at you,' I said candidly. 'I was told you were the loveliest of all the fae,' I went on, hugging my knees to hide their trembling. 'And I was warned that I might only adore, but never dare to love. Yet how can I help myself?'

She laughed out loud – a silver sound that filled my senses with ecstasy 'Oh, August, August, my poor love-hungry swain! For two whole days you mourned Hyllis. And but an hour ago you were singing the song of longing to me. But for whom? Who was on your mind when you sat dabbling your feet in the water and chanting "*White Wand! White Wand! Wyn me my wiccy, Wand!*"?'

'That's unfair!' I cried.

'Unfair? Unfair that I should remind you of your purpose for coming here? Did you not call the one call that a Wych may never disregard?' Her glorious eyes widened for a second in simulated surprise. But as I squirmed inwardly at her reminder, my soul floundered in rapture at the glowing vision of loveliness leaning over me.

'Would it soothe your stricken soul, dear sorcerer of love, if I brought Leila here and placed her in your eager arms? It may not yet be too late. Perhaps I can perform the miracle and snatch her from her doom. Speak quickly, time is short – shall I call her?'

She raised her Wand and I groaned, then set my lips firmly, determined not to give her the satisfaction of hearing yea or nay escape them.

She tossed the glittering Wand high into the air and cried, 'Go then, dear Leila! Wise was your choice, indeed! Your lover so soon has gone a-seeking compensation!' She caught the Wand as it fell and laughed. 'Poor August! You do not need to voice your choice; it is written in the depths of your yearning eyes! But it will be no easy thing, I warn you, O Weaver of Lies. No miserable hag of your fanciful imagination ever devised the exquisite torment that *this* wicked Sybil shall inflict upon you. Shall you be content then to sit just where you are and feast your eyes on a form that inflames you with unrequitable desire, and on glances that agonise with unattainable promise?' She laughed again, and the richness and depths of the sound made me feel faint with its thrill.

'So be it, then,' she said when I made no reply. 'I too will be content, and content shall be the lacerated hearts of my wiccies.'

She drew the garment she had been embroidering back onto her knee and continued her work, leaving me speechless and immobile at her side. It was only when I came to move and could not, to speak and dared not, that I knew what she had done. I was condemned by my own foolhardiness to sit there in silent adoration, like a graven image. From her silver-sandaled feet to the flashing crown on her head, my gaze could wander at will, yet never see enough of her exquisite form through the transparency of her robe.

Hours passed this way, while I sat enthralled with the inescapable delight of my eyes and filled with excruciating longing. Sometimes she would cast me a glance and a smile. Sometimes, as she adjusted her work, the rippling fabric would lightly brush my clasped hands, or her foot carelessly but briefly meet mine, to evoke such agony that I could have screamed. But I had no voice.

The needle stabbed endlessly and her hand plucked ceaselessly throughout the day as the crystal ball ebbed and flowed at her side. Sunné set and Mona rose. And silence grew between us.

CHAPTER 14

GWENDOLYN

I learned afterwards that because the story sessions had become such an established source of amusement, my disappearance caused enormous dismay. Discordant rumours shattered the tranquillity of the Weal: I had spurned Dina's love and incurred the wrath of the White One, who had swept into the forest like an angry goddess and despatched me to the nethermost regions of mortality in the twinkling of an eye. But Smye thought otherwise. He said it was obvious that the Wych had become enamoured with me and had drawn me to The Wandle where I would be powerless to resist her charms – even if I wanted to. This was received with a lot of respect – and even greater dismay, for they all knew what it meant to be a recipient of a Wych's love. They would never see their dear August again. No more stories; no more laughing at the antics of Fizzlebane or Fumingwort; no more cheering the furious Dreadful on his way.

None of them could bear to pass Great Oak, where the effigies reminded them of what the White One had taken from them. So they had to take long and circuitous routes to get anywhere at all.

As the hours lengthened and apprehension grew, the jangled lines of the forest communications suddenly vibrated with news: *Black Wand is in the Weal!*

Loy discovered it to be true when he met the imposing figure striding along the path towards him. The wicca stood respectfully to one side and gave the traditional greeting.

'Hael and wyn, Black Wand.'

The Black One stopped. 'Hael and wyn, brother Loy! Tell me, what ails my people?'

Loy replied with single-hearted sincerity. 'We mourn for our brother August, Black Wand. He is gone from us never to return. Despite his often bad humour and his fatal charm over the wiccies, we loved him. We have never known a brother so amusing, so merry and so wise.'

'And where, say my people, has this paragon gone?'

'They say he has gone to The Wandle, Black Wand. That White Wand has taken him for herself …'

Black Wand surprised him by laughing gently. 'Grieve no more, brother Loy. Fear not for your friend. Go tell all our people that no harm shall come to him. He will return, and *that* I promise! Let the forest ways be reunited and all abide in peace. Farewell!'

*

In the half-light of The Wandle, I saw the Wych lift her head at someone's approach and move her Wand gracefully as if acknowledging a silent greeting.

'Sister Wand,' came Black Wand's voice quietly, 'the Weal is distraught. Our people pine for your love-bound prisoner. Is it wyché to hold him thus and have our people mourn? What would you with him?'

'I would preserve my wiccies, Brother Wand! They wither like moths in the hot breath of his flame. Better he should be here, enclosed, than so many of my wiccies go prematurely to mortality.'

'I have sworn, Sister Wych, that he shall not depart. And in truth he is not meant for dispatch. I have promised our sorrowing people that their idol shall be restored to them. Would you have me break a Wychy promise?'

'But, see – he does not wish to go. He has chosen his weird. To release him will not avail, for he will not leave. Nothing now will satisfy him but my love … and that, as you know, would be disaster for him.'

'Perhaps not.' Black Wand's tranquil voice was soft. 'Like ourselves, he is not wholly fay, Sister Wych – this much you have already divined. He is wyché also, and has magic of a contrary kind.'

'Where does he come from then, that he is so unlike our own? What is his mystery?'

'Ask of *him*, Sister Wych. My mission is done. Hael and wyn, White One!'

The Wych began a gesture as if imploring him to stay, but checked it. Several minutes passed before she sighed and looked down at me. 'So, my patient prisoner, I am bidden to enquire of you the cause of all this wrack. Well, I am a good listener, so say on.'

I found myself released, able to move and speak, so I told her the sequence of events that had led to the fatal climax a week ago. As I did so, I suddenly remembered the gold and jet black Wand that had written the fateful words: *Mrs Mye, I am going to disappear.* I had utterly forgotten it until that moment, but as I spoke about it now its significance made me stop and gasp. The Wych and I stared at each other; me in wonder, she in delighted amazement.

'O, incomparable Wychy!' she cried aloud to her Brother Wand. 'Truly thou art the greatest of all Wands!' Then she leaned forward eagerly. 'But that cannot be all, August – say on!'

When I told her about finding myself inside my shirt, she interrupted me incredulously. 'Then you are not half born! You have left no mortal shell!'

'White Wand, I am *not* dead!' I exclaimed.

She gazed at me for a while with a baffled expression. 'A Wych is a sorry creature at times, August,' she eventually continued. 'She knows wisdom in many guises, yet misreads the greatest of all redes. The youngest wiccy has proven wiser than her Wych. "August is mortal," they said. And August *is* mortal; mortal and immortal both – a miracle of the enchanter's art. What said my Brother Wand?' She raised her head as if addressing him. 'Truly, O Peerless One, he is *incapable* of dispatch.'

She flung the garment over the crystal ball once more and knelt before me, her bright face level with mine, contrite yet radiant. 'Lo! An immortal kneels to a mortal, August – something that aeons of time have not seen. And she craves his forgiveness.'

I seized her hands and covered them with kisses. 'No, no,' I rambled. 'Wrong me again, O White One. Imprison me every day by your side.'

Her arms came round me, drawing me into her ethereal embrace, and unimaginable bliss swept over me.

*

How it came to pass that I should find myself capering through the Weal at sunrise, only a Wych could explain. I had plunged into unconsciousness with the moon's setting and woken again at day-spring – but not on The Wandle. White Wych had ensured I would keep the Black One's promise, for nothing would have made me leave her of my own accord.

I was in a state of intoxication. 'Behold the lover of White Wand!' I carolled as I gambolled across a glade. 'My shackles are the silken tresses of a Wych's hair,' I sang.

Her lips they are the moisture
Of the scarcely falling rain
Caressing, warmly touching
Pressing swiftly on again
And dimly coming scented
From between the magic twain
Her breathing is the night wind
As it murmurs on the plain

Her skin is softest twilight
When the very heavens fawn
Its freshness waking cowslip
'Mid the meadow-moss at dawn
Her presence is the stirring
Of the rising life at morn
Which calls a joyous answer
From rowan, oak and thorn!

I loved the Wych! And that fabulous being loved me!

*

The fifth instalment of my serial was a memorable session, and quite unlike any of the others. There is no privacy among the little people. All knew the truth. August had achieved the impossible – he had made love to the Wych and lived!

Dina and Sylvie remained faithful attendants, but a little apprehensive and not a little proud to be so close. I hugged them both as if nothing had occurred and received their delighted kisses in return, but in good fellowship. Beyond it, they knew, lay an impassable barrier. The White One herself had clearly indicated her preference for this wicca of wiccas. I was thankful for the accidental disclosure a few days earlier that my story contained no Wych, otherwise my embarrassment would have been complete.

When the session began to break up in its usual hub-bub, an unexpected murmur of surprise rippled across the crowd, and silence fell. A lane opened up before me, and down it came a figure in a tabard of gold, blue and red, bearing a trumpet on his hip. There was such dignity in his bearing that I rose and doffed my cap as he arrived. A flourish of the trumpet greeted this.

'Hael and wyn, noble August. I am Kye, the Royal Herald, come to proclaim an edict of Alder, our noble King!'

I blinked at the announcement. Was there really a King of the little people? I somehow found the presence of mind to respond. 'Hael and wyn, Royal Herald! Pray exercise your duty.'

He gave a quick smile before turning to execute a fanfare. 'O, my People ancient from of eld!' he declaimed. 'Heed this edict that none may disregard. Know that upon this coming eve Our Lady Mona shall be taken from us for a spell, that she may pay her eternal tribute to our enemy, Dragga. Wherefore we do command ye, one and all: Be not abroad from Mona's first arising until our noble Wychies shall declare the evil Wreak to be waned and Mona returned to hold the night enthralled. Remember and obey, beloved people. Hael and wyn!'

The Herald concluded with a final crescendo and strode away.

I saw – and felt – that his words had cast a cloud of fear over the assembly. The little people shivered and crowded together, and I was conscious of foreboding. Before I could ask any questions, however, another sensation swept across the crowd.

'Tis Rosynose!' exclaimed Dina, clapping her hands with joy. Everyone else beamed their pleasure at the arrival of a shallow dray, heavily laden with barrels, jacks and crates, drawn by six gaily caparisoned spotted fawns.

Beside the scarlet and gold clad coachman, and in even more resplendent livery, sat a rotund little figure who threw up his hat and opened his arms to the crowd.

Everyone rushed forward to greet him. Before I could catch anyone for an explanation, the individual himself emerged from the crowd with a wiccy on each arm.

'Hael and wyn, August! I am Rozyn-Who-Knows, the Royal Vintner, and yonder is largesse from our Liege who bids me dispense to all who stand in need of comfort and joy on this day of portent and dread omen!' He laid a finger alongside his nose and winked. 'If, therefore, your story be at its close, I will proceed to regale our brethren with refreshment.'

'Hael and wyn, noble Rozyn,' I returned. 'It is so concluded. Pray proceed.'

As he returned to the dray, I overheard Loy asking, 'Fizzy, what's he mean – this day of portent and dread omen?'

'It only happens now and then, Loy. It's to do with High Moon. Sometimes Mona's light disappears while she is still there in the sky. The Wreak from Dragga takes over the Weal and we dare not be abroad.'

'Oh, you mean a lunar eclipse,' said Loy. 'There's nothing in that, old man.'

'Oh, but there *is*, dear Loy,' Dina assured him. 'It releases the terrible Wreak.'

'So there'll be no fun and games,' I joined in, disappointed that I was to be denied another meeting with my fascinating Wych just because of some natural phenomenon.

'But there *will* be, August,' she assured me. 'When Mona's light returns and the Wreak is gone, we shall hasten to The Wandle. Rosynose brings us special potions before the doom occurs so that we do not suffer so dreadfully in the darkness, for we do not fall asleep at these times – that is what makes it so awful. But see, Rosynose is beckoning us.'

I watched as casks were tapped and goblets of gold and cups of crystal were distributed. Loy held one out for me to sample and the taste was honeysuckle sweet. A glow tingled through me to my fingers and toes. In another moment I would have slid rapturously into the inviting arms of Sylvie, had Rozyn not intervened.

'Come, come, brother,' he chided, passing me another concoction. 'We've enough trouble with Dragga without you doing his work for him. What you need is a foxglove-fix-me-up!'

'Perhaps I don't want to be "fixed up", Rosy,' I said, ogling another wiccy behind him.

'Try this,' he advised, passing me another cup. I drank, then drifted off into unconsciousness.

When I opened my eyes, I found myself lying between two barrels of highly polished oak bound with silver hoops. Fronds of bracken sped past above me like serrated green clouds. The sound of tiny galloping hooves made me sit up and stare at the backs of Rozyn and the coachman. We were speeding along a broad track-way.

'That was some knock-out drop, Rosy!' I said. 'Are you my guardian angel, or what?'

He turned round with a broad grin. 'You could say that I am, August. Had I not countered the honeysuckle rum, a certain one-who-shall-be-nameless might have been very displeased. And, as you may know, her displeasure can be most disconcerting.'

I felt no resentment towards him for the trick, nor disturbed that he appeared to be in my Wych's confidence.

'Where's your hideout, Rozyn?' I asked.

'By the Brook of Wynn, brother,' he said. 'Its magic water is a tonic in itself.' He gave me a whimsical glance.

I understood the meaning of his look. It reminded me of Leila and the night we'd spent together beside the moonlit water. I switched my thoughts away.

'Where does the King live?' I asked.

'At Alder's Stede, northward of his Weird. You will be presented to him this night when we all forgather on The Wandle.'

The vehicle slowed to negotiate a piece of rough ground.

'And where are we going now?'

'To the Wynn, to dispense comfort to the gnomes. They too are subject to Our Lady Mona and the King, you know.'

'Is there no queen?' I asked.

He looked astonished for a moment. 'Is there not Our Lady Mona of the skies?' he replied enigmatically.

Before I could comment, he let out a delighted guffaw. 'Pull up, Colly,' he ordered. 'Here's Skinney, the siren of St John's Wood! What shall we prescribe, I wonder? Essence of nectarine? A juniper jolt? Or a flagon of oak apple ale?'

The driver obeyed and halted before Miss Kinney, who was signalling us to stop with a primitive umbrella of folded beech leaves.

Rozyn rose, doffing his cap, and saluted her with an elaborate bow.

'Hael and wyn, fair one! We are agog to know your pleasure?'

'Don't be impertinent,' she said primly. 'Kindly inform me where I can find Mr Baddenham.'

'My lips are sealed, O virtuous one! I dare not assault such virginal ears as yours with any telling of his present occupation.'

'You mean he has, er, *gone native*?'

'Alas. He is lost forever, O rose petal whom even the lovely fauns must envy.'

'Don't be so ridiculous, you absurd creature. He must be returned at once. Do you understand? At once, I say! You have no right to hold him prisoner.'

I stood up, doffed my cap and bowed. 'Good morrow, Miss Kinney.'

She gave a frightened little scream and stepped back, presenting her umbrella defensively with a trembling hand. 'Mr Autrey! I didn't realise you were there. D-don't you dare come near me. Keep away, please. Stay where you are …'

'My dear Miss Kinney,' I said reproachfully, 'is that the way to treat an old friend? Have I not eaten your salt? Were you not anxious to take me into the bosom of the St John's Wood intelligentsia?'

'After the way you've been behaving the last few days?' she said scornfully. 'Barnsley has told me every-thing. Yes – *everything*! You … you wretched man.'

'I very much doubt it,' I said cheerfully. 'Even *his* purple imagination wouldn't be capable of that!'

'You are positively disgusting, Mr Autrey. I don't know how you can stand there and brazenly admit your shameful profligacy. Is no one safe from your prurient attention?'

'*You* aren't fishing, are you, Miss Kinney?' I asked.

'How … how dare you!' She backed away, waving her umbrella menacingly in my direction. Her suddenly wide open – and unexpectedly lustrous – blue eyes abruptly made me realise that beneath her outrageous appearance was a rather beautiful fay. The coachman was holding his sides. Rozyn borrowed his whip to deliver a surreptitious dig in my ribs with a wink and a chuckle, and I crammed his cap down over his ears in retaliation.

'You're mad, Mr Autrey. You're all quite mad!' Miss Kinney squealed. 'Jeremiah warned me this morning. He said you sprang out at him like a fiend from hell.'

Whatever had been in Rozyn's first potion still appeared to be working, for I jumped down from the dray and approached her with outstretched arms.

'Like this?' I asked.

She gave a piercing scream and ran into the undergrowth – and immediately fell foul of a network of brambles that held her fast.

'Here goes!' I cried, and dived after her.

'Get away, you ... you *monster!*' she screamed, trying to hide portions of her anatomy that the thorns had exposed.

'Do you *really* imagine that I am about to assault your virtue, Miss Kinney?' I asked patiently.

'Wh-what are you going to do to me?'

'Free you from these thorns if I can. Now, lie still. I can't get at them if you keep squirming around like a demented eel.'

'I'm being torn to ribbons,' she moaned. 'I shall die from loss of blood.'

'Rubbish,' I said. I pulled aside a portion of her skirt to release it and she gave a terrified gasp, which I ignored. 'Haven't you discovered that elfin flesh can't be punctured?' I asked. 'You may *feel* the thorns, but they won't even scratch you.'

The victim examined her hands with surprise. 'Oh,' she said, then surveyed the rest of herself. 'But look at my clothes.'

'Not very much left *to* look at!' I answered.

She blushed. 'Must you be so personal, Mr Autrey?'

'If you can tell me how to untangle this mess without exposing your nether limbs to knee height, please do so by all means. But why worry anyway? They're rather well-shaped calves – and I *am* a bit of an expert on these subjects, as you may have gathered.'

'I-I used to have rather nice legs, Mr Autrey.' There was certain breathlessness in her tentative reply.

'They're still worth a second look,' I agreed heartily.

'Mr Autrey, how *dare* you! You really mustn't. You're taking advantage of me when I am defenceless.' But her voice lacked any real conviction, and then softened. 'You know, Augustus, I think Barnsley must have been exaggerating. You don't appear to be half as dangerous as he says.' She sighed, and continued meditatively, 'Do you know, it's really quite comfortable here – and the thorns don't hurt at all.'

I rose to my feet.

'Aren't you going to set me free, Augustus?'

'You're as free as the air already,' I said in as disinterested a tone as I could manage. 'There's nothing clinging to you now – not even me. But as long as you insist on wearing these physical clothes, Miss Kinney, you will get tangled up again. Elfin garments are impervious to injury and slip right through obstructions. You should get a proper faerie wardrobe, then all your troubles will be over.'

'But they can be *seen through*, Augustus,' she said apprehensively. 'And besides, I don't know where to get them.'

'It's not difficult,' I promised, giving her a hand to her feet. Somehow she contrived to rise too quickly, and over-balanced into my arms.

'Oh, Augustus!' she exclaimed, holding on tightly.

'Miss Kinney!' I gasped, surprised by the beatific smile that had transformed her features into almost regal beauty.

'Do call me Gwendolyn,' she breathed.

'Well, blimey O'Riley!' said a voice behind me. I saw a shade of the old Miss Kinney return as her eyes narrowed in mortification.

'Barnsley! You horrible little eavesdropper.'

I looked over my shoulder to see a study of amazement.

'Oh, hullo Barnsley,' I said casually, disengaging myself and stepping aside. 'Uncanny knack you have of dropping in when you're not invited.'

Barnsley's mouth gaped as his ogling eyes swept over Gwendolyn's suggestive disarray. Then he turned to me with a look of undisguised admiration.

'Aug,' he said, lifting his cap, 'I have to hand it to you. You're a ruddy caveman. Phew! And she can't say I didn't warn her!'

'*Augustus*,' said Gwendolyn, intimating with all the authority of a well-bred woman that I was required to offer my arm in support. I bowed, crooked an elbow and, with her hand resting on it, we swept past the dumb-founded interloper. I had a momentary vision of an exquisitely beautiful face above me, examining the ever-moving depths of a large crystal ball with quizzical amusement.

I looked down at the strange scarecrow of femininity beside me. Gwendolyn was so exactly the glowing picture of a butterfly emerging painfully from its broken chrysalis that I felt a dangerous impulse towards compassion. But then Sylvie and Dina made an unexpected appearance from round a bend in the path and stopped to stare in astonishment.

'Augustus!' whispered Gwendolyn sharply, shaking my arm insistently.

'August!' cried Dina, as she and Sylvie hurried to examine my charge. 'Whatever have you been doing to this poor wiccy?'

'It's Skinney!' cried Sylvie. 'Oh, poor you. Really, August, you are so clumsy. Just look at these garments – you've torn them to pieces.'

'Skinney, dear,' said Dina, 'we're sorry we've avoided you for so long, but we had no idea how very beautiful you are.'

To my relief, they disengaged the bewildered Gwendolyn from my arm, petting and patting her, and I was able to vanish quietly into the bracken.

CHAPTER 15

THE WREAK

It seemed that I had taken another step forward thanks to the Royal Vintner's beverages, for now I found that I could tap into the delicate and intangible threads of understanding which spread from elf to elf throughout the forest. Thinking of Gwendolyn's dramatic transformation brought me awareness of Dina's and Sylvie's help in selecting a robe for her. Elsewhere, Barnsley was scandalising St John with an account of how I had ravished the lady, and his account had of course been picked up on by all and sundry on the network for an updated edition of *The Exploits of August*. The one thing I really wanted to discover, and couldn't, was what was happening on The Wandle. Try as I might, there seemed to be no way of piercing its silence. All my yearning evoked not so much as a whisper from my lovely Wych.

I spent the rest of day wandering the Weal, lost in lovelorn pondering – 'She loves me, she loves not' kind of fashion – and wondering whether White Wand was as hopelessly infatuated with me as I was with her. And what *was* the secret that had so suddenly turned her from a dispassionate flirt into such an overwhelming lover?

August is mortal! That's what they said of me. But how could I be mortal in this elfin form? I knelt beside a pool and considered my reflection. The sprite that looked back at me had no trace of mortal about him – except his eyes. For the first time, I realised how darkly human they were; not at all like the clear, limpid eyes of the true fay. For a long, long time I held an unsatisfactory communion with my eyes, until they began to grow unrecognisable and unreal.

At last, a faint chill warning groped ghostly fingers over the ether, and I knew the Wychies were sending their urgent reminder that Sunné was setting and the earth's shadow would soon obscure Mona. The elemental in me shivered and would have gone to cover, but the mortal said stay, and stared back defiantly in the mirror of my gaze. Was I to scuttle like a frightened rabbit at the first sign of danger? On the other hand, ought I to defy a solemn warning that struck fear into my soul?

I had begun to rise, the dilemma still unresolved, when a voice intoned softly, '*Therefore do we command ye, one and all: Be not abroad from Mona's first arising.*'

I crouched on hands and knees, frozen in amazement as the benign face of Black Wand looked up at me in place of my own reflection.

'Are you unmindful of the edict, my son?' he asked.

'N-no,' I stammered. 'But what do edicts have to do with it? An eclipse is an eclipse, a lunar eclipse – a perfectly natural occurrence. I don't see why –'

'A natural occurrence to *mortals*, yes,' he interrupted evenly. 'But Mona's light is essential in sustaining us. Normally, when both Sunné and Mona are down, there is no consciousness. But when Mona is above us and her light is obscured, a psychic vacuum is created. In that nothingness, substantial seeds of fear and dread are sown. The little people are not as humankind, August.'

'Yes, but that doesn't apply to *me*,' I argued, although his words had raised the hair on my head under my cap. 'I'm an anachronism; neither mortal nor immortal. I know

I find it difficult to hold on to *all* the elements of my mortality, but I'm too undeveloped a fay to rise to ecstasies – even of the Mood.'

'Are you so certain?' he asked, smiling. 'Methinks I heard only this morning as free and exalted an elemental as any in our Weal! "*Her eyes are holy star shine, undefiled and crystal clear!*" Only an elfin soul could carol such a paean of praise, August.'

It took me aback, even though I knew there were no secrets in the forest.

'Yes … well … that was different – an aberration of the spirit,' I answered with embarrassment.

He nodded his understanding. 'And what has mortality to offer that is more perfect, more complete, than elfin ecstasy?'

We continued to regard each other for a few seconds. His gaze was no longer veiled, as it had been two days earlier, but wide and frank, his eyes grey-blue and similar to my own. Then the image disappeared and the pool reflected only the darkening sky. I stood up, feeling that I had been ticked off by this kind, paternal spirit. He certainly knew the weak spots in my defences. But I was still in doubt about what to do. Or was I …?

I looked around at a deepening twilight that was becoming tinged with an odd greenish glow, and knew that by now I was the only representative of my kind abroad in the forest. It was time to be going. But where? To skulk and shiver in the old oak that Loy and I used for shelter? I was a long way from my haven of rest, but where else to go?

I tapped into the ethereal web, but only fragments of whispers came back to me. Barely distinguishable whimperings from holes and nooks, caves and crannies throughout the trembling Weal pleaded: '*Wychies! Wychies! Weal us, Wychies!*'

I shivered in sympathy with their piteous little moanings. But was I going to do the same? Was I going to add such pitiful appeals to my beloved Wych? Pride asserted itself. Never! Yet still I hesitated – until a wringing appeal came over the gossamer wires.

'August! Beloved August! Why are you not with us? Where have you gone? Come with your comfort, dear August. Spread the wings of your wisdom above our troubled spirits.'

In my mind's eye I could see the unhappy forms huddled together, eyes once luminous with laughter, now bleak with terror. I was profoundly impressed that they should now turn to me, the mysterious misfit. I longed to gather them in my embrace and change their naïve *'August is mortal'* into a devout *'August is magic'*.

My resentfulness deepened with the growing darkness. Where were the mighty Wychies? I thought bitterly. Safely ensconced on their Wandle, heedless of their distraught charges, and no doubt content that I should deputise for them. I was suddenly furious. So *that* was their cunning plot! That was the meaning behind Black Wand's gently teasing homily.

'To hell with you all!' I cried, and began to zigzag like forked lightening through the undergrowth and up to Wandleside. I knew exactly what I was going to do: I was going to defy this mythical Wreak. Dragga be blowed! I was going to prove once and for all that this soul-destroying yarn was mere superstition. It was nothing but a carefully built up threat, designed to keep the cowering hundreds obedient to those all-powerful twins.

The frenzy lasted until I reached the cliff top and began to realise what lay in wait for me. At first, as I stood on the edge, I saw no difference. I looked down at the untroubled surfaces of the lakes, like purpled mirrors, and found only beauty there. Then I turned my gaze to the black silhouettes of The Wandle's firs and saw a pale, ghostly green mist trembling above it like some kind of St Elmo's fire. As the shadow grew across the moon's face, so the green phosphorescence tumbled from the treetops and rose in depths of gaseous luminosity.

My senses thundered: '*Get out you fool! Get out before you take root! You can't stand this!*'

No! It's only an illusion; the failing beams of the moon's light distorted by the setting sun.

'*It isn't, you know. It isn't. It's unnatural. It'll creep over the top of The Wandle and over the Weirds. It will reach out for you and swallow you.*'

No, it won't. The Wychies are on The Wandle. It can't pass *them* – the legend says so. Stop panicking.

'*I can't help it! I'm scared.*'

The darkness deepened. The cloud of evil vapour flared higher. The tips of the trees bristled with spears of phosphorescence that danced on them like tongues of green flame. I could no longer see the Weirds below, only the ghostly green holocaust that was beginning to sweep across The Wandle like a pall of smoke; a ghastly, rolling, flickering presence. Fear petrified me as the very grass at my feet began to shimmer.

All too late I realised that the Wreak *was* a monster; an essence of evil that would draw me into it. Claw-like tendrils unfurling from the creature's body were already groping across the Weirds and crawling up Wandleside in my direction. Exultant streaks of green shot upwards from the burning nightmare and I threw myself on the ground gibbering with terror.

I frantically sought some anchor holds for my toes and fingers, but my tiny hands clutched wildly at grass and roots I could no longer feel as the first curling tendril poised ready to drag me to extinction. If I wasn't dead before, I was certainly going to die now.

Knowing that I was done for, I let go … and in that split

second before it could take me, something else took hold …

I had become a weightless sprite, cradled in the invisible arms of a blissful calm. Two strong hands were holding mine. I rose between them like a faerie toddler, supremely happy with a godlike parent on either side. The smiling faces of the Wychies flanked me like two pillars of shining white and blinding black. The jewels of their crowns and vestments burned like fire. Their eyes dazzled me with beams of love and strength. Their Wands were swords of molten light, blazing against the pallid phosphor doom.

I stood between them facing the Wreak. Its immensity left me breathless. There was nothing left now beyond the edge of the cliff. Wandle and Weirds were gone, replaced by a vast gulf of verdant fire roaring silently into space. I knew then that this was the moment of totality, when the Wreak roamed free, pouring its baleful essence over Weal, Woe and Wandle alike – a sentient evil seeking its prey. It hurled itself against the cliff, crashing against the unyielding granite; an angry flame-spitting monster blasting searing spumes of venom into our faces.

Belatedly I now realised that this was what the Wands had been fighting to keep on the other side of The Wandle. I felt ashamed and angry at my obstinacy, for they had had to leave their posts to rescue *me*, the witless traitor. I could only imagine how they must have felt when they realised I was on the cliff, wondering if I would take cover in time before they would have to surrender their stronghold in order to save me. Yet their eyes shone on me and their hands tightened on mine with loving assurance as they thrust, parried and repelled, wielding their bright Wands with the deftness of fencers.

With the wreathing tentacles dodging, darting, and feinting to contrive a stranglehold, the pace quickened, bringing a silvery laugh from my left and a deep answering chuckle from my right that sent a wave of courage through me.

'Nay, respected Dragga!' Black Wand cried, flicking a tendril from around his head. 'You bind me not in such untimely fashion. When I come to make my homage, it will be without the Wand. But lo! The Wand is with me yet!'

'Well spoken, brother,' laughed the White One. 'Whilst ever the Wands are one, noble Dragga, their wielders will be worthy opponents. Strike on, ageless father of evil. Give us valiant sport.'

As if in answer, the inferno heaved with increasing wrath. The lashing, virulent tentacles swirled even higher in fury, but the Wands never faltered in their flickering, swishing circle of defence, until the battle was fought to deadlock. Then the Wychies laughed again.

'Thy day is done, Dragga!' Black Wand cried. 'See, he falters, Sister Wand.'

'Weal and wyn, Lady Mona!' answered White Wand, jubilantly pointing to a tiny splinter of silver striking downwards into the heart of the Wreak.

Before us the green murk began to writhe in agony. The mass rolled backward, thinning quickly at its nearest edge, and the Wands fell motionless.

'Hurry, noble Dragga!' White Wand mocked. 'Our Lady Mona's Eye is opening again. Away to your lair, you death-riddled wraith!'

We watched the reappearing Weirds, and soon the shadowy bulk of The Wandle came into sight. Ragged trails of pale greenish-white vanished back through the conifers to Dragga's Weird. The Wychies arms were around my shoulders now. I looked into their starry eyes, and my own filled with tears. Then White Wand, whose lips I could no longer see, sealed mine with healing warmth and love.

'You have suffered your fiery baptism valiantly, my son,' said Black Wand. 'Now it is time to be gone. Hasten to Great Oak and tell our brethren the joyful news that Mona has returned to hold the night enthralled.'

Seizing his hand, I kissed it fervently before racing off to do as he bid.

CHAPTER 16

BLACK WAND'S WOE

It was a new August who obeyed his Wychy's command, singing out the glad news from the foot of Great Oak. Loy appeared at the entrance to our common hideout with a whoop of delight and jumped down, followed by Jean, Fizzy and another wiccy.

'August, you're as welcome as the flowers in spring,' said Jean. 'We don't want to go through anything like that again, do we, Loy?'

'We were petrified,' Loy admitted. 'But who cares, Mona's herself again. We missed you though, August. Where did you get to?'

Being hemmed in by a flurry of little people laughing, kissing and dancing saved me from having to answer.

Baddenham was staring open-mouthed at a stately vision in honeysuckle orange and cream that had just appeared. She came towards me with outstretched hands – it was Gwendolyn.

'August,' she said quietly, 'I just wish I knew how to thank you.' Her smile was dazzling. 'Everyone has been so kind.'

'It is more than enough to see you looking so wonderful,' I answered truthfully, bowing and kissing her hands. Her eyes surprised me because I could see that they were as wyché as my own – yet different.

Her face dimpled with pleasure. 'When do we start for The Wandle?'

'Right now, Gwen,' I answered, as Dina appeared at my side.

'Come on, August,' Dina said, taking my arm and urging me forward. 'We must hurry.'

Wiccas and wiccies were now streaming by us, all headed in one direction. With Dina snuggled contentedly on my right arm and Gwendolyn on my left, we pressed forward after them.

'You don't mind me calling you Gwen, do you?' There was a remoteness about her that made it only polite to ask.

'*You* can call me whatever you like, August,' she whispered, pulling my arm close in companionship. 'What do you think of my perfume?'

For the first time, I realised that I had no sense of smell, for we did not breathe like mortals. Her perfume was whatever I imagined it to be – and I was able to assure her quite truthfully that it was 'heavenly!'

Just in front of us, Smye was bobbing along with an arm around Sylvie. He kept glancing back over his shoulder with round inquisitive eyes, clearly anxious not to miss a move in my latest apparent entanglement. Ahead of him, tree-filtered beams of moonlight flashed brilliant ribbons of yellow and green, blue, white and gold across hundreds of hurrying wiccies and their twinkling escorts as they scampered onward and upward over the moon-whitened pathway to Wandleside. Trills of laughter and song tinkled on the breeze as we all hurried to the rendezvous. Other happy strands of little people joined us from all over the forest where they had been in hiding, including a jubilant troop of gnomes who capered and gestured with whoops of delight.

The united stream flowed out at last between the huge beeches and onto the cliff top where I had been such a short time ago. I half expected to find the scintillating figures of the Wychies waiting for us, but they were gone.

'Oh … how beautiful!' exclaimed Gwen as we arrived at the head of Windaway in brilliant moonlight. 'It's perfect. But what a tiny path.' She drew back, still clinging to me. 'There's only room for one to go along it at a time.'

'You'll be quite safe,' I assured her.

'Hurry up, Gwen,' called Dina, who had already gone ahead on the heels of Smye and Sylvie.

'Oh, no – I couldn't,' she protested. 'I'll lose my footing and fall over.'

I could tell that she was only feigning alarm – and was very naughtily using the argument to cling on to me. We were holding everyone up, so there was nothing for it but to swing her up in my arms and bound down the elfin stairway, with the vixen holding on tightly and giggling ecstatically.

Halfway down, the coiling line of people snarled to a stop in some kind of traffic jam. The forefront, along with Rozyn's dray, had come to a halt at the meeting of the Weirds. I set Gwen down and, like everyone else, we sat on the narrow path dangling our feet over the edge. I realised then that a new feature was being added to the scene. Spanning the narrows, and growing ever more solid as we watched, was a glittering crystal bridge, arching gracefully from the nearest edge to the far bank of The Wandle.

'Why, bless my soul!' said Baddenham. 'Will wonders never cease? Who on earth built that wonderful thing?'

'The Wychies of course, my dear fellow,' he was informed. 'But only ever at High Moon.'

Gwen looked round quickly, apparently recognising the speaker's voice. 'Why, it's Mr Pwyll, isn't it?'

'Pwyll the Pad, if you please, dear lady,' he answered. 'And delighted to welcome you to the fold at last.'

Gwen turned to me and explained excitedly: 'This is Canon Pwyll – he used to live with us at *Mens Sana*. You might remember Edmund spoke of him?' She laughed. 'Pwyll the Pad – what a curious name. Oh, Pwyll the *Padre*, of course! I wonder what Edmund's doing now? And Barnsley? They wouldn't be here, would they, August?'

I assured her that they would not, and wondered why we weren't going over the bridge now that the way lay open. Someone began to sing, and the words were taken up by others. A plaintive chant came rolling down to us:

> Dragga dree'd a mortal Weird
> And Alder dree'd another
> To separate the wreak from wrath
> The Wychies dree'd another
>
> And that our people be not wiled
> The foreign Weird to fondle
> 'Tween Dragga's Woe and Alder's Weal
> The Wychies made The Wandle

'What are they singing, August?' Gwen wanted to know. She was nestled so precariously at my side, her flashing sandals swinging to the rhythm, that I was forced to hold her more closely for fear that she would go sliding down into the Weird below.

On the other side of her, Smye answered soulfully, ''Tis the Legend of Weal and Woe.'

Dina, who had cradled her head comfortably in my lap and had been watching my face, asked, 'Why do you laugh, August?'

'I was reminded of another version of the legend, my dear.'

'Please sing it.'

'But it's a false one, Dina – just a garbled version that the children are taught in Three Weirs.'

'Then we want to hear it, please!'

'Silence for our noble August,' bellowed a bulky gnome. 'August will sing us a new song.'

'Very well then – but don't blame me if it doesn't make sense,' I warned. And so, adapting the words to the melody, I gave them the version I had first heard in The Green Dragon:

> The Dragon made the Dragon's Weir
> And Adder made the King's
> The Witchett made the other one
> That from the Adder springs
>
> The Dragon and the Adder strove
> The forest to ensiddle
> But neither won full half of it
> 'Cos Witchett stole the middle
>
> So Dragon wards the woeful side
> The King the Wale doth hondle
> While Witchett sits atween the two
> A-laughing in The Wandle

The last verse was taken up lustily as a chorus. The words echoed back and forth across the shining waters with what seemed to me such garish impudence that I wondered what the Wychies must be making of it. And yet, now that I thought about it, the words didn't seem so far from the truth.

Snatches of the song continued to drift around us for a while, until a lively wag broke in with the now almost unending ditty of Chrysobel:

> … who cuts the wood
> That feeds the fire
> That heats the oven
> That bakes the cakes
> To keep them from star-va-tion!

The anthem concluded with a thumping acclamation: 'Fi-zzle-bane and Fu-ming-wort!'

Suddenly all the chatter ceased and an expectant thrill swept through the waiting throng. Every head turned to the north.

Loy leaned over my shoulder. 'What's to do, August? Can you see anything?'

Several voices answered him: 'The King is coming! See, his barge is on his Weird.'

A glittering vessel had come into view, propelled swiftly by long sweeps of its oars.

'*There!*' said Dina, who had shot upright and was pointing. 'Do you see? There's Alder himself!'

While I strained my eyes to take in every detail of the craft, the precision of the twelve oarsmen caught Loy's professional eye.

'Grand show,' he murmured appreciatively.

'Oh, oh! Look, August!' cried Sylvie. 'There are the Wychies!'

The two splendid figures had materialised on the far side of the bridge and stood like black and white pillars awaiting the arrival of their sovereign. Excitement grew in Wandleside. Every fay quivered with pleasure at the spectacle, and the air was filled with whispers and comments. I reflected that it was quite logical that Alder should approach The Wandle from his own King's Weird. It was strange, though, to think that this scene had been enacted for hundreds of years without a whisper of it reaching human ears. As for the fae's excitement, I now know that the difference in time between the little kingdom and the world of mortals could make it appear like some huge bi-annual event.

'... and those people with the King are the court officials,' Dina was explaining sotto voce. 'The Chamberlain, the Herald, the Master of Gnomes, and the Pilot.'

The lovely jewelled craft drew into The Wandle side of the bridge, the oars flashed upwards amid glittering spray, and a liveried figure sprang out to tie it up. After him came the Chamberlain and Herald, who bowed to the Wychies. Then the Herald turned and raised his trumpet and sent golden notes pouring out over the water as a blazing presence rose from the centre of the barge and stepped ashore. The Wands sank gracefully before him and a thunder of shouts echoed across the narrows from the watchers. The King passed between the two magical figures and disappeared with his attendants into The Wandle.

The assembly on Windaway was on its feet again, a wriggling mottled snake that looped itself to and fro all the way down the side of the cliff. The Wychies signalled with their Wands, and Rozyn and his dray rolled quickly and smoothly forward over the fragile highway, leading the way into the dark mystery beyond.

When our little party reached the bridge and raced across, I had eyes for White Wand alone. Every wicca bowed to her as he approached, while his sisters curtsied to her fellow. I tried to meet her eyes as I made my obeisance but had no time to speak, for Gwen and Dina seized my arms again and hurried us forward.

'August, she's too impossibly lovely for words,' gasped Gwen. 'Oh, isn't this wonderful!'

We hurried through the majestic twilit scenery of the track-wiled island and arrived quite suddenly at an enormous circular clearing into which the little people were pouring helter-skelter. I looked up at the moon and knew that the place must be at the very centre of The Wandle. It seemed impossible that barely an hour earlier I had seen the island engulfed by Dragga's virulent malevolence. The memory made me look up and around with a shudder, wondering how nothing of its evil presence remained. Surely it could not have escaped entirely from being tainted?

'The trees go up for ever and ever,' breathed Gwen in awe, following my eyes to the tops of the encircling conifers.

Then the Chamberlain was standing before us, smiling and indicating where we should take our places to one side of the circle. Loy, Simmonds and Pwyll soon joined us, and then Baddenham arrived looking bewildered.

'What's the drill?' he asked anxiously. 'Aren't we being allowed to join the party?'

'Later, we shall,' Pwyll answered him. 'But first, I believe we're presented to the King.'

'Of course. Quite right too,' approved Loy, who began adjusting a non-existent tie and straightening his already perfect attire. 'Really must get a fresh outfit. Don't feel at home in anything but gold and blue. Wonder why?'

'It's the sailor in you,' I joked.

'Eh? Oh, yes, of course!' he said in pleased surprise. 'Association of a lifetime. What about you, Pwyll, old man? Do you feel at home in that lovat green and hazel get-up?'

'Oh dear, yes,' answered the Pad with a smile. 'I really don't miss the old black and white at all.'

Loy regarded him with renewed interest. 'Often wondered – if it's not a rude question, Pwyll – how do you feel about things? I mean, about Our Lady Mona and magic and all that …?'

Another fanfare from the Herald interrupted the discussion. We had been stationed exactly opposite the King on the other side of the circle. To each side of him, and facing each other, one black and one silver seat suggested where the Wands would sit.

The last of the little people hurried in; fragments of colour hastening to find places near favoured friends.

Then we grew quiet and tried to spot the better known faces in the crowd. I saw Smye whispering to Jean, and Fizzy gazing up at the moon as if unwilling to embarrass us with his stare. Dina and Sylvie had their heads together, watching silently, but gave little waves of acknowledgement when they saw that we had located them. During the fanfare, I became aware of the Wands' reappearance. They stood together silently where the path joined the ring. Gwen nudged me from my silent worship of White Wand as the Chamberlain signalled us to follow him across the great arena.

There was a slight hitch when Simmonds took a step back to allow his ex-commander to go first, while Loy courteously motioned for me to precede him. I put a stop to all this by signing that we should all proceed abreast, although I allowed Gwen to go first. She inclined her head and stepped forward with such composed serenity that it drew whispers of admiration from the crowd.

Each of us was then called in turn, and we went forward to kneel before the King and kiss the jewelled hand held out in welcome. As I found myself moving towards the gold-robed figure, I noticed that he held a Wand of gold in his left hand, and saw in the contours of his features an agelessness and unmistakeable authority. Here truly was my noble lord and liege, my King! I knelt in homage and kissed the slender hand held out to me.

I hardly remember how I returned, except that a jovial gnome eventually dragged me down forcibly with a hearty and affectionate pat on the back, saying, 'Masters of Crafts should sit together – Threadgold the Master of Rings and August the Master of Love, eh?'

I returned his attention with a good-natured jolt in the ribs before the Wychies, gliding across the arena side by side, drew our eyes back to them. The crowd became silent again as the two knelt before the King, crossing their

Wands together in front of him. Alder raised his own and lightly touched the pattern, evoking a brilliant flash from all three that brought a satisfied murmur of approval from the watching hundreds.

The Wychies rose and went to their separate places. They did not sit, but stood facing each other with their Wands poised above their crowns, as if waiting for a signal. That signal came with an imperious shout from the entire assembled company that seemed to shake the very trees.

'Wed the Wands, O Wychies! Wed the Wands!'

And the two hurled their Wands towards each other.

I realised that I knew what should happen – an astounding Catherine wheel of spinning light, and then ... But it didn't. The whirling Wands flashed towards their centre and the white one made a brief, complicated circle before returning to its owner's hand. But the other – the one belonging to Black Wand – fell inertly to the ground before the King.

The wizard folded his arms and bowed his head, and there was a moment of stunned silence before the truth sank home and wails of dismay rose from the circle.

'The Black One's Wand has cast him away!'

'Black Wand has withered his Weird!'

As if unable to witness the humiliation of one who had been her beloved partner for so long, White Wych flung her mantle across her face. My heart turned cold. I found myself refusing to believe that the lonely figure who now approached the King could possibly be Black Wand. But undeniably, his once magnificent Weird now hung in grey, drab, lifeless folds from his shoulders. He bowed to White Wand as he came abreast of her before going to lay his glittering jet crown gently at Alder's feet. He then rose, turned, and passed swiftly out of the circle.

CHAPTER 17

THE DREAMER

As Black Wand vanished into the darkness of The Wandle, I couldn't believe that this was the tall, strong, confident figure who had baited Dragga.

'*You bind me not in such untimely fashion. When I come to make my homage, it will be without the Wand. But lo! The Wand is with me yet …!*'

Now he was gone – without the Wand – to surrender himself to the reeking monster. I felt a sense of utter shame. If it hadn't been for me, the Wychies would never have left The Wandle and Black Wand would be with us still, for Dragga could never have invaded their home while they were there. The sobbing and wailing of the little people only served to deepen my sense of alarm and dread.

I saw Alder incline his head towards his Herald, and Kye strode to the centre of the arena. The cries hushed. He turned to face the King and executed a curious fanfare; a melody that vibrated in tones of reassurance and hope. He repeated it in turn towards the other three points of the compass, and then returned to the King's side.

The golden figure of Alder rose and we all stood. He stepped forward and addressed the assembly in a loud, composed voice.

'Be comforted, O my sorrowing people. That our beloved Wychy should have lain down his Weird and crown is a calamity which must befall every Wychy in the fullness of time, when his Wand lays claim to another's hand.

'Be comforted, O my people. The wisdom of Our Lady Mona is unfailing. It is her law that sorrow shall give place to joy. For every loss there shall be gain. The Black One's Wand has already marked one among you who is destined to take the place of its departed servant. Therefore, beloved people, I command that all wiccas now present shall test the Wand. He that the Wand elects shall henceforth be our faithful Wychy, to ward and wield it in his turn.'

As Alder resumed his throne, a sigh of relief went round the gathering – including a heartfelt one from me. But the grief remained. Although it seemed that no Wychy could last forever, I still felt instrumental in having caused a premature departure in this case.

The Chamberlain and Herald now took up positions on either side of the abandoned Wand. As soon as Kye had repeated his fanfare, the Chamberlain raised his staff to signal each wicca to approach. The officers of the court were to go first to demonstrate procedure. The only exceptions would be the gnomes, including the Master. The wiccies all sat down, leaving us wiccas standing.

Kye was the first. He stepped to the side of the Wand and stretched out a hand directly above it. Nothing happened. He bowed to the King, stepped back, and the Chamberlain summoned the next wicca.

In every case nothing happened, and I began to wonder if this was a mere formality that would ultimately lead to Alder making the appointment himself. But excited anticipation and stifled comments rose as the circle began to straighten out into a dwindling line of apprehensive spirits and the Wand still lay inert. Who was it to be?

Winzy was so nervous that he had to be reminded of what to do. 'Raise your right hand and hold it level, palm down above the Wand, brother.'

The trembling elf obeyed, held his arm out for second, and then at a shake of the head from the official, gave an audible sigh of relief and fled to the opposite side of the circle.

During our slow movement forward, tiny hands kept reaching up into mine with messages of hope. I had to suppress a surge of hope that also welled in me at their unspoken wishes.

Smye left the ordeal, patently overjoyed that the honour was not his. He looked back, singled me out, smiled and winked knowingly. I looked across and saw Loy giving the thumbs up sign. Baddenham too made an irreverent gesture as if putting a crown on his head. Long before I reached the head of the queue, voices were whispering 'Au-*gust*, Au-*gust*, Au-*gust*' with such fervency that I realised with incredulous awe that they wanted *me* to have the Wand!

Standing with an outstretched hand and watching the magic thing rise up towards it, I admitted something to myself that I had already guessed: my predecessor had intended that I should succeed him. A torrent of sound, including a flourish from the Herald, whirled like a hurricane through my being as my fingers closed around the Wand and I looked into the smiling face of the Chamberlain. The little people were going wild with delight.

'A *Wychy*! A *Wychy*! O Black Wand, O Black Wand!'

The Chamberlain stood to one side and there before me was the Wych, her expression remote and serene. In the ensuing silence, we went together to kneel before the King, where I received the Black One's crown on my head. The fastening of a splendid new Weird about my shoulders completed the transformation. I felt changed into a giant of wisdom and power.

My first official duty was to present my Wand to the King, just as Black Wand had done earlier. White Wand crossed mine with hers and we watched Alder's golden one gently descend to evoke the vivid spark of response from all three.

When we rose, we returned with measured steps to our respective stations and turned again to face each other. My Wych's appearance was remote and stately, a silent reminder that I was her partner in a still incomplete ceremony.

'Wed the Wands, O Wychies!' came the cry, sounding even more thunderous than before, if that was possible. 'Wed the Wands!'

We raised our arms like combatants, our Wands poised, and then threw them straight towards each other. The wheeling objects sped forward to meet and spin about each other in a brilliant radiance of light, then returned to our waiting hands a moment later.

Under the benign but ever-watchful eye of the Chamberlain, and to the music of flute and bassoon, White Wand and I then led our people in a fantastically tangled dance known as Wandlewile, which opens every High Moon festivity. An effortless instinct guided my feet through a winging pattern that wove in and out of the trees like the ribbons of a maypole. The maze of The Wandle was now an open book to me as we tripped ahead of our whirling minions, the joyful wiccas following White Wand and the happy wiccies following me.

During one of the patterns, I looped back on myself and came face to face for an instant with a wiccy whose presence I knew to be alien. This was surprising enough, but I recognised her brown eyes – as wyché as my own – from somewhere I could not remember. Yes, dear Ann, it was *you*! But why your eyes should flash in amazed recognition of me was a mystery.

I passed you like a meteor hurtling through a spiralling nebula of star dust. Your gasp at the touch of my flying Weird went through me like a scented gale. But the very next moment, my Wych reappeared from the spinning mist of figures to take my hand, and we raced together to end the dance at Alder's throne. Consumed with curiosity as I was, this was not the moment to question her about the astonishing encounter, for another ceremony was about to begin.

The assembly returned to its circle as we resumed our seats. From the opposite side the Royal Vintner entered holding a golden loving cup that glittered and flashed streams of living colour from the countless tiny jewels with which it was set. He knelt on one knee to present it to the King.

'Sovereign Liege of Mona's immortal kin. I bear the magic mead, the wine that never wanes, that you may honour us with your loving pledge.'

Alder rose, accepted the chalice and raised it high as he proclaimed his response. 'O my people from of old. Bear witness that I renew my ancient pledge to love and to lead, to defend and to guide, the destiny of our kin.'

He drank from the cup and returned it to Rozyn. The Vintner then turned to White Wand, knelt before her, and made the same presentation, addressing her as 'Lady of Wisdom'. She also rose and held it out to the circle.

'O loving ones, I pledge that I will always wyn your love and Weal your woe and ward the welfare of our kin,' she said, and drank.

Rozyn then presented me with the chalice as 'Lord of Wisdom'. I repeated my Wych's action and words, drank and returned the cup to the Vintner. As I watched him leave, I was aware of my mind opening with a new understanding of my role, and, when I looked across to White Wand, we seemed united in mystic complicity and knowledge.

It was several dances later before I managed to secure White Wand for a partner.

'There is a stranger in our midst, dear Wych.'

She smiled at me reassuringly. 'None but a dreamer, Brother Wand. 'Tis not unusual.'

'Then she is a mortal?' I asked

'In her waking state. But why are you asking? What meaning has she for you?' Before I could find a diplomatic answer, she laughed. 'Oh, August, my deplorable Wychy! Is your love for me already so wearisome that you must seek fresh adventures?'

I couldn't bring myself to tell my Wych why I needed to know who you were, Ann. But I wanted to find you again. And although I was now capable of knowing the location of any wicca or wiccy at will, I couldn't trace you.

But why had I had no knowledge of your presence? And why had I responded to you so intensely? Surely even a dreamer couldn't penetrate our mysteries without the Wychies – or one of us at least – knowing about it and allowing it? And if it hadn't been me …

*

Later on that night, I came upon the Royal Vintner standing on a cask surrounded by a bubbling multitude of little people. He was holding up a goblet.

'A golden cup of Rozyn's Rapture!' he was bidding. 'A golden cup for the first kiss from a pair of rosy lips amongst this merry lot …'

He disappeared beneath a wave of bidders, only to emerge laughing uproariously, minus cap and goblet. He reached for another potion from his assistant.

'And now for a nymph of my own choosing!' he declared, his amorous eye roving over the throng.

'Who has the brightest eye? The rosiest lip? Whose feet are fleetest?' He interrupted their squeals of delight by suddenly pointing. 'Who else but the vision with the shining nut-brown eyes, yonder?'

He leapt down and headed through the crowd towards the very person I was looking for – *you*! I knew this would never do; to feed a dream-wraith with potions of power that Rozyn had devised was dangerous. My Wand seemed to twitch with a life of its own at the very thought, and the Vintner halted in his tracks. He stared about him looking confused, then seized the nearest fay, who happened to be Gwen, and kissed her.

'Rosy, old man, you're high!' yelled Baddenham gleefully. 'Her eyes aren't brown, they're blue!' This raised gales of laughter from the throng. The Vintner drew back, examined the surprised Gwen at arm's length for a moment, laughed happily, kissed her again, and pressed the chalice upon her. Gwen looked at me as if apprehensive of what might be in it, but the Vintner was not to be denied, and joyous voices insisted that she should drink. She closed her eyes and obeyed.

The voice of my Wych murmured in my ear. 'Well done, wizard. 'Twas wise to deflect him from the dreamer. And doubly wise to wile an irksome worshipper from your path.'

I ignored the irony. 'Is Rozyn's Rapture *so* potent, then?'

'A specific, my love. He has a magic all his own. Perchance your Gwendolyn will hunger less longingly for forbidden fruit this night.'

She moved away before I could reply. Surely a Wych is too noble to succumb to jealousy? Or was the remark prompted by the old warning that one may not love a Wychy and live?

I glanced back and discovered Gwen's eyes fixed on me. Her eyes were not quite as translucent as a normal fay's; their depths contained a pale blue iris, which was wyché. An almost reproachful look came into them for a moment. Then she walked towards me, composed and purposeful.

'August ... or should I say Black Wand? How does one express oneself on these occasions? Should I congratulate you or ...?'

' ... say the words that are really in your heart?' I said, breaking in on her conventional phraseology with a laugh.

She looked baffled. 'If only I could see your eyes for a moment, I might know,' she complained. 'I was just getting to know August. I don't think I'll ever know Black Wand. Are they even still the same person?'

A Wychy's problems, it seemed, were not as remote as I thought. There was a radiance about this transformed creature that I found increasingly difficult to ignore.

*

The sun was close to rising before I saw you, the dreamer, again that night. We had partied on through hours of unrestrained enthusiasm, and we had danced, sung and mimed without a moment of tedium. Numbers had sauntered off in twos and threes without a care of becoming lost in The Wandle maze. Four of us at least kept a measure of dignity: the King and his Chamberlain, and White Wand and I. We each performed individual duties – for the most part putting a brake on the effect of Rozyn's potions or heading off the irrepressible gnomes whose heavy-handed pranks might have turned the revelling into a riot.

The King and his party were soon to make their ceremonial departure – and with them our tireless revellers – so I wandered off in search of stragglers, rousing a number of couples sighing dreamily in each other's arms without embarrassment on either side. A group in the north-west were happily singing the un-ending roundelay of Chrysobel. They did not know of my approach because the faerie telegraph does not operate in the Wands' domain, so it looked like witchery when they suddenly found me standing by. Honeyball, lying with his head on a wiccy's shoulder, had paused for metaphorical breath before inventing a new line. He opened his eyes and looked straight into mine, then sat bolt upright and exclaimed: 'Oh, oh!'

Loy looked up. 'Black Wand! No, it's only August! I mean it's ...'

It was then that two luminous figures slowly passed nearby, their heads close together and so absorbed in some deep exchange that it seemed neither had seen me. But I was growing to know my Wych, and I knew it was intentional, the message plain. You, the dreamer, were her concern, not mine.

You weren't among those who followed us back to the crystal bridge, which everyone capered happily over once the royal barge had swept majestically on its way.

At last only we of the Wands remained behind to watch the crystal bridge begin to fade. Like melting ice, its arches diminished into threadlike traceries ... and a moment later it had vanished into nothing in the rays of the rising sun.

There was no interregnum with that phase of moon, but I felt a deep need to be on my own after the tremendous events of the last day and night. When we turned to face each other, I knew that White Wand recognised it. I bowed, she curtsied, and we went our separate ways to either end of The Wandle.

CHAPTER 18

A WYCHY, A WEIRD AND HIS WAND

Slowly following a path that I knew led to my new dwelling, I thought hard about all that had happened. I knew I had a lot to learn, despite the knowledge that had already come to me through the crown, Weird and Wand. At that moment, the Wand was my greatest mystery. It seemed to have a personality of its own, yet never left me for an instant. As I walked, I found it impossible to drop it or throw it away; it simply returned to my hand. It also responded instantly to my thoughts, just as I had witnessed when I needed to divert the Royal Vintner's attention from you, the dreamer.

The movements I made while experimenting with the instrument disturbed the folds of my Weird and reminded me of the pigeon blue clothing I wore beneath it. Not quite right for a Wychy of The Wandle, I decided. I wanted to keep the jewelled belt given to me by the Master of Gnomes, but I would need to find something more suitable in colour. Immediately, and to my amazement, my garments altered to the dove grey and silver I had imagined, while retaining the master's gift.

I arrived at an open doorway framed in shimmering black stone that appeared to be inset in a large irregular block of sandstone. I knew I had reached my new home, and was not surprised. When I stepped through the entrance, however, I froze in astonishment, wondering whether I had crossed into another dimension.

Scintillating blackness enveloped me, its depthless intensity flashing with a million points of coloured light, like a starlit infinity of precious jewels. I moved one foot cautiously forward and spangled galaxies hurled themselves into terrifying cascades of light. Then I realised I was gazing at the reflection of countless tiny gems sewn into my Weird. A movement of my arm confirmed it, and I wondered how the effect had been engineered.

I felt the Wand move and illumination sprang into being. I was standing at the entrance to a large dome-shaped room with walls and floor of polished black crystal. In the centre stood a massive black glassy table and a chair of the same shining stone. On the table lay a huge open book, the whiteness of its pages contrasting sharply with their background.

I sat down slowly. The reflections had disappeared, but the light – which seemed to be coming from me – made me feel like some luminous mind suspended at the heart of an infinite darkness. I recalled the world I had just left. At once, as if in an enormous concave mirror, I saw The Wandle and the path I taken from the water's edge. I saw the expanse of Wychies' Weird rippling beneath a gentle breeze, disturbing the reflection of clouds above. I looked upwards at Wandleside, and directly before me was the scene I had come to know so well.

I thought of my now deserted companions, and the image changed to show the Weal. Jean and Loy were tripping irresponsibly along to the Wealspring; Smye was holding forth on the power and wisdom of Wychies Black and White; Gwen and Pwyll were sedately pacing the grass; and Baddenham and Dina were in a highly compromising position ...

I switched my thoughts away. I had seen enough to convince me that I could see at will everything that was happening in the Weal. It occurred to me that my new home worked on the same principle as my Wych's crystal ball. Except that she looked *into* hers from the outside, and I looked *out* of mine from the inside.

I looked for her and immediately had a vision of her exquisite face looking down on me, as if at that moment she had turned to gaze at the Wych globe. She remained a few seconds, then vanished – a reminder that I had no power over her realm of responsibility. I sighed happily and turned my attention to the book. The open page read:

> It is not often that an elemental may inhabit both mortal and immortal kingdoms at the same time, but this is the Weird you now wear.
>
> Attend well, Wychy, for this is the essence of the second of the three wishes I promised you – that when your humanity can no longer be denied, you may resume your mortality. The choice will be yours: either to drink of oblivion and remain in your restored mortality, or surrender that estate forever and return to the little kingdom. It is necessary that you should know this, but unlawful for me to write more. Neither I nor any other has the right to presuppose any decision that only you can make.
>
> Hael and wyn, brother! May the peace of The Wandle long be with you.

So the way was still open – that was my first thought. But why? Why should I *ever* want to return to mortality? I had the Wand, the Wych and a wonderful existence. What more could life as a mortal offer me?

I wondered at the author's tremendous foresight. Discovering that his end was imminent, he had somehow magically created an elemental existence for me with a choice of returning to mortal existence if I wanted. And in one concentrated week he had enabled me to be fit enough to succeed him. This begged the question, however, of where *I* would find such a successor if I ever chose to return to mortality. And why was such a situation necessary?

Although I was happy, I would have been happier still without such a choice hanging over me!

*

Some hours later I went in search of my Wych for some answers, and came upon her sitting in the same little clearing where I had first seen her. We greeted each other and she waved me courteously to a carved stool nearby. I sat and regarded her with undisguised delight, my fascination unchanged despite the alteration in our relationship. This lovely creature was my acknowledged Wych, my partner in love and magic – my consort. But were we *really* equal? Could I ever lose the impulse to adore her that set her on a pedestal above me?

'Why am I imprisoned in the Weird of another's design, Sister Wand?' I asked.

She shook her head, the gems in her hair radiating fire. 'Not imprisoned, Brother Wand – constrained. In the course of his Wandship, *he who is gone* devised new symbols for the Weird that you now wear – as his predecessor did for him, and as you will do for whoever follows.'

'But *he who is gone* – what of him? Was he not your Wychy?'

'There is only one Wand. Wychy and Wych are always one in spirit, Brother Wand.' She rose and held out her hand in a delightfully feminine gesture. I took it gladly and we sauntered away from her retreat into the trees.

'Do not fear your fate, timorous one,' she chided. 'You have the powers of heaven and earth in your hands. Why do you doubt yourself? Look to your Wand; it will guide you.' Then she took my arm and looked at me askance. 'Why do you fear your Wych, brother?'

'I love you beyond my understanding, sister. Our people truly name you the loveliest of all the fae.'

'And *you* truly are the most desirable of Wychies!' she returned softly in way that set my heart racing. "Tis small wonder that all our wiccies sigh for you. And well they may, for Black Wand is the unattainable mystery of all their living. Be warned, their little hands and hearts will draw at you without respite, yearning for your smile. Yet your heart must be firm towards them, for you know they may not love their Wychy and live.'

'But why is this terrible curse laid upon them?' I asked.

'Not a curse, Brother Wand. It is an inevitable result of an emotional apotheosis too great for their fragile nature to bear.'

'I wasn't a Wychy when Hyllis and Leila –' I began.

'Ah, but you were – and still are – *mortal*, dear heart. It's that dark part of your nature that destroyed them.'

'Yet I – a fay – loved you, Wych?'

'And that same mortality spared you,' she said with a mischievous twinkle. 'How could my love destroy and dispel a mortal into mortality?'

'Then logically, my mortality should have injured you,' I argued.

She laughed evasively and placed a delicious salute on my cheek. 'By every canon our lore, a Wych is invulnerable to all save Dragga, my poor confused wizard.'

'Then why –?' Before I could finish, she stopped, turned and set her lips on mine in an embrace that effectively put an end to all further questions.

*

All those who had held the office of Black Wand before me appeared to have helped compile the great book, which I began to browse through in search of all the answers I wanted. Intense curiosity made me want to find the spell by which my predecessor had engineered my appearance in the forest. But magic is not something that can be read and pronounced mastered. One can learn principles and memorise means and methods, but success, like a musical composition, will always remain the result of spontaneity and genius. My Wych had called her Wychy 'incomparable', which it seemed he was, for I could find nothing in the book that spelt the mystery out for me.

There was plenty more to learn, however. It appeared that the *Woe* – the weed that restores the little people to their immortal existence – is known as *Wizard's Woe* because they have no control over it, and its action is impartial. The illustration in my book showed a tiny, dragon-like, virulent green weed with feathery appendages. I pondered its growth and distribution, and found it propagated by some agency of the Wreak, principally in the marshes of Dragga's Woe, but it could be transmitted anywhere with ease. One thing was certain, though: *I* had never ingested it.

I looked at '*wandling*' and discovered a great deal about how to wandle a wraith out of its mortal body during sleep. I read this with especial interest, but there was not a word on how wraith and body could be wandled into one …

Someone was plucking urgently at my Weird.

'*Black Wand! Black Wand! Help me!*'

I looked up, the darkness of my walls vanishing, to see the grotesque figure of Barnsley clasping a frightened wiccy whom I recognised as Lettice.

'No need to scream the place down, you silly bitch! I'm not hurting you, am I?' he gloated. 'Only want a kiss …'

I raised the Wand and cried out severely: '*Lay off, you lecher!*'

It would be difficult to say which one of us was the more surprised – Barnsley, who reeled back, tripped and fell as if he had been invisibly punched on the chin, or me, who hadn't given a thought as to what might happen.

Barnsley sat up and looked around angrily. 'Spoilsport!' he howled. 'Want 'em all for yourself, do you? Well, you just show your ugly mug for half a second and see what I'll do to it!'

I left him bellowing and turned my attention to the ethereal web of communication. I learned from its incessant chatter that the new Black Wand's exploit was already ringing round the Weal. Lettice had run to the arms of Dina, who was murmuring words of sympathy and appealing to White Wand in the same breath. I could relax and be thankful that my Wych would take care of her while I reflected on how to deal with the bad man of St John's Wood. It would need solving sooner than later, I thought. Such a pestering rogue was as capable of wrecking the wiccies' happiness as much as that other erstwhile menace August had been. I wasn't entirely unsympathetic, however. The poor fellow could hardly help being tormented by the frustrated demands of his warped libido. I wondered if I should enlist the Royal Vintner, but then I remembered that Barnsley had already met Rozyn once, to little effect.

So perhaps the Wand could effect the transformation? I leaned back in my great chair and looked at the beautiful object now poised horizontally between the middle fingers of each hand. (I had found a treatise entitled '*Shewing best how a Wychy may handle his Wand*' and learnt that this was the right way of short-circuiting one's thoughts.) But no; such a gesture would be a vulgar exhibition of force. Far better an insinuation of ideas ... I closed the book, feeling a sudden urge to visit the Circle of Rejoicing.

*

So much had happened there barely eighteen hours earlier that I paused a few moments when I arrived to relive those unforgettable scenes. A barely perceptible touch on my Weird made me turn swiftly. A dainty figure was running across the grass towards me. Beyond it, a white and silver presence faded back among the trees.

'Black Wand! Black Wand! Oh, thank you, Black Wand!' It was Lettice. She kissed my hands and hugged my Weird gratefully. 'The White One has bidden me come to you to heal me of my hurt.'

And there was I thinking that it wasn't my problem! I led her towards one of the many polished wooden benches that surrounded the circle. 'Come sit beside me and tell me your woe.' Her amber eyes were anxious.

'I am full of such strange unease, Black Wand. I'm afraid I have the Sickness.'

'But Lettice, there is no longer any cause for distress. Barney is gone. Didn't I send him away?'

'Indeed you did, beloved Wychy!' She began to smooth the folds of my mantle with one of her delicate hands, which I found somewhat disconcerting. 'But ...' her voice sank to a whisper, ' ... how can I hide the truth from your all-seeing eye, Black Wand? *I did not want him to go!*'

She raised her head again with a troubled glance that sent a chill through me while I took in the implication of her words. The terror of a violent embrace had impelled her – a fully born – towards the very thing she would normally abhor. This was surely one of the most deadly symptoms of the Sickness. I folded her close in my ample Weird. My Wych had sent her to me to be healed of this hurt, but what could *I* do that White Wand could not? Had Lettice asked for the Bane to anaesthetise the gnawing terror? No – I had read in my book that once it had been asked for, no Wych could refuse it. *The Sickness is the deadly fever of the immortal kin*, it had said. *The Malady is also infectious. Eventually its course must culminate in a rabid desire for the Bane, against which no argument or coaxing can prevail. A supplication for the berry is the final symptom of the Sickness that only dissolution and a full cycle of mortal existence can dispel.*

So what could I do to counteract the baleful influence?

'I would seek your love, like Hyllis and Leila –' Lettice murmured.

'And pass on, like them, to seek the Bane?' I interrupted, with a mental wince at the memory.

'But they were glad to go!' she whispered dreamily. 'They went with shining eyes immersed in love. But I … I fear to go. Their dream was one of beauty. But mine is ugly – a horrid fascination that I cannot understand. I shrink from it, yet yearn to know.'

'To know what?' I asked her gently.

'How mortals live. Their loves and joys. The pain and anguish of their wiccies when they bear new lives. The little ones that smile so happily with the wisdom of their kind … Oh, Black Wand, my thoughts are so tangled – they're like a broken web.' She clasped me tightly, burying her head in my shoulder and sobbing in distress.

'Sleep, little one!' I commanded softly, as a possible solution occurred to me. She sank down in my arms at once. I carried her quickly towards the meeting of the weirds, glided over the water, and laid her on the far bank. I then returned to wait among the trees. After a short while two figures appeared above Wandleside.

'Look!' cried Pwyll, pointing. 'There's Lettice. Fallen asleep beside the Weirds.'

'How did she get there?' asked Gwen.

'It'll be Wychy work,' said her escort. 'I remember Jean and Loy saying they had to deal with August in the same way not so long ago. Come on, we must get her back to the Weal.' And he began to hurry down Windaway.

'Well, I must say it's a most unchivalrous thing to do!' exclaimed Gwen, following him. Her criticism made me smile. 'Dina sent her to the Wands for comfort, didn't she? Not to be thrown out like a piece of useless baggage.'

They arrived at the foot of the winding path and Pwyll stooped over the sleeping fay.

'White Wand hasn't given her that awful Bane, has she?' asked Gwen.

'Lettice wouldn't be here if she had. She's simply fallen asleep, that's all. Look's more like the Black One's work if you ask me.'

'Oh, not *again*!'

'And the same remark applies to *that*,' said Pwyll as he lifted Lettice in his arms. 'Surely you have heard that one may not love a Wychy and live? Or haven't you heard about Hyllis and Leila?'

'That's unkind, Pwyll. I'm sure he acted most honourably towards *me*.'

'Meaning you had a narrow escape.'

'Now you're making it worse!'

'Gwen my dear, I wasn't teasing – it was meant as a statement of fact.' He began the long climb back with his burden.

'This tangling with Wychies is all very mysterious and I don't understand it,' said Gwen. 'Dina said that August wasn't a wizard when he first found the Wych … By the way, is it true that he went flying through the Weal shouting the news the next morning?'

Pwyll laughed. 'Shall I ever forget it? I'd have done the same if I'd had his good fortune.

'But what an unspeakable thing to do!'

'Really, Gwen!' Pwyll stopped and turned, inadvertently holding the unconscious Lettice over a fifty foot drop to the Weird below. 'You can't be jealous, surely? One doesn't have that feeling in the Weal. I mean, you don't think it upset me that you and Loy went rambling through the brambles this morning?'

I decided I had overheard enough. With the moon rising perceptibly later than the sunset, Lettice would have a healing period of unconsciousness before waking up with everyone else later. And I felt that she would be safe with Gwen, whose memories of mortal existence and *Mens Sana* would provide convincing arguments to dispel what remained of the infection.

*

When it came, the Weal's reawakening reminded me of my morning sessions at Great Oak – even if the faerie morning would now be moonrise. The sessions had become routine; and routine, I realised, was important to the little people. Was it possible for me to continue them? Could a Wychy amuse his people with absurd inventions that concerned the very core of their existence and beliefs? Dare mighty Black Wand masquerade as Hellbane Harry simply to make his audience laugh?

'If you do not,' said White Wand appearing at my side, 'then I for one shall be grievously disappointed. Pray allow my awesome wizard to leave his Witchery Wood for a space and enthral his faithful audience with his stories. I positively tremble with terror at the prospect of poor Chrysobel's fate.'

I looked around at her laughing eyes. 'I have already

made it clear, beloved, that the damsel's honour is not really at stake.'

'I know, dear weaver of dreams. But I fear your worshipping audience will find it impossible that such a wicked wizard would accept her "no" as an answer.'

'Ah, but,' I argued triumphantly, 'is it not true that one may not love a Wychy and live? Wouldn't that be too appalling an ending?'

'Much too drastic,' she agreed, putting on such an air of mock solemnity that I wanted to kiss her. 'I'm afraid you have talked yourself into a pretty pickle, my learned wizard. I am intrigued to know how you propose to get out of it. Your Wand will be of little use this time.'

I took her hand and pressed it to my lips. 'Perhaps from the well of *your* wisdom, my peerless pearl –'

'Not for a thousand Wands, Brother Wychy! Is it not the law that we may not wile each other's wills? Why else did I send Lettice to *you*?'

'I did wonder. Did I discharge my duty well?'

'Eminently well, Brother Wand. Your wisdom increases by the hour.' She suddenly stopped bantering and drew me closer. 'The Sickness is a terrible scourge, brother. I have known it rage like a plague over our people, wringing the Weal with appalling woe. Our people have withered like leaves in autumn and Dragga's greed is never sated. The breathing of the Wreak is never wholly absent. You know it appears again on the night of the new moon – when Mona is wedded with Sunné?'

'So I have learned,' I answered. 'I marvel that The Wandle isn't still saturated with its presence.'

'Perchance it is,' she said, so calmly that I stared at her. 'It had existence over all, did it not?'

'And you allowed it to happen in order to rescue me,' I pointed out shamefacedly.

'Is that so hard to understand?' she asked. 'If August had been taken, would I have had a Wychy today? But come, Mona is about to shed her gladdening beams and our people will be stirring. You should not tarry.'

'Come with me,' I begged.

'No – that may not be, my adorable wizard. Our Weirds wind other ways.'

'But surely it is fitting that we who are one should act together?'

'Wear your own Weird, Wychy! Seek not to wandle mine! I shall not walk the Weal with you.'

I must have looked crestfallen, for she stepped back laughing. 'Oh you Wizard of Woe – be gone with you! I shall return to my lair and hear what I shall have to hear.'

CHAPTER 19

MONA'S EYE!

It seemed like years since I had last trodden the Weal, but I could instantly hear faint whispers from every quarter as the faerie telegraph began to wake, seeking assurance that all was well and asking what was new. My presence was discovered in seconds and sparked electric thrills in all directions.

'Black Wand walks the Weal. The Wychy is with us!'

Within moments, streams of hurrying feet began approaching from every side. Caps were doffed and curtseys swept the pearl-dewed grasses as wiccas and wiccies arrived in ones and twos, their faces alight. Soon the scene swelled into a lively procession of joyful followers tumbling in my wake.

We arrived at Great Oak to find a growing crowd gathered before the seat of honour with the evergreen effigies beside it. Swept along on a wave of love, I took my seat and gave the traditional greeting. The response was deafening, with an excited scuffling for the nearest positions of vantage. Dina and Sylvie hovered expectantly, their expressions hopeful. I nodded and they descended like a pair of lovely pigeons, nestling on either side of me. I knew without looking that Gwen and Pwyll were sitting together. Baddenham was nearby, gazing at me in undisguised wonder. Fizzy, Loy and Jean formed a happy trio. And Smye's round eyes were staring at me so speculatively that I had to give him a special smile to transform his awkwardness into a beam of gratitude. I made no bones about commencing as if there had been no interruption.

'Well, Dragon Dreadful, who was ferrying the wizard's two familiars ...' and I paused to indicate that the ritual would remain unchanged.

'Fi-zzle-bane and Fu-ming-wort!' they yelled.

'... high above the rolling forest through magic storms of sea-green lightning and rose-red raindrops ... yes, Gwen?'

'I was wondering, Au ... I mean, Black Wand, wasn't it uncomfortable for the poor things, sitting on the creature's nasty spines?'

'Indeed no, Gwen,' I assured her solemnly. 'The artful dodgers had lashed themselves *alongside* his uncomfortable encumbrances.'

'Ah, nautical types!' exclaimed Loy with a triumphant wink at Simmonds.

'Inflated fenders!' chortled Simmonds with an unexpected humour that I was glad to hear.

'But they weren't in the sea,' Jean objected. 'Black Wand said they were flying through the air.'

It was all good fun and I thought the gently carping interruptions were better than ever. As soon as I was able to, I continued with a description of Dreadful's arrival at Chrysobel's village, disguised as a storm cloud.

'Please, Black Wand, how did he manage to do that?' asked Smye.

'Simple, my dear fellow,' Baddenham answered for me. 'What Black Wand is describing is one of the most basic of physical phenomena: the introduction of heat to cold water. Dreadful's hot, the rosy raindrops are cold, thereby producing a cloud of steam in direct ratio to the quantities of water and heat present at the precise moment of contact. Thus, if the calorific content of Dreadful's fiery breath be symbolised by x and the quantity of rose-red rainfall in its proximity during any given time be defined as y, then the –'

'Then the unfortunate familiars would be reduced to boiled turnips in two shakes of a lamb's tail!' said Loy with such an air of innocence that the assembly rocked with laughter.

I had to rule out the equation firmly. 'Your assumptions are both wide of the truth, dear wiccas. It was not possible to boil the familiars because they were both lineal descendants of water sprites on the maternal side. And in fact the cloud was not made by fire and water. It was actually a *dust* cloud that had been thrashed out of the earth by the tremendous beating of Dreadful's wings.'

They all cheered at the unexpected explanation.

It was an assurance that my personal popularity and official dignity remained unscathed. If anything, the Wand had received an immense boost. Clearly, August wasn't exactly the same fellow as he had been, and it would have been disrespectful to question the pros and cons of his arguments directly. But this was offset by his indulgence in allowing them to debate the finer points amongst themselves, as of yore.

Their clamoured speculations became so drawn out that I was thankfully able to adjourn the problem to a later date, leaving the dragon and familiars still suspended in mid-air. This time no one drifted away before me. Everyone stood respectfully to one side to let me pass, although a succession of loving hands fingered my Weird with awe as I went by.

I wandered off to look into a project that had recently occurred to me, and which I wanted to have ready when the time came – I felt that I needed a residence within the Weal. Not because my own dwelling on The Wandle was gloomy or depressive, but because I thought it too remote. I wanted a place where the little people could look in for a chat whenever the mood suited them. I had no fear that they would abuse the amenity. I had made a practical survey in my mind's eye. It had to be accessible, yet not too near the beaten track. I had a vision of a large and ancient beech in which the weather had hollowed out a natural recess at its foot. It was not too far from Great Oak and quite near the highway from Three Weirs.

I had considered the possibilities and visualised its design. It would be enclosed within a durable façade of natural features to deceive the human eye: brushwood and leaves and a doorstep of lichen. A job for the gnomes, I thought, forgetful that the mere desire would ensure when and where I wanted to meet them. So I made my way unhurriedly towards the beech tree, thinking over the details of its interior, and arrived to find a little band of respectful figures observing me.

'Hael and wyn, Master!' I greeted the Master of Gnomes, and 'Hael and wyn, merry craftsmen,' to the rest of them.

The gnomes pressed forward with jovial returns and eyed me expectantly. A Wand would never summon them from their subterranean home without a pressing need. I explained my plans to the Master. Immediately, his half-dozen followers began swarming eagerly over the site, elbowing, arguing, proposing and jesting with the greatest excitement.

'A ferrous matching exterior, Master!'

'Embellished with a veneer of old gold beech leaves!'

'And jade lichen! It must certainly be jade, Master!'

The Master nodded approvingly. 'Whitegold and Ironwright shall put it in hand at once. What size the portal, Black Wand? Four Wands high is the common measure – but what of the width? One and half? Two?'

'Two Wands,' I told him, realising that his measurements were based on the length of my Wand which was three mortal inches. 'It will look more generous and hospitable.'

'Twelve Wands depth to the chamber?' queried another gnome, peering cheekily out from the cavity. 'We can easily excavate to provide height in proportion, Black Wand.'

We held an earnest conference on materials and furnishings. It needed tact, however, to overcome their desire for the magnificence their fingers itched to provide. But I didn't want my guests overawed, I wanted them to feel at home and comfortable with its wholesome simplicity.

'And what, Black Wand,' asked the Master before I left, 'is to be the name of your new home? The lintel can be so cunningly contrived that no mortal eye will ever read it.'

The idea of a name had not occurred to me. I thought of my Wych's last words and adjusted them slightly. 'I shall call it *Woe Begone!*' I answered.

Back on The Wandle, I outlined my intentions and hopes to my Wych and told her that I would eventually invite the forest to a comprehensive house-warming.

'Such an occasion would hardly be complete without your presence as guest of honour,' I pointed out.

To my surprise she shook her head and answered without raising her head from the glittering garment on which she still worked.

'A mere Wych of The Wandle is no match for a Wizard of *Woe Begone!* my brother.'

'But beloved, the Weal is for *all* – wicca and wiccy and Wych alike. My people are your people and yours are mine. Why hide your grace from their yearning hearts?'

'Wandle your own Weird as you will, Wychy,' she replied. 'My secrets are my own and even you cannot know them.'

There was no persuading her and I took my leave sadly. It hardly seemed right that I should enjoy the sunlight of the little people's joy while she remained aloof. I had to come to terms with the fact that this was no longer the Wych of my first encounter. Then I remembered that I was hardly the Wychy she had known and loved for so long before me. For now, I could only bow respectfully and take my leave, sad at the shadows I could see in her lovely eyes, such was the wistful longing of her parting look as I returned to my end of The Wandle. And the look troubled me greatly. I had seen that same yearning so often before in the gaze of a languishing wiccy for the unattainablility of August.

But why for *me*? To my Wych, I was wholly attainable – a glance, a smile, the slightest movement of her finger, could bring me to my knees. And yet I sensed that behind the warmth there was this growing reserve. Had my impetuosity become a threat to the deeper mysteries of her nature?

'Truly,' I said to myself with a sigh, 'a Wych is an incomprehensible being.'

*

Before I was ready to open *Woe Begone!* in the manner I had planned, I needed time to study the mysteries of my calling, while keeping an eye on the activities of all my charges from afar. Most of all though, I wanted to be near my Wych, who so mystified me.

From time to time within the black dome of my home, I was appealed to by wiccy and wicca alike with the song of longing. I would identify the owner of the voice and then, if their desired one happened to be already 'booked', would cast around for someone else, inspire them with the Mood, and direct their feet towards the singer.

I found one exception, however. Gwen was fast becoming a mystery. She had no partner, showed no sign of pining for one, and nor could I wile her into the Mood for anyone else. Pwyll and Baddenham both sang of their longing for her, and I had to find others who willingly came to their rescue. Gwen was fond of me, I knew. And she had flirted with me outrageously on the night of High Moon. But she now seemed perfectly able to resist the longing for fulfilment that had been the kiss of death for others – and which now appeared to have affected my Wych. I therefore resigned myself to thinking that Gwen's singularity was perhaps just as well.

Occasionally new half borns appeared, still stunned by the impact of their liberation. Their capacities to adapt themselves varied a great deal and called for tact and patience – and just the right choice of companions to place in their paths. Like those before me, I directed the more recent inhabitants to sponsor them. Loy, Baddenham and Simmonds were of constant help, and Gwen was a star performer. She had beauty and dignity, and her long submission to the doctrines of *Mens Sana* made her eager to forestall any straying in that direction.

I was also watching the two who remained at St John's Wood. Its physical composition laid it open to discovery at any time, and the state of its occupants nagged at me. St John and Barnsley, anxious to preserve their hold on their previous existence, were roaming far and wide seeking new companions. My Wand itched many times to send a wave of shattering conviction upon them, and I hardly know what held me back.

A new turn of events looked promising, however – particularly the arrival of Henrietta Wick.

'She is a curious person,' said Gwen. 'Been rather fond of the fleshpots, I fancy, and probably hasn't spent an altogether moral life. But I rather like her, and think I can help. I'm afraid of Edmund's influence though. He can be very convincing, and if he contacts her –'

'He already has,' I told her.

'Oh, no!' She was aghast. 'I'll go and fetch her away.'

'I'd rather you didn't, Gwen.'

'But you can't leave her in that kind of imprisonment!' she said in dismay. 'After all, I should know, Au ... I mean, Black Wand.'

For the first time, I began to doubt the wisdom of being so informal that I had to assert my authority.

'Doubt you my wisdom, wiccy?'

She returned a troubled stare. 'Well, perhaps you have some other plan in mind, Black Wand. But I cannot understand the need to inflict unnecessary pain.'

'Hetty won't see it that way,' said Loy, who was also present. 'Or if she does, she won't know it because it'll not be that much different to what she's always known –'

'The pain, dear Loy,' Gwen interrupted, 'will be mine.'

Loy looked at her with concern. 'You are a queer one, Gwen. I thought you'd come over completely. Last evening in the Brambles, you even said –'

Gwen rose and walked haughtily away. Loy made to follow her, but I shook my head.

'Gwen must learn to wear her own weird, Loy. It is the law.'

'I know, but I'm worried now, Black Wand. I shouldn't have reminded her about the brambles. But I forget so many things nowadays. She's such a sport, I wouldn't offend her for worlds.'

*

One of the most important duties of a Wychy is to assist his Wych in guarding The Wandle against the Wreak during the hours between sunset and moonrise. Its reflection is a baleful light we call the Scathe, and for this reason the little people seek their protection in the woodland nooks and crannies, where the lightest covering will shield them from its penetration during the interregnum.

Wychies are eternally wakeful and need no rest. On the night of the new moon, a fortnight since the eclipse, I felt I could risk an investigation of the horror at close quarters. It occurred to me as I walked through the dense mass of firs that The Wandle was a major fortification, yet it had two gaps in its ceiling: one over the Circle of Rejoicing and the other over my Wych's retreat. I was wondering how they were shielded, when White Wand appeared at my side, wrapped tightly in her gleaming Weird.

'The refraction of the ancient ball of beryl guards mine,' she said.

Her sudden appearance and her ability to read my thoughts puzzled me. I stopped and we faced each other.

'How is it, beloved,' I asked, 'that you can still discern my ways and thoughts, yet yours remain as far removed from me as ever?'

'Have you not learned from your book of lore that the Weird is an impenetrable cloak?' she asked lightly. 'While ever you insist on going with your Weird unclosed, The Wandle and the Weal are in clamour with your errant moods.'

I quickly drew in my Weird around me. The likelihood had occurred to me but, foolishly, I liked the swish and freedom of its rippling folds.

'And now my valiant wizard goes unheeding to his doom,' she continued, sighing in mock sorrow. 'Are you already so disenchanted with your office?'

'I am only going to *look* at the Wreak, beloved, not defy it,' I answered.

She shook her head, her diadem flashing cascades of colour. 'To look is to invite, dear wizard. Were we not all three scarred by Dragga's claws up there on Wandleside? And The Wandle is now tainted and doomed. Its destruction may be delayed, but it cannot be averted.'

Her words filled me with dread. 'Surely there is a way –?' I began.

'Come!' she said, 'I have something to show you that only wyché vision may reveal.'

She led me to the Circle of Rejoicing, and to the great throne of Alder still draped in its richly embroidered scarlet covering.

Drawing back the huge drape she revealed a chair carved from a single block of rock crystal, the solid cube of the seat forming its foundation.

'You wanted to see how the Circle of Rejoicing is protected,' she reminded me.

'It is a marvellous piece of work,' I said, frowning at her doubtfully, 'but how does this do it?'

'Look again,' she said. 'Look as you would look beyond the confines of your secret chamber.'

So I did, and became aware of a huge and superb moonstone fashioned in the likeness of a shining eye, set within the cube.

I was awestruck. 'What is it?' I breathed.

'The Eye of Mona,' she answered in a low voice as she covered the throne once more. 'It is not wise to gaze too long. Doubtless your book of wisdom has something to say of its tradition and consultation. For the moment, rest content that its power to resist Dragga need not be questioned.'

In tacit agreement, we wandered away from the circle. Soon her arm came around me as we walked slowly through the spruces.

'There is so much that I don't understand,' I said. 'What of our Liege, the King? What kind of fay is he – if indeed he is?'

'He is wyché like ourselves, Brother Wand. But we do not know his Weird – nor does he know ours. In Alder, however, resides the ultimate welfare of our race under Mona's Eye.'

'Does *he* return to mortality from time to time?'

'I have no knowledge of it, brother. His Weird is his own mystery. It is not recorded that a King has ever begged a Wych for Bane – or that a new King has ever been.' She turned her lovely face to me and asked, with apparent naivety, 'What says your own book, Brother Wand?'

'It is silent,' I admitted.

'And rightly so,' she agreed quickly. 'Each to his own Weird. Yours to welcome the half born and mine to speed the fully born.'

'And both,' I reminded her promptly, 'to preserve the balance of our people's happiness and despair. Your retirement from the Weal puzzles them and they turn to me instead of you.'

'I answer every call –' she began evasively.

'Yet not always mine,' I interrupted.

'You are no longer an innocent wicca, Brother Wand. And I have heard no song of longing from your lips.'

'Then you shall now, Wych!'

I put my arms around her and was about to commence the mournful lines, when she pressed her fingers against my lips and cried breathlessly, 'No, no! That lament will wither me more speedily than the dreadful Wreak!' She drew away from me, the gems on her mantle dancing tremulously. 'How shall I ever make it clear to you? Your mortality is a *terrible* enchantment! It runs like a river of pain throughout my being. I pray you, do not beguile me now when my heart is so rung with sadness.'

The rebuff took me aback. I couldn't understand the sudden switch from indulgent love to this rejection. What had she, so wise and understanding, to fear from me, who loved and worshipped her with all the elemental simplicity of my being?

Before either of us could say more, I heard a voice like a trumpet call inside my head.

'The waters of my royal Weird are wiled, my Wychies. What unwonted burden drifts upon the ways where none but my barge may wyn?'

I knew from White Wand's instant alertness that she had heard it too. Her eyes resumed their normal self-possession, and she called in reply: *'We hear and will attend, O King!'*

CHAPTER 20

THE WIZARD OF WOE BEGONE!

Without stopping to explain, White Wand turned away and we hurried in the direction of the Weirds. At the narrow neck of their meeting we looked northwards over the star-spangled waters of King's Weird.

My Wych pointed, and I saw through the gloom a small white shape travelling silently down its centre.

''Tis strange to see a boat upon these waters,' she said in a troubled voice. 'Yet boat it is – though not of a kind I have ever seen before.'

I looked more intently – then laughed. 'Sister Wand, it's a toy! A piece of paper folded to look like a boat. Little mortals make them. Some child must have set it afloat below the bridge in Three Weirs and the wind blew it out of reach. It can't be uncommon for objects to get carried here by the current, surely?'

'By no means,' she answered with a shiver of repugnance. 'Many unwanted things come floating down the river; bottles, tins, dead animals – even dead mortals. But none of these float upon the royal Weird. Our united arts deflect them at the branching of the current into Dragga's maw. I tell you, brother, yon toy is fraught with omen. My heart tells me that it brings unfriendly magic to our peace.'

'Oh, come on!' I argued, amused. 'What sinister magic can there be in a child's innocent plaything? It was probably too fragile to divert into Dragga. Anyway, it'll sail out of King's and into ours. There's really no concern, dear Wych.'

'So speaks your mortal half,' she said softly but scornfully. 'I tell you, that thing is ominous to have penetrated our magic. Our Liege desires it not upon his Weird – and I certainly do not want it on ours. Go seize it, Wychy, and destroy it.'

She was so insistent that I knew I had to humour her. I glided over the narrows and caught the thing easily – it was three-quarters my size stood on end, but light enough to carry.

'See!' I said, showing it to her triumphantly as I returned to the bank. 'Nothing more than folded paper from a school exercise book.' I held it out to her but she shook her head.

'You act unwisely, brother, to bring *anything* of mortal making onto The Wandle. I dislike its weird.'

'It's an inanimate object!' I laughed. 'How can it have a weird? It has no intent –'

'Say you, indeed?' she interrupted, indicating it with her Wand. 'Your "innocent" and "inanimate" object bears writing – see?'

'It's just scribble,' I protested, unfolding it and holding it out for her to see. Her wyché vision, more speedy than mine, raced across the faintly pencilled page while she held her Weird tightly about her.

'*Dear Mr Witchett …*' she began. (I'll not repeat it all, Ann, for you already know its content.) My Wych read it aloud to me to the end, then raised expressionless eyes to mine.

'It's from the grandchildren of my housekeeper,' I explained lamely. 'I told you about them at our first meeting. But it means no more than the letters they write to Santa Claus begging for Christmas presents.'

'And what manner of wizard is Santa Claus?'

I told her the legend and she considered it gravely for a moment.

'And their prayers are always answered?' she asked significantly.

'If their parents can afford it. But only so as not to disappoint their belief. When they are six or seven they're old enough to understand the truth.'

'And how old is Stella?'

'Twelve,' I admitted uncomfortably.

She smiled superiorly. 'But she still has faith in her Witchett?'

'As do all the mortals on our fringe – and certainly the older ones.'

'And how shall you answer this … *innocent question*?'

'How can I? Mr Gus can't go back. He's unmortal, now …' The argument died on my lips. My mortality seemed to be a matter on which we never saw eye to eye. Nevertheless, I could not dismiss the problem. The children's implicit faith touched me deeply. To them the Witchett was a very real – if very terrible – being who had stolen their Mr Gus and had the power, if he could be so persuaded, to send him back. The idea of ignoring them aroused a sense of shame. But what could I do to reassure them, yet not give too much proof of Mr Gus's continued existence?

An idea occurred to me. After my moonrise story session at Great Oak, I announced my house warming invitation to *Woe Begone!*

I arrived at my new home in time to see the Royal Vintner's dray roll into view with his excited fawns. His round form fairly tumbled off it to greet me.

'Hael and wyn, Black Wand! At the behest of Alder, I am come provided with the rarest liquors from the royal cellars that this occasion will not wither for lack of good cheer!'

I was staggered at the speed with which the news had spread to bring Rozyn so quickly. His two helpers unloaded a cabinet from the dray and brought it over to set down before me. Rozyn opened it with a flick of the wrist to reveal an array of crystal bottles with richly tinted contents. Another flick and a store of miniature barrels were shown in a lower compartment.

'Accept this humble gift, dear Black Wand, to adorn your new abode,' he said with a flourish.

'I shall treasure it, good Rozyn, for the entertainment of future guests,' I answered gravely. 'Please convey to our Liege my thanks for his generous gift towards our celebration this night.'

With a touch of my Wand, I opened the door into the beech tree and the cabinet was taken in.

The little people began to arrive, singing:

'Hael and wyn, Wychy, walking the Weal
Bright is thy Wand! Be thy Weird in the wind
Starry in moonlight, flashing in sun
Wielder of wonders, weaver of fun!'

Because no one could remember what a house-warming was, they took it upon themselves to devise a celebration of their own. With their usual speed of imagination, and with Honeyball acting as master of ceremonies, they began with the inescapable roundelay of Chrysobel and her cakes. Next came a grotesque hornpipe by Loy and Simmonds, and then a more relaxed rendering of *Greensleeves* by Pwyll for Gwen. The bubbling throng then milled around the Royal Vintner's inviting casks for refreshment. Rozyn was in his element.

When everyone was assured that I had been warmly welcomed to my new abode in the Weal, they drifted off happily, leaving me with a small group consisting of Gwen, Loy, Jean, Pwyll, Baddenham and Simmonds, and two or three recent arrivals who felt in need of guidance regarding their new surroundings. I sat on a low stool within the beech where there was plenty of room for them to gather.

'Baddy,' I said, 'you remember the toy tea set that is used in *Mens Sana*?'

Baddenham grinned at Gwen as he answered. 'I should say I do! Barney and Simmo pinched it from some children in Wychy's Mead as a surprise for Gwen –'

'And wished ever since that they hadn't,' interrupted Gwen calmly. 'Do tell me, George, was the brew really as horrible as you all made out?'

He laughed. 'Worse! We used to pitch it away when you weren't looking. But didn't you know how awful the stuff was yourself?'

'I never liked tea, dear, so I never tried it. I thought you all liked it though.' She looked at me. 'Why did you ask about the tea set, Black Wand? Do *you* want tea?'

'No, Gwen – I want the tea set. And the doll's dress and bonnet you used to wear. I want them all returned to their owner.'

The party became very still. This sounded like a new departure.

'But the dress was terribly spoilt by the thorns, Black Wand,' Gwen reminded me. 'I don't know where it is now. Or the bonnet.'

'That's all right, Gwen,' I assured her. 'Sylvie and Dina know, and are bringing them to us now. Since you were once at *Mens Sana*, Baddy,' I continued, 'I'd like you to help fetch the tea set. And Loy – will you supervise?'

Loy smiled delightedly. 'Wizard show!' he said, and turned to Simmonds. 'You'll give a hand, won't you, Simmo? Larceny at *Mens Sana* and housebreaking in Three Weirs? Oh, boy! Hope Sin's at home. I'd love to see him try and stop us. Simmo, you've got a pretty decent left hook ...' he said, and broke off to look proudly round at the rest of us, '... Simmo was inter-services champion in his day!'

'Use a modicum of care, Loy,' I warned. 'Direct action should not be needed. Both St John and Barnsley are absent at this moment. You only have to walk in and remove the things.'

'Okay!' Loy jumped to his feet. 'Bags I the teapot and milk jug. Baddy and Simmo can grab the cups and saucers. We'll want someone else to help with the plates ...' He looked around expectantly.

'Jean and I will manage the plates,' offered Apples, a new boy so named for his surname having been Appleby. The others, with the exception of Gwen, also begged not to be left behind. I nodded, and the crowd streamed off, screaming, 'Hush, hush, hush! We're coming to burgle you!'

Sylvie and Dina arrived with the dress and bonnet, at a loss as to what I could possibly want with them. Gwen explained while I restored them to pristine condition with the Wand.

The raiding party returned dancing with glee in less than half an hour and set everything out before me.

'All present and correct, Black Wand,' Loy announced smugly. 'And no casualties to either personnel or stores.'

The report sounded sufficiently innocent but, even if I had not known what had really happened, the grin on Simmond's face would have given it away.

'It was a pity you deemed it necessary to dawdle so long showing Jean and the others around the place, Loy. If you had come away at once, as I intended, you would have been well out of sight before St John and Barnsley returned, wouldn't you?'

'We-ell ...' growled Simmonds unrepentantly, '... they had it coming to them anyway.'

'You don't mean you've been fighting?' demanded Gwen, scandalised.

Pwyll coughed apologetically behind his hand. 'No option, my dear. We tried to reason with them, but Edmund is so impetuous, poor fellow.'

'It was all fair and above board,' said Loy. 'Nothing so low as a brawl.'

'Heavens no!' said Pwyll. 'Just a three-round contest between Simmo and Sin.'

'Properly refereed by Pwyll,' put in Loy. 'With Baddy as timekeeper. Barney seconded Sin, and Apples seconded Simmo.'

'Went the full three rounds too!' enthused the new boy. 'Simmo was most considerate. Saved the knockout for the last moment so as not to disappoint the customers.'

I sent them off to return everything to Stella Mye, with strict instructions for absolute secrecy and silence.

*

As the days sped by it occurred to me that my tasks were becoming inconsistent with my traditional duties. White Wand never entered the Weal, and I noticed a growing unease among the wiccas who were her especial responsibility. Although nothing was said, they were bringing their spiritual aches and pains more and more frequently to me – often diffident and apologetic.

''T'will be excellent practice for you, Brother Wand,' was all my Wych said when I asked her.

'But is it wise, beloved?' I begged. 'Your wiccas need you and your loving sympathy as much as I do.'

We were sitting in her clearing in brilliant sunshine.

A flash of the old Wych returned as she replied, 'I would not have your love waning with over-loving, Black Wand. We Wychies are not all fay.'

Then her hand went out to me and I went to sit at her feet, resting my head against her knee. I thrilled with love and desire for her embrace.

'But, Wych, do you love *me*?'

'Much too much,' she admitted readily, but through veiled eyes.

'Then why –?'

She kissed me. 'Oh, my brother ... beloved Wychy! I am no longer wyché when I look into the worlds of wonder that lurk behind your eyes. Once I could read them, but now I have no sight. Once I held you powerless at my feet and revelled in your love and adoration. But now I am the one who is enthralled and enslaved!' She kissed me again passionately.

I drew her nearer and she sank at my side, her arms around my neck and her head bowed in weeping. My queenly, unattainable Wych had entirely disappeared.

I held her close and kissed her head, wondering what possible explanation there could be. After a few moments she raised her head and I found myself looking into melting eyes that shone with quivering tears.

'Does your love-bound captive please her lord?' she asked.

I answered her with a longing kiss, but was still unable to understand what had happened to her. She clung closer and continued, 'Truly you are the wicked Wizard of our Witchery Wood. You have utterly bewrayed my heart –'

Sudden tensions pulling at our Weirds broke the spell. *'Black Wand! White Wand! There are mortals in the Weal!'*

She gave a sigh, slipped from my arms and crossed the grass to her ball of beryl.

''Tis the Lord of the Weirs ... and another,' she whispered back to me. Then called out reassuringly, *'Fear not, little people! All is well.'*

'Who walks with him?' I asked.

'The dreamer,' she said casually.

The dreamer! The memory of two astonished brown eyes made me rise and go to stand beside the Wych to look. Sir Edward We'ard and you, Ann, were walking up the sunken track from the Mead in slow motion. The difference in our timeframes makes mortals appear slow and heavy, and their speech ponderous. It's also why we are invisible to you. I looked at you with interest. You could hardly be from the village or I would surely have recognised you. And yet … there *was* something vaguely familiar about your face.

'She is beautiful, is she not?' asked White Wand softly.

I made no reply. I was trying to fit your mortal features with the ethereal counterpart I had seen previously; but I couldn't recognise them. I thought that if I had ever met you in the village, though, I would have found you very attractive. Then you turned your head, attracted by some sight or sound, and looked straight at me, and I was thrilled by the instant recognition.

'Ann Singlewood!' I exclaimed, amazed that it was the same you that I had seen at the window the night I had fled to the forest.

'You know this mortal?' asked my Wych.

She listened intently as I told her all I knew and had somehow completely forgotten until now. She seemed perplexed and indignant.

'What said *he who is gone* about this matter?' she asked.

'Nothing, Sister Wand. I had no memory of it at that time, so I never told him.'

'I do not like this,' she said, turning her attention back to the ball. We continued to watch.

Sir Edward indicated the bench-like seat among the roots, and you both sat. I could see that he was not happy about something he thought you had done. It was to do with the return of the doll's tea set, frock and bonnet. He seemed to think you had written the letter to the Witchett. Then you explained how you had helped the children float it down the river to the Weirds, and had been going to find replicas so they would not be disappointed. And then you showed him the letter you *had* written – the Witchett's apparent reply.

My Wych was furious with its content. 'So! It seems my unweaned wizard already outgrows his Weird! What wandling is this? Know you not that the wiling of mortals is unwyché?' she demanded.

'As well as I know that the wandling of dreamers is unethical,' I answered.

'Seek not to unravel my Weird, Brother Wand!' she warned. 'That which I have done is needful and lawful.'

'How was it needful to parade Ann Singlewood's phantom before my bewildered eyes at High Moon?' I returned. 'She was the last mortal I saw … a woman who was no more to me than a face and a name.'

'It was needful to *me*,' she said, dismissing it with a gesture. 'Your earlier knowledge of her is something only *he who is gone* could explain. That is not part of *my* mystery.'

I tried to remain patient. 'In what way do you say *I* have wiled her?'

'Because of your mortality, her presence so beguiled you that you were set on finding out what hidden plan I had in mind for her. So you wiled her into sending a written message to you upon the Weird.'

I caught my breath that she could accuse me so unjustly. 'That is untrue, my beloved! You heard her for yourself. She was not the author of the letter, and she expected no answer, which is why she wrote one herself for the children. I did not know until this day that she was either the dreamer or the person I had seen at the window. This I swear by Mona's light.'

We stared into each other's wide eyes. Then she relaxed. Her sternness melted and her tightly drawn Weird fell free again.

'Brother Wand, I have been unwyché and misjudged you. Can you forgive me?'

'For what?' I asked, relieved that we could kiss in peace and understanding once again.

She leaned against me for a while. 'Oh, beloved! So much misunderstanding overtook me. I was almost resolved to cross my Wand with yours – and that must never be! It seems *he who is gone* had some other secret destiny that I may not know.'

'He wrote –' I began, eager to heal the rift even more, but my lips were silenced with another kiss.

'Say it not,' she implored. 'I could be tempted to unmake it.'

We returned our attention to the crystal ball, and you, Ann, were saying, '... Stella thought it was the Witchett because he was wearing a shining black cloak, had a tall black crown on his head and carried a black Wand. She also dreamed that there were stuffed figures of the dragon and Hellbane Harry's two assistants behind him. But – and this is the amazing part – she said the Witchett was telling the fairies that these two assistants had discovered where Chrysobel lived and they had called on her. They were very respectful and raised their hats, just as gentlemen should when meeting a lady – though these particular hats had been specially made for the occasion. But although they were polite, they were also very firm and said that she had to go back to the castle with them and have a chat with the Wicked Wizard, who wanted to show her his etchings.

'Stella said the fairies all began to laugh at this point, and interrupted the Witchett with all sorts of funny questions. But he didn't answer them because other fairies shouted the answers back instead. And it was all so funny that some of them rolled in the grass because they were laughing so much. Stella didn't know what all the questions meant, but she had to laugh too. And her special friend Rosynose was laughing loudest of all. When I asked her why he was special, she said that when he had first met her and asked her what her name was, she couldn't remember it, so he said she was to be his Star Maiden. He was always very kind to her.

'There was a lot more of the story that I won't go into now, but when it ended all the fairies went away singing and dancing, and her friend Rosynose let her ride with him up on the front of his little cart. Then he kissed her and said that if she was a very good girl and went back to sleep he'd let her come back again another night to hear the rest of the story. And then she woke up.'

I turned to my Wych. 'So what is Rozyn up to?' I exclaimed. 'Is he allowed to wandle mortals?'

'Rozyn-Who-Knows always knows what he is doing,' murmured White Wand, keeping her attention on the ball. 'But be comforted, Wand; the dreamer shall not know what she should have guessed already – that Black Wand and "Mr Gus" are one and the same.'

At this point we could see St John, Barnsley and their latest companion, Hetty, scrambling down the bank close to where you and the Weir Lord were sitting.

'I know *him*,' Barnsley was saying. 'He's the lord of the manor round this neck o' the woods. Potters round the forest quite a lot. The gobs don't seem to mind him. They say he's a "friendly", so they don't run for cover. But I don't know *her*. She's new.'

'His daughter, perhaps?' St John suggested.

'Dunno. Nice pair of legs though!'

'Do you ever think of anything else?' demanded Hetty tartly.

'Yes – yours sometimes!'

Barnsley dodged an unladylike backhander.

St John growled, 'Shut up, Barnsley! We don't want to attract their attention, do we?'

'They won't see us. We're all dead, remember? You don't see ghosts in daylight.'

'I wish I had a costume like hers,' sighed Hetty. 'These ghastly rags aren't even fit for throwing away.'

Barnsley leered. 'Pity!' he said meaningfully, preparing to dodge again. 'Still, it's all we've got. And you wouldn't even have them if dear Gwendolyn hadn't gone and joined the enemy.'

They had just reached the other side of the path, when you and Sir Edward spotted them.

'You infernal liar, Barnsley!' St John exploded. 'They *have* seen us!'

'You beast, Barney!' squeaked Hetty. 'Oh, what a sight I must look. Get out of my way!'

The three disgruntled misfits hurried away, arguing and bickering. As I watched them go, I thought that a more perfect condemnation of human frailty would be hard to imagine. But even White Wand acknowledged at last that there was a need to do something about them.

CHAPTER 21

MENS SANA SEES THE LIGHT

Returning to my end of The Wandle, I picked up on the trio from *Mens Sana* just as Hetty was wailing: '… I've lost one of these horrible shoes now … and here goes the other!' She kicked it from her foot and it sailed into St John's back.

'You'll get thorns in your feet!' he shouted.

'So what? I can't be any more miserable than I am now. Go and get me some of those wonderful goblin garments you're always drooling about, Barney.'

'Not a hope,' was his gloomy reply. 'They've a rooted objection to being undressed. Better ask Aug – he's a bleedin' expert at it, blast him!'

'Who's he?'

'Autrey – the fellow we told you about,' St John said severely. 'The one who assaulted Miss Kinney.'

'What?' Hetty plucked incredulously at the drab, ill-fitting flannel blouse. 'When she's wearing stuff like this? The fellow must be a moron.'

'She wasn't wearing as much as that when I saw her,' Barnsley sniggered. 'He's a ruddy wolf, that Autrey fellow.'

Noting that their route would take them in the direction of *Woe Begone!* I looked to see who might be there, and found Gwen. She was sitting with her back to the door, listening happily to Pwyll playing a lute and serenading her in concert with Baddenham.

'Oh, no,' Pwyll said, stopping. 'Here comes that *Mens Sana* crowd. Better disappear hadn't we, Gwen?'

'No, dear Pwyll,' she said. 'I'm not afraid of them any more. And besides, I've a bone to pick with Edmund.'

'But Gwen,' warned Baddenham, 'remember what Black Wand said –'

'He said I wasn't to go out of my way to meet Hetty. He didn't say I had to hide from her if she ever came *my* way.'

The two wiccas settled back doubtfully, but lute and voice remained silent.

'Well, well, well!' cried St John. 'If it isn't Gwendolyn and George. And surely that's the Padre?' He pointed at Pwyll. 'What luck! *Mens Sana* reunited at last! How *are* you Gwendolyn? Delighted to see you again.'

'Personally,' replied Gwen, looking curiously at Hetty as she spoke, 'I've never felt better in either of my two lives, Edmund. But please don't delude yourself that I am ever likely to return to the fold, because I am not.'

'What? After the way that Autrey fellow treated you, my dear?' But St John spoke mechanically. He couldn't take his eyes off her.

'Of course, if you prefer to believe that tale-bearing liar on your left, Edmund,' Gwen waved a careless hand in Barnsley's direction, 'then you will never be capable of believing your own eyes. Do I *look* as if I am being badly treated?'

'I'll say you don't,' said Hetty, eyeing her enviously. 'I'm green! Where did you get it?'

'This?' Gwen glanced down at her dress with its girdle of opals, and shrugged artlessly. 'There's dozens better than this.' She looked at Hetty's appearance with sympathy. 'I *am* sorry you had to wear those awful things. They're terrible.'

'You didn't think so until a few days ago,' said St John, darkly.

'Quite true, Edmund. But that was down to you and your absurd notions about keeping the flag flying and having nothing to do with the goblins. I didn't have much chance of learning anything different, did I?' She turned swiftly to Hetty. 'Hetty, dear, do I *look* like a goblin?'

'You look more like an angel. Are those earrings real?'

Gwen removed them. 'See for yourself.' She threw them over to Hetty, but St John caught them before she could move and put them in his pocket.

'Oh, no, you don't, Gwendolyn. You are not enticing Hetty away like that. *You* may have lost your morals, but *she* hasn't.'

'Look who's talking!' said Hetty incredulously. 'Who's just pocketed some priceless jewellery that doesn't belong to him? Those earrings were for *me* to look at.'

'No, Hetty,' Gwen corrected her gently. 'They were for you to *wear*. I felt I owed you them for the indignities you've inherited from my mistakes. Now you see the sort of people you're associating with.'

'But I don't want to associate with them!' wailed Hetty. 'I'd much rather live with you.'

St John quickly interrupted her before Gwen could point out the obvious. 'What about you, George?' he asked Baddenham. 'You can't possibly feel at home amongst these morons. You'll die of intellectual starvation.'

'I'm looking forward to that with fervour and hope,' Baddenham answered with a laugh. 'You can addle your own brain with pointless speculation if you like, but I prefer simple reality. You see, old man, I've discovered that I really *am* dead ... and I quite like it. You can't be any deader than dead, can you? And if this is hell, then commend me to that wonderful black devil with the Wand who saved me from sending myself back to heaven!'

Pwyll chuckled softly and began to pluck at his lute again. St John rounded on him with a sneer. 'Bit of a let down for you, isn't it, Padre? I mean, after spending a lifetime qualifying for the harp, it must be a heck of a knock to one's self esteem to find you're fobbed off with a mangy old lute?'

Pwyll smiled serenely and drew golden notes from the instrument. 'I fear my poor theology has suffered a chronic attack of spiritual enlightenment, dear Edmund. I have at last discovered tongues in trees, books in the running brooks, sermons in stones, and good in everything – with sin nowhere to be found.'

'What about lust?' St John sneered.

'I have not discovered it.' Pwyll's smile became radiant.

*

I began to feel grateful then that I hadn't used my Wand to convert the inmates of *Mens Sana*. And in the days that followed, I grew even more thankful for *Woe Begone!*

The unconventional haunt that made me available in the Weal proved wise, for White Wand retired still further in her reserve. *Woe Begone!* helped dispel any sense that all was not well on The Wandle, and Gwen was becoming a passable substitute for my absent Wych. There was a hidden strength about her; a quiet dignity such as I had seen in the King – which led me to wonder whether I should take my troubles to him. I felt sure he would know what to do but I shrank from such a drastic step, for it seemed a betrayal of my Wych. So my problem remained. What could I – or should I – do if anyone went looking for the Bane and couldn't find her?

Meanwhile, there was still St John's Wood to deal with. I directed Dina's thoughts to where she and Gwen would find a faerie robe of pastel blue. Gwen agreed to cooperate, as I knew she would, with Dina's idea of smuggling it into *Mens Sana* during its occupants' absence.

As soon as Hetty discovered it in her room, she threw her rags away with a whoop of joy and came downstairs to demand the return of her earrings. St John raged. Barnsley goggled. But the wiccy stood her ground.

'Hetty, I forbid you to wear that immoral thing!' St John shouted. 'Change back at once!'

'I won't! And you have no right to order me about. I'll wear whatever I like, and if you don't like it you can look the other way. Now give me back my earrings, you thief!'

'You will do as you are told, my girl!'

'Oh, will I? And how are you going to make me? Strip me?'

St John shrank at the challenge and fell back on hopeless bluster. 'It's indecent, I tell you. Do you want to be mistaken for a goblin's whore? Haven't Barnsley and I got enough on our hands without having to watch you wherever you go?'

'You do that already!' She said scornfully. 'I've been taken out like a dog on a lead ever since I arrived. Do I get those earrings or not?'

'You do not … unless you'll exchange them for that film of indecency you call a dress.'

'Then it's no go, Edmund. We'll leave things as they are. I expect Gwendolyn will be kind enough to find me some others.'

'Oh, no, she won't. From now on this house will never be left unoccupied. There's no chance of anyone sneaking in here again. You hear that, Barnsley? Hetty's not to be left alone.'

Barnsley looked rather interested at the possible opportunities the instruction provided. 'Yes, of course, Sinjy. You want me to look after Het when she goes out, while you stay here and hold the fort. Good idea. Come to think of it –'

'Never mind thinking, you fool – if you seriously think I'm going to let her out with *you*, you've got it all wrong. *You'll* do the staying behind.'

'So's *you* can have high jinks with Het? You're joking! Fair's fair.'

'Don't mind *me*,' Hetty murmured, sitting down demurely on a bench. 'When you two satyrs have decided who's going to seduce me, I'd like to get a word in.'

'How dare you say a thing like that!' exclaimed St John, scandalised. 'I, at any rate, have always treated you with every consideration and courtesy. Do you really think I'd be so unchivalrous as to take advantage of you?'

'Yes!'

Barnsley guffawed and Hetty flicked a look in his direction. 'At least Barney's honest,' she said. 'He knows he's got a one track mind and he doesn't try to hide it. I know where I am with him. But you've just started to wake up, Edmund my boy. The only reason Gwendolyn was safe here was because of her awful appearance. But you couldn't take your eyes off her a day or two ago – and you can't take your eyes off me now. If I was a prude I'd have blushed long ago.' She rose and assumed a pose, mischievously smoothed down the transparent robe, and beckoned Barnsley over. 'Take a bet, Barney?'

He obeyed willingly. She whispered in his ear while keeping her eyes on St John, who was glaring with unconcealed jealousy. Barnsley tittered with glee and took advantage of her proximity to squeeze her anatomy quite brazenly.

'It's on, baby!' he declared enthusiastically, then laughed fruitily at St John's murderous expression.

'Well, I'm off for a stroll,' said Hetty. 'Bye-bye, you two.'

She had reached the door before St John sprang to his feet. He stared suspiciously at Barnsley, who grinned back, smugly unperturbed. 'I'm going to escort her, Barnsley,' he said aggressively.

'No one's stopping you.'

Barnsley sat himself on the bench, drew out one of his abominable cigarettes and selected a match from a neat stack on the floor.

'Don't light that in here,' he was angrily told. 'You know the rule – no smoking in the house.'

Barnsley raised a derisive eyebrow, the match poised in mid air. 'I'm watching the joint, ain't I? Better hurry, Sinjy, or she'll give you the slip and hook up with the gobs.'

St John dashed out. Barnsley laughed heartily, struck the match on a stone beside the hearth and lit the weed. He was still chuckling some minutes later when Hetty returned, but his amusement faded into amazement when he spotted the flashing gems swinging below her ears.

'Blimey, Het, you're a fast worker! How'd you manage that?'

'Mind your own business, Barney. I won the bet, that's all you need to know. Now it's your turn to scram – go and ask Gwendolyn to get me the girdle to match the dress. That was the arrangement, remember?'

Barnsley jumped up joyfully. 'And when I get back with it … well, you know what you said …?'

'Yes, I know *exactly* what I said,' Hetty answered enigmatically. 'Now hurry up before Edmund returns. I warn you, he's as mad as a hatter, so keep out of his way.'

Barnsley stared at her in disbelief. 'You don't mean you got them off him without …?'

She gave him a withering look. 'You don't think I'd let him put anything across *me*, do you?'

Barnsley roared with laughter and made to slap her playfully across the bottom, but she deftly eluded him. He looked at her suspiciously. 'You aren't going to pass *me* up too, are you Het? I mean, no monkey tricks. You know what you promised – as soon as we got a chance to get together …?'

'I've already told you, I remember *exactly* what I said.'

'Yeah, but come to think of it, you didn't say *exactly* –'

'Look, I'm not giving it to you in four-letter words, you fool! Oh blast, it's too late – he's coming across the lawn now.'

They waited in silence for St John's arrival. He rushed in breathing heavily and looking like a storm cloud. 'You … you …!' he spluttered, shaking his fist at Hetty.

'That's enough, Sinjy,' Barnsley ordered, with an unconvincing air of offended virtue. 'All's fair in love 'n war, y'know. No need to call her names 'cause she didn't want to play.'

St John turned on him furiously. 'You dirty skunk! You fixed it up between you, didn't you? That's what all the sniggering was about. That's the dirty bet you took.'

'Nothing wrong with the bet, Sinjy. Het said she'd have those earrings off you in half an hour. And she did. It was all a joke, see?' Barnsley said defensively.

'*A joke!*' St John fumed. 'There's two sides to a bet like that. What were *you* going to get if she'd lost?'

Barnsley shot a guilty look at Hetty, who smiled back provocatively. St John began to tremble with rage.

'You disgraceful little bitch! You're nothing better than a tart! You tricked me with false promises. You said if I gave them back you'd –'

She cut him short with a laugh.

The inflamed dupe lunged towards her. 'I'll have those earrings back if I have to tear them off you!'

Barnsley lunged too, and struck St John on the arm. They crashed to the floor, cursing and clawing at each other.

Hetty moved unnoticed towards the door to make her final escape – and stopped abruptly as she opened it.

'May I come in?' I asked politely from the threshold. The battle ceased and two astonished faces looked up at me.

'It's Autrey, curse him!'

'Aug, by Gawd!'

'Black Wand, if you please,' I corrected them gently.

'What are *you* doing here?' St John snarled.

'Paying a belated call in response to your invitation, St John.'

They stared me up and down, trying to make sense of my appearance.

'Won't you take a seat, Mr, er, Black Wand?' Hetty invited archly.

'Thank you.' I moved to sit on the bench and motioned that she should sit at my side, which delighted her.

'Things getting you down, boys?' I asked affably.

'Clear out!' shouted St John. 'Or we'll throw you out.'

'Hear, hear!' Barnsley agreed. 'I owe him one for that clout on the ear he gave me.'

I took no notice, but from under my Weird I produced a girdle of sapphires and diamonds and offered it to the incredulous wiccy at my side.

'With Gwendolyn's compliments, Hetty.'

'Oh, oh!' she gasped. 'How did she know?'

'Allow me?' I asked, and took it from her to fasten around her waist. It brought a yell of rage from Barnsley. St John looked as if he was about to have a fit.

'Comfy?' I asked her.

'Perfectly, thank you, Mr Wand,' she said, her eyes dancing. Leaning closer she asked curiously, 'Aren't you supposed to be the big bad wolf of the forest?'

'The biggest,' I assured her. 'Feeling scared?'

'Not in the least. I could fall for you in a big way, gorgeous! Are you going to take me away from here?'

'Naturally, my dear Hetty.'

'Hear that, Sinjy? The swine's going to take her away!'

'Oh, no, he isn't!' St John shouted, leaping to his feet and grabbing a rickety chair.

Hetty fluttered her eyelashes coyly. 'Where are you going to take me, Mr Wand?'

'Sinjy!' yelled Barnsley. 'What's in Gawd's name is stopping you? Sling the ruddy chair at him!'

'I can't – the blasted thing's stuck to the floor!' St John said, pulling at it vainly. 'Why don't you do something yourself, you fool?'

'Because I'm gummed to the ruddy floor too!'

I continued my talk with Hetty. 'I shall take you to fairyland, my dear. To a place where there is only laughter and love. Where the little people dance on star-studded grass and the trees look down on their revels with joy.'

'Then you must be a wizard,' she said.

'I am.'

'Then do something to prove it,' she challenged.

'Such as?'

She gave a sidelong nod towards St John and Barnsley and whispered in my ear: 'Turn them into toads, of course! That's what wizards are supposed to do, isn't – oh!' she broke off with a shriek as I waved the Wand in front of her eyes and deluded her vison. 'Oh! They *are* toads! Ugh! Oh, the horrid things. Don't let them touch me! I shall die if they –'

'But they are what you wanted to see,' I reminded her.

'Yes, but I *hate* toads. And I didn't really think you could ... oh, please, Mr Wand, change them back again. I ... I think I preferred them as they were after all.'

I lifted the illusion and she relaxed, regarding me with awestruck eyes.

'You really *are* a wizard!'

'What's all this rot about toads?' St John demanded apprehensively. 'We've been here all the time, you idiot.

Look here, Autrey, we've had about enough of this tomfoolery. What are you doing here anyway? What do you want? We haven't interfered with you.'

'But you have, very much, my dear fellow,' I said. 'You are a *constant* source of interference. You betray your existence to innocent mortals by wearing these travesties of human garb. You've caused endless concern by living in this doll's house. I'm tired of having to divert wandering mortals from entering this part of the forest. Can you imagine the stir if its existence became general knowledge? I have therefore decided to dispense with the danger by removing *Mens Sana* – and *you*.'

'Remove *Mens Sana*?' St John shouted. 'You can't do that! It's our home. We've nowhere else to live. If you're thinking of sending your band of goblins along to tear it down –'

'Nothing so crude as that, old fellow,' I cut him short. 'The means are already to hand.' I lifted my Wand suggestively.

'I see,' St John sneered. 'Going to wave the old magic wand, eh? And hey presto, it'll all disappear in a flash, I suppose?'

'You'd be surprised,' I said. 'Edmund, you've rooted your ideas so deeply into this rustic hideout that it's become a plague spot to our people. It really does have to go.'

'Oh, *does* it? Well I'm here to stay, whatever else goes. Isn't that so Barnsley?'

Barnsley shifted uncomfortably.

'I dunno, Sinjy … Gussy's a crafty beggar. We were going to sling him out, but we don't seem to have managed it yet, do we?'

'Because you couldn't,' said Hetty scornfully. 'And don't forget, you'd still be the couple of loathsome toads you really are if I hadn't changed my mind.'

'You're nuts,' St John dismissed her rudely. He turned to me: 'All right, Autrey. I've had my say. Now let's see what you can do.'

'Very well.' I dipped my Wand carelessly towards Barnsley's bundle of matches at my side. The flaring gasses from the match heads hissed out, streaming in all directions, firing flames that licked at floor, walls and ceiling. Barnsley gave a yell of horror at finding his trousers alight, and rushed for the door. St John stayed only a moment longer, before diving out of the open window. Hetty screamed in alarm and would have followed, but I pulled her back.

'We'll be burned to death!' she shrieked.

I calmed her struggles. 'You're already dead, sweetheart. The fire has no power over us.'

'But Barney and Edmund were a mass of flames.'

'Because they were wearing physical garments,' I reminded her patiently. 'Look at me – not even singed.'

She relaxed and looked around with wide eyes at the vast ball of fire. 'It's beautiful,' she sighed, nestling back in my arms as streams of yellow, green, red and mauve roared up in tall spires to consume the tinder-dry walls.

As I picked her up and carried her out through the wall of fire to the back of the crumbling house, I felt a passionate kiss on my cheek.

'Darling wizard! If this is really being dead, don't ever let me live again, will you? I want to stay dead for ever and ever.'

When we reached the trees I set her down, and we walked away, my arm and my Weird around her shoulder, and her arm tightly around my waist.

'What a couple of fools they are!' she laughed. 'With all this wonder around them, they chose to live in that ghastly hovel.'

'Habit, dear child. But I think you and I have been able to shock their decadent systems, don't you?'

'You mean *you* have!'

'Only after you prepared the way. Your wicked little plot to play one off against the other shook poor Edmund to the soul.'

'Serves him right.' She nestled closer. 'Snooty old hypocrite!'

'He's not a bad fellow really, Hetty. Everyone finds it difficult at first. It's just that Barnsley feels the elemental desire for love too keenly, so he goes after it like a bull in a china shop. Edmund, of course, thought he had strangled his libido completely – you very cleverly spotted that he hadn't.'

'And me?' she asked.

I laughed. '*You* aren't fighting at all! You're grabbing at your new life with both hands, bless you.'

She rubbed her cheek against my shoulder. 'Mmm … what a wonderful wizard you are. Where are we going?'

'To meet Gwen … and here she is! Now get along with you, and listen to *everything* she tells you.'

'Black Wand!' Gwen came running towards us. 'The Weal's buzzing with the most alarming rumours about *Mens Sana*. What's happened?'

'No one's hurt, Gwen, I assure you. Least of all the imp of depravity I have under my Weird.'

I removed my arm and disclosed Hetty's laughing face.

'It was wonderful, Gwen!' she cried, running to her. 'And thanks for the girdle – look, Black Wand fixed it for me.'

'And you're sure you're all right, Hetty?' asked Gwen solicitously.

'Of course I am! Although …' she glanced back at me mischievously, 'if you hadn't come along just when you did, I *might* not have been!'

'*Hetty!*' said Gwen severely. 'There's one thing you need to learn here and now – Black Wand is taboo. He has a heart of stone where we poor wiccies are concerned. You'll get your fingers burnt, I warn you.'

'No, I shan't!' Hetty laughed. 'He's just proved to me that nobody *ever* gets burnt here. He's the most wonderful wizard that ever was. And you needn't look at me like that, Gwen – I've just told him so.'

'Please be quiet, Hetty. I'll explain the facts of life to you later … Black Wand, where is Edmund?'

'Running for dear life in a state of nudity, along with Barnsley. But worry not, my dear, for Pwyll, Loy, Baddy and Simmo are all in hot pursuit of them with clothing – before the forest can become too scandalised!'

But if that little problem was on its way to a solution, a far worse dilemma was closing in on me.

CHAPTER 22

THE WEIRDNESS OF A WYCH

It arrived a week later when the forest and its inhabitants seemed to have recovered their usual harmony. The two fugitives were still causing one or two problems, old convictions dying hard.

'Barney has quietened down a lot,' said Gwen at one of our 'at homes'. 'If I could only persuade Hetty to take him in hand. It needs someone who's still pretty tough; someone who'll stand no nonsense from him. But the little minx is too intrigued by the trinkets the gnomes have been showering on her to notice his existence. So Barney remains a potential menace.' She paused, looking at me hopefully. 'I suppose *you* couldn't get them together?'

I shook my head. 'Unless one of them sings me the song of longing for the other, I can do nothing, Gwen. But I *could* mention the name of another ...' I looked at her enquiringly.

'Oh, *I* can't do anything, Black Wand! I've so many wiccas to look after already ... there's Baddy and Loy and Pwyll and Fizzy, you know.'

'On the contrary, Gwen – everyone thinks that *they* are looking after *you*! Now, had you mentioned Edmund ...' The forest had taken to using St John's given name now that the rebel had been accepted into the fold. The contraction of his surname was felt to be too harsh and needed softening.

'Well, yes, Edmund is a responsibility too, of course,' Gwen replied. 'Why are you smiling?'

I made no answer.

'You've grown into a very curious person since High Moon,' she said with a sigh. 'When you were August you always seemed ready to try anything. But now, nothing! Black Wand is beyond me.'

I raised an eyebrow. 'Pardon me?'

She came and sat by my side and took my hand to kiss it. 'You are a wonderful person, dear Black Wand. Too wonderful for a half born like me. I know you can't love me, but I can't help feeling little nags of mortal jealousy. Tell me, please,' her voice fell into a solemn whisper, 'is she as beautiful as they say?'

'You saw her at High Moon,' I reminded her, stroking her hair gently. The contact helped soothe the deep uneasiness that her words had aroused in my heart.

'I mean, in herself. Her mind, her … love.' She sighed. 'You must be the happiest wizard alive.'

I kissed her hair to hide the pain that I felt so acutely. She tilted her head to gaze up at me in wonder, but I veiled my eyes and she saw only the wizard she found so hard to understand.

'I'm sorry,' she said. 'That was naughty of me. I'm trying to understand who you are, Black Wand. You're fascinating; everybody says so. Hetty openly declares that she is infatuated. All the wiccies adore you.'

'As they should,' I reminded her. 'Is it not the law that the Wands shall epitomise our people's unattainable ideals?'

'Yes … but if you can't – or won't – love them –'

'Ah, but I do! I can't help myself. But the ultimate end is inevitable.'

'So it's really true, then? You can't love a Wychy and live?'

'It's beyond question, Gwen.'

The hurried arrival of Smye put an end to this absorbing conversation. 'Black Wand,' he panted, 'there are mortals in the Weal!'

'Is that *so* unusual, dear Smye?' I asked mildly. 'Do you think they intend harm?'

'I don't think so, Black Wand. They are only small mortals. One is very small and very fat.'

I closed my eyes, the better to see as I could in my home on The Wandle. I smiled with delight as I recognised Stella and Edie wheeling little Johnny up the sunken track in his pushchair.

'*Be at peace, little people!*' I called for all to hear. '*These are good mortals, and my friends.*'

'Your *friends*?' Smye's eyes grew even rounder than usual, and he ran off to have a closer look at them.

'How do you know who they are, Black Wand?' Gwen asked as I continued to watch with my eyes closed. 'How can they be your friends?'

If it had been anyone else – apart from my Wych, of course – I would have discouraged them by saying something wyché and hard to understand. But Gwen was different. I opened my eyes to answer her.

'I knew them in mortality, my dear. And so did Smye; he was their grandfather. Only he's happily forgotten that he came back to the little people when they were infants. He was known as "Mus Mye" in Three Weirs – hence "Smye" here. His widow is … *was* my housekeeper.'

'Yet he still seems concerned about them, and curious?'

'There is more empathy with children among the fae. And little Johnny is so young and still attuned to the little people; he would be able to see Smye – if Smye showed himself.'

Gwen nodded. 'Yes, children often see things that they forget in later years.'

'B-Black Wand!' Smye came running back to us, agog with news. 'Th-the White One! She's in the Weal!'

Gwen clutched at me in guilty fright. I soothed her at once, assured that my Wych would understand our closeness.

'It's the little one – the f-fat one!' Smye stammered. 'White Wand has … she's taken him …!'

But I had already seen it for myself. Little Johnny Mye was sitting on the track where his companions had placed him, and was now gurgling with delight at the Wych who stood before him laughing and talking to him like a fond mother. Stella and Edie had disappeared and I found the chattering pair happily pushing the buggy back towards Three Weirs, oblivious to the fact that it was empty.

'The Wych has wiled them so they forgot their brother!' Smye wailed. 'And when I asked her what she would do with the little fat one, she bade me, "Begone!" So I came to find you, Black Wand.'

I moved Gwen gently aside and rose. She wanted to follow, but I gestured at her to stay. Crisis was in the air. Something unheard of had happened: a human child had been abducted.

*

When I arrived, the Wych was sitting beside Johnny playfully teasing him with her Wand, which he was trying to grab with eager hands. I knew she was aware of me standing on the opposite bank. All around us were many little faces watching fearfully.

The Wych rose and motioned to the child: 'Stand up, little brother.'

The infant levered himself unsteadily on to his feet, towering over his new mistress. She made inviting noises, bidding him to follow her up the track.

I leapt down and strode towards her. 'Wych, what is this?'

Her eyes, bright with wonder, met mine. 'I wyn me a wicca, Brother Wand. One that shall be mine beyond measure!'

'Sister Wand, he is mortal.'

'So? He has a faerie wraith within him – see how he laughs.' She turned back to the toddler. 'Come, smiling one.'

I stared in horror at the baby, nearly three times our size, staggering towards us, with the ethereal elfin figure within it joyously acknowledging the beckoning Wand. In his eagerness to reach it, the child stumbled in a rut and would have crashed down on top of us had we not both staved off the fall with our upheld Wands.

'Isn't he wonderful?' my Wych cooed fondly.

'All babies are wonderful,' I agreed sourly. 'And baby he is, Wych. He has no place alone in the forest.'

'Alone? Foolish Wand! He will live with me forever on The Wandle.'

'Impossible. His mortal frame will die –'

'Not at all. Our people will gather herbs, roots and leaves as he desires.'

'That will kill him,' I said flatly.

'Indeed? I had forgotten. Then you shall advise me.'

Without a doubt, my Wych was utterly obsessed and there was no reasoning with her. Once she had him on The Wandle, no one, least of all me, would be able to release him from the preposterous fate she would weave for him. I threw up my Wand and halted the infant.

'You cannot do this, White Wand.'

Her eyes flashed. 'Would you command me, Wychy?' she challenged, and raised her Wand to beckon little Johnny.

I crossed it immediately with my countering will.

'Beware, brother!' she cried. 'Shall Wychy clash with Wych? Our Wands were fashioned for weaving, not for war. Be warned – you may not wile your Wych's will!'

'Let my Wych be wise and forbear to wile a mortal's will,' I returned intently.

She withdrew her Wand and held it horizontally between her fingers, and I did the same. We faced each other watchfully, like two cats, each waiting for the other to spring.

'Two other mortal children have also been wiled,' I reminded her. 'When they return home, there will be fear and consternation in the village. The children will be punished for their apparent negligence and their elders will come swiftly to the forest to find their babe.'

'Then more's the need for action, Brother Wand. There are a thousand places here he can be hidden – but none shall find him on The Wandle. There my little one shall be safe for all time.'

'The wrong will be irreversible, my Wych,' I argued. 'Can you not conceive the anguish of his mother?'

With a slight movement of her Wand, she waved it aside.

'Mortals beget many such. She can bear another – my Wand shall command it. But I cannot beget. With all my arts I am condemned to be barren. Why should I be begrudged this incomparable delight?'

'And what shall you say to the Lord of the Weirs when he comes seeking his own?' I demanded.

She smiled evasively. 'Your mortality argues falsely, Brother Wand. I know our Weir Lord's lineage and his descendants. This child is not his.'

'You know very well, Wych, that *all* the people of Three Weirs are his concern. He is *their* Wychy and wise administrator. What will he tell them? That the forest will no longer preserve and restore those who are innocently lost here? Is it not our law that such strays must be guided back to the haunts of men?' I lowered my voice. 'This is a *mortal* fascination, Wych; a symptom of the Sickness ... surely you can see that? I beseech you, beloved, act with care. Your people and your Wychy need your love.'

I could see from her expression that it was a hopeless argument, and I could not divert her by force, nor countermand her orders. In our people's eyes, no quarrel could exist between the two of us. Even now, I dared not think of the apprehension they must be feeling. I had to find a way out of the dilemma. Then something I had read in my book of wisdom came back to me.

'Sister Wand, you must know that none may cross over to The Wandle without our united consent,' I reminded her firmly. 'Then know also that I shall not lend my Wand to its invasion by *this* mortal.'

She met my gaze with a look of reproach and disappointment. 'It must be so, then. He shall live in the Weal,' she said resignedly. 'But I know others who are knowledgeable and willing to do my bidding,' she added, brightening. 'They will ensure the babe is nourished. And should that not be enough, I will wandle mortals to bring proper gifts of food and clothing. So in some ways, it will be even better.'

I knew she could do this, and prevent anyone from finding him. I might refuse to participate, but I could not place obstacles in the way of providing Johnny with sustenance. I was back to my last-ditch attempt.

'Better for you, perhaps, Wych. But not for our people. The searchers will begin beating the forest soon and send our people flying in terror to their hiding places. Their freedom will be lost, their intelligence warped and their peace completely withered. And how shall you answer to our Liege Alder for the unlawful wandling of mortals, and the derangement of his people?'

'It is my Weird that I wear,' she replied with finality, and turned again to the teetering babe.

I stood aside to allow his plunging feet to pass unhindered, and could only wonder at how she intended coping with the enormous problem he presented. I guessed that she would liberate his wraith in sleep to talk and play with him, then return him to his body to eat and rest. It was too awful to contemplate.

I made my way back to The Wandle, only half aware that the forest telepathy was thrumming with discord. Wiccas and wiccies were cowering away in holes, nooks and crannies like frightened creatures in a hurricane. I pulled myself together a little when I came across Gwen standing in my path, trying to comfort a trembling wiccy.

'Black Wand! Thank goodness you're here. Whatever has happened? This poor child, Clee, is frightened to death. The whole forest is flying for cover like scared rabbits!'

I caught at my flying Weird and folded it securely about me, calming the waves of anger that surged within me. The storm cleared, and the sun even came out from behind a passing cloud to press a leafy pattern of light and shade on jangled spirits.

'All is well, little people,' I assured them. 'Come, shelter beneath my wings and be at peace.' I opened the Weird again, and placed an arm around each of them.

'Oh, Black Wand! How comforting you are,' the wiccy sighed, nestling close.

'Your Weird has the sureness of a shield,' said Gwen. 'How fortunate you are to have such magical protection from these hellish hurricanes. But you haven't explained what caused it.'

I kissed them both, told them where they would find Pwyll and Baddenham, and continued alone to my secret chamber where I turned to my book of wisdom. But it was dumb. No one had ever imagined the care of human children in the past. On the wandling of mortals there was a great deal, though in that respect my Wych would be more adept than I. She would have no difficulty in heading searchers off in the wrong direction.

I leafed through to the end of the volume with the feeling that I needed some other source of inspiration – and fast. It was nearly six o'clock and the two children were nearing Three Weirs. I was about to close the book when its last entry caught my eye – my predecessor's last communication, and the granting of my second wish:

'... *That, when your humanity can no longer be denied, you may resume your mortality ...*'

Wasn't that exactly what I needed now? As a mortal I would be bound to act with mortal motives and could therefore counteract my Wych without breaking Wychie law. And I would remain mentally immune from her wiling, for I would still have my Wand. The book also listed a third and final wish:

'*Even then, a third choice will be yours: either to drink of oblivion and remain in your restored mortality, or surrender that estate forever and return to the little kingdom.*'

Surely that would be easy, I thought. I'd need no more than a brief hour to get the little child out of his fix, and then I'd come back to the forest. I certainly had no intention of remaining mortal for the sake of little Johnny Mye. All I had to do now was to work out how to take human form again. After several minutes of thought, I suddenly sent my Wand spinning into the air with triumph as I remembered: 'The Wealspring!' I blessed the memory of Leila for telling me too late that its waters held the magic power of granting wishes, for had I known that at the time I might have used them all too wrongly.

But first the Woe, which I would need if I was to return safely. Despite its miniscule size, it was simple enough to find when I reached the marshes. There was no mistaking the tiny, bright green feathery fronds that so closely resembled their undoubted progenitor. I pressed the tiny phial I had brought into the smelly mud to gain a fibre of the root. Even as I did so, the mud sucked at my feet.

'No, no, respected Dragga,' I said, echoing my predecessor and pulling myself free. 'I have my Wand – you do not bind me yet!'

A soundless voice seemed to answer from the depths of the Weird:

'*Your time will come, Wychy! Dragga binds all – mortal and immortal. My power lies yet on The Wandle, for my breath seared all three of you. Three is the number of my lawful victims, and only one has yet surrendered. Before Mona's face is full again, that number must be whole. It is the law, Wychy. Fail me not.*'

I repelled the sound with a derisive gesture of my Wand. The ancient monster would have his second victim this very night, for I had enough of the root to kill me a hundred times over. But what of my Wych? The moon would be full again in only three days' time.

In the little grotto of the Wealspring, I removed my crown, Weird and clothes, for I was taking no chances that they might not expand to fit my human form. The Wand, of course, I could not lay aside, and nor the phial of Woe.

I knelt, filled the golden cup and drank, saying, 'O eternal spring, I wish to be restored to my human frame.'

At once, a blanket of leaden weight seemed to drop on my shoulders. I lurched to my feet in a swirling, blinding red mist that thickened and gelled around me. I staggered painfully away, before losing consciousness and collapsing in the undergrowth.

CHAPTER 23

'UNCOO WUG!'

I was lying face down in crushed vegetation, my hands clenched like a drowning man and a great weight pressing me into the ground. But my nose was filled with such a mixture of earthy smells and scents that I felt intoxicated. I was human! I was solid and so love-hungry for the earth that I couldn't get enough of it … until growing soreness and discomfort informed me that I was also cold and my naked body was scratched and bloodied all over by brambles.

I lifted myself carefully onto my knees, a slow-moving, heavy, ungainly giant once more, in a world that had none of the vibrant sounds and colours I had become used to. It was alive however with breeze and movement, and I wondered how it was possible that I had never missed the animal sense of taste and smell that made me feel so hungry – starving would not have been too strong a word for it. But first I had to find Johnny.

When I climbed clumsily to my feet and looked around, though, I had a shock. The brambles and bracken were shoulder high and I couldn't recognise where I was. As a mortal, I had never trodden this part of the Weal. I found it unbelievable that I should have lost my bearings so easily, and a wave of panic crashed over me when I realised that I could wander for hours and be none the wiser. Had I really taken this huge step of becoming human again only to be immediately defeated? I forced myself to think. I knew I had to avoid going west – that way lay Dragga's Weird – so I turned my back on the setting sun and set off, shivering with cold. I stubbed my toes painfully on fallen branches, stumbled over rocky outcrops, and cursed when stray brambles whipped around my feet and tore at my legs.

Eventually the ground started rising, and my spirits rose too. I toiled on, knowing that I was at least heading in the right direction. Then, quite without warning, I found myself standing on the brink of the sunken trackway. I jumped down to the rutted path, nearly twisting an ankle as I did so. It was somewhere along here that I had last seen Johnny and my Wych, but I had no idea how far she might have lured him before his baby strength gave out.

I ran onwards until I reached the trail striking off at a right angle up to Wandleside. My feet rustled in the decayed leaves, and again fear struck at me: suppose she had covered the exhausted infant's body with them? I could search until dark and not find him. I needed to think … think … think … and then I remembered my Wand! I relaxed my grip on the three-inch device clenched in my right hand and concentrated hard: *point to where the child lies and make him cry.*

To my relief, I felt it move to the right, though sluggishly because of my dense form. I followed the direction quickly and clambered out of the shallow track. Johnny was whimpering fretfully from a spot not many yards distant. I picked him up and cradled him in my arms.

'Now then, Johnny boy, what's all this? Don't you remember your Uncle Gus?'

His small balled up fists left his eyes and recognition beamed through the tears. 'Uncoo Wug!' he sobbed. Then his tired little arms crept round my neck and he fell asleep. The trusting embrace awoke a flood of emotion that brought a lump to my throat and tears to my eyes. I had never held a little child in my arms before, and the benevolent compassion of a Wychy paled in comparison to the rich, deep, heart-tugging feeling that was almost passionate in its exhilaration. This was real, solid and worth every bit of my ordeal.

'So, Brother Wand, you would rend my Weird!

I turned with glad eagerness in the direction from which the tiny voice had come, but could not distinguish her form.

'Beloved Wych, I can't see you,' I whispered. 'Where are you?'

'Where no mortal eye will ever see a Wand,' she replied in bitter reproach. 'Here in the heart of the Weal, in the kingdom of my people.'

'I could see no other way, my beloved,' I begged. 'The child is mortal. His family must have him back or their searching will overwhelm our people. I have not deserted you, my Wych. I shall be back by moonrise –'

'Be not so certain, Wand,' she warned. 'You are mortal now – the glamour of it is already in your eyes. Unwholesome shadows fall between us. There is Woe in the Weal where none was before. The dark stain of your loving is in me. How else should I have suffered this terrible delusion of the child and brought such misery on us both? Go … go now! Return the little one to his rightful weird.' She sounded drained, her voice resigned.

'That, and no more,' I promised fervently, and headed away quickly down the deeply worn track.

*

A medley of distant voices rising from Wisher's Lane brought me to a halt. There would be women with the search party, and I was naked. I had to hide. Calls floated up from below: 'John-ee! John-ee!'

I placed the sleeping infant gently beside the track as if he had curled up there for rest, then scrambled up the eight-foot bank and lay beside a massive overhanging beech. I would keep watch and, on discovery of the child, would swallow my Woe and, in elfin form, return to the Wealspring for my clothes.

But it was you, Ann, who came around the corner, holding Stella Mye's hand as she lead the way. Sir Edward We'ard followed alongside Ted Hoathly and Police Constable Beale. Behind them I could see Johnny's parents and Mrs Mye senior.

Heavens above, I thought, what if one of them scaled the bank and began searching the slope behind me? There was nowhere to hide – I couldn't even make a run for it.

'… For the hundredth time,' Sir Edward was saying, 'I tell you no harm will have come to the child. We are in the Wale. It is quite impossible for anyone to come to harm here.' He stopped suddenly and pointed. 'Ann, your eyes are younger than mine … what's that bundle at the foot of the tree there?'

'It's him! It's Johnny!' screamed his mother, running towards you as you picked the little boy up.

'Pass up a blanket, somebody!' called Sir Edward. 'And pass word back that Johnny's been found!'

I had just relaxed back with a sigh of thankfulness when I heard Johnny wake and start calling for 'Uncoo Wug' … and you recognised who he meant, Ann. I had not expected that. Nor had I expected the irresistible desire that had come over me to hear your voice again. You were looking around and nearly saw me. I had to duck away quickly.

I could just spy Ted Hoathly shaking a finger at the constable. 'What I says is, if we were to make a proper search we'd find him safe and sound, same as young Johnny here.'

'And if you think I'm going to do anything like that, Ted Hoathly, then you're crazy,' came the constable's reply. 'If Mr Gus is alive and wants to live here alone, that's his business – so long as he doesn't go scaring people, of course.'

'I reckon he's out of his mind!' panted old Joe Harmer, arriving late and flourishing his knobbly walking stick. 'It's like I've always said: he's been wandled! Mark my words. You can laugh at me, Charley Beale, but the old Witchett bain't dead. He be alive much as you and me. He's mazed Mr Gus, that's how it is, and no amount of looking will bring him back.'

'What you mean, Joe,' said Constable Beale severely, 'is that he's suffering from amnesia –'

I heard Joe snort derisively. 'He bain't suffering nothing, Charley. He's been wandled – and don't you dare tell me you don't know what I mean by that.'

'You can call it what you like,' said the policeman, 'but the force knows it as amnesia. And if you don't stop waving that stick in front of my nose, I'll book you for common assault ...'

Their voices faded as they followed the rest of the search party back down the path. I half rose, only to duck back down again when I saw you were still there with Sir Edward.

'... it's a lovely evening, Ann,' Sir Edward was saying. 'Shall we walk on, or ... bless my soul! Surely this is the very spot where we held our last tête-à-tête?'

'I wondered when you were going to recognise it,' you said, smiling. 'And look, someone's left a blanket behind. It'll make a more comfortable seat, won't it?'

Sir Edward took the blanket from you and laid it over the bench-like roots. I could see you better when you were seated, and I couldn't take my eyes off your lovely face.

'How do you think the children came to desert little Johnny up here?' you asked. 'How on earth could they have pushed the buggy all the way back to the village without realising it was empty? And what made them bring him up *here*? Stella once told me they were never allowed further than Wisher's Mead.'

'You tell *me*, my dear. I really can't explain it.'

'Do you think they could have been "wandled" as they call it round here?'

'For what purpose, Ann? To bring the whole village charging into the Wale to look for them? It doesn't make sense. It seems a pointless prank for such wise guardians to play.'

'Sir Edward, do you remember I told you about my dream of how sad the White One was? I felt that it was somehow my fault, as if I had come between them, and you said it would be a calamity if that happened. I can't help feeling that this is all tied up with that. I'm going to concentrate on dreaming about the White One tonight; I want to find her again.'

'Well, if you do succeed in finding her – or young Autrey for that matter – perhaps you could remind him that I will have to inform his relatives eventually. *And* there's the question of his estate, whatever that might be.'

You laughed; a lovely, gentle sound. You told Sir Edward that from what you had seen of me in your dream at full moon, you didn't think I was dead. And nor would *I* think I was dead. 'I don't know how I know this, Sir Edward,' you said, 'but I know August is coming back. You said if I followed my heart it would bring us together ... so I *know* he's coming back because I know it in my heart.'

My own heart skipped a beat when you said that. Watching you from my hiding place, I no longer wanted to return to the little kingdom. I was no longer an elemental. I was a human being, young and virile, who had just fallen passionately in love with you.

Forgive me that I needed to wandle you both into forgetting the blanket – I needed it desperately. It's here in the house and will be returned to its owner. When I pulled its merciful warmth around me, I was minded to catch up with you both then and there. But I remembered that I was not only smeared with mud and bloodied with scratches, but I would have to account for my movements – and some questions were bound to be embarrassing and difficult to answer.

I waited until dark before making for the village. I skirted the outlying buildings and reached the cottage via footpaths and back gardens, vaulting the garden wall. As ever, the key was above the lintel and I let myself in. It felt strange to be back and confined after the freedom of the forest, but here I would find food and clothing – and a bath, which I needed even more.

I turned on both taps. The 'hot' water was of course cold, but the bath filled quickly. I had to find somewhere safe to put the invisible phial that I still held in my left hand, and chose my cufflink box. Why putting it somewhere safe should matter, I didn't know – I wasn't going back, was I? To throw it away, though, would mean losing the Wand, which I still held tightly. How could I be content to lose it and forget everything? I suddenly felt angry. Why should I have had this laid upon me? *Forget!* The word hammered at me so much that it helped over-come the excruciating effect of the cold water on my body's soreness. How could I forget everything that I so poignantly remembered?

After my bath, sheer hunger sent me back to the kitchen where I found a small store of tinned food. Tins of baked beans and sausages promised heaven. I ate the first one cold and heated the second, and never did I enjoy a meal more than that. Over a cup of hot tea sweetened with condensed milk, I thought about what faced me.

If I did not drink the Woe soon then the next full moon in three days' time would bring a full mental lobotomy. But I had fallen in love with you and I wanted to meet you and tell you how much I loved you. If I looked beyond that, it was logical to suppose – if you would have me – that I would then settle down to, hopefully, a happy married life, children and earning a living. And all as if nothing had happened. It seemed so absurdly matter-of-fact and presumptuous. I could keep my cherished memories and lose you. Or lose my memories and be an empty shell. Would that be fair on you?

I went into my study and stood staring around, and a possible answer came in a flash. I could cheat the Woe if I wrote everything down, just as it had happened; the good, the bad, and the impossible. Then I could give it to you in the form of a letter-cum-manuscript and wait for your answer.

And that is what I have now done. I've held nothing back. And if, when we meet, I'm a witless moron who can't remember a word of what I have written, then please, dearest Ann, help me to remember and assure me that it was all true.

Hael and wyn, beloved. I love you so much, now and forever.

PART III

WYCH

CHAPTER 24

THE SCATHE

It was well past midnight before Ann finished reading the manuscript and gave way to tears.

'Oh, August, how *could* you?' she cried in anguish, beating her fists on her bed in frustration. 'You've said it – you *are* a witless moron! Don't you see what you're doing? You're throwing away the very thing you've passed on to me. How can I say I love you, knowing that it's robbed you of all you have in the forest? It isn't fair! *You* won't know, but *I* will. Oh, I wish you'd go away, you witless wizard. Go away – anywhere!' She sobbed, heartbroken. 'Anywhere on earth … where there'll … never be … the slightest chance … of us ever meeting!' She buried her face in her pillow and cried herself to sleep.

*

She woke early. The morning felt oppressive. Unable to get back to sleep, she went down to the kitchen. A door slammed shut. She glanced out of the window towards the cottage next door, and saw Mrs Mye hurrying down the path to turn into her aunt's. She looked distressed, and Ann raced to intercept her at the kitchen door.

'Mrs Mye, what *is* the matter?'

'Oh, Miss Ann! It's Mr Gus! He's … he's dead!'

Ann shook her head, half laughing in disbelief. 'That's impossible, Mrs Mye. You're mistaken. He *can't* be dead.'

"'Tis true, I say, Miss Ann … I touched him. He's quite cold.'

A chill of fear touched Ann's heart. It *had* to be a mistake. She went next door with the housekeeper to see for herself.

It was an odd sensation, looking down on the young man in the armchair. He sat leaning comfortably against the sloping back, head to one side on his shoulder, jaw slack, and his eyes half open. There was no doubt that he was dead; his body was already stiff with rigor mortis.

She managed to recover her composure and asked quietly, 'Who is his GP?'

'Dr Winter, Miss – in the village.'

'Find his number for me, will you? I'll call him.'

Left alone for a moment, Ann bent and gently kissed the cold, sweat-beaded forehead. An unexpected bitter-sweet taste on her lips surprised her, but thinking no more about it, and with tears welling in her eyes, she breathed, 'I'm *so* glad you went back.' Then she stood upright, blinking the tears away as Mrs Mye returned with the doctor's number on a piece of paper.

She made the call as calmly as she could, though her mind was whirling with questions. Had he drunk the Woe? Had something else killed him? Perhaps it was the effect of sheer fatigue and starvation on an already weakened body? The bulky envelope on her bedside table also worried her. The author had died – unexpectedly and in mysterious circumstances. No doctor would sign a death certificate in that situation. There would have to be a post mortem and an inquest. The court would want to know the deceased's last activities; his state of mind, and what he had been doing immediately prior to his death. The thought of them examining the manuscript made her flesh crawl. No one else must be allowed to see it … except, perhaps, Sir Edward We'ard.

She suggested that they should both return to her aunt's house to wait for the doctor, then ran lightly upstairs to her room while Mrs Mye made a cup of tea. There was still no sound from her aunt's room, and she did not intend to disturb her yet. She grabbed the envelope and quickly dropped it into the depths of her suitcase. Even in dying, she reflected, the well-intentioned August still carried on his blunders.

When Mrs Mye brought in a cup of tea, she found Ann kneeling on the floor by her bed, tears running down her cheeks.

'Oh, Miss, I'm so sorry. Here, take my hanky. It's quite clean.'

But then Mrs Mye began to cry herself, and Ann passed the hanky back and fetched a clean one from her drawer.

'We're both being silly,' she told the housekeeper firmly, between sniffs. 'After all, these things happen every day. And there really isn't any reason for *me* to be upset – why, I never even met Mr Autrey. You'd better get back next door; the doctor will be here in a minute.'

'But you'll come with me, Miss, won't you?' said Mrs Mye in alarm. 'I think you should be there too, seeing as how he sent you that last book of his. You might be able to help the doctor discover what happened to him.'

'I'll stay with you 'til he comes, Mrs Mye, of course I will, if that will help you. But I'm afraid Mr Autrey's document was just a rather long fairy tale … and not an entirely new one at that. It included some of the children's manuscripts you sent me to read. He wanted to ask my opinion of them. I expect he was too shy to approach me directly.'

The housekeeper looked relieved. 'I don't know what I thought he might have sent you – his life story or something. But I know you'd have helped him if you could.'

'I'm only sorry that I shan't be able to discuss it with him now, Mrs Mye.' She breathed in sharply, controlling her tears, and let her breath out slowly as her shoulders sagged. 'Let me get dressed and I'll be with you in five minutes.'

*

Ann took a notebook with her to jot down anything the doctor might say that her aunt would need to know about. By the time the formalities were over and her aunt had woken up and been made aware of the situation, she realised how tired she felt. She needed space and time to think, but her stomach was a tight knot of exhaustion, while her brain seemed to have been replaced with cotton wool. For a fraction of a second her eyes closed in mental torpor.

'Wisher's Barn!'

She jolted alert at the clear yet voiceless summons that sounded inside her head. Wisher's Barn, the place that grew Wych's Bane – the counterpart to Wizard's Woe. What did it mean? Was it really a call, or just her imagination? And if it was a call, how was she supposed to answer?

'I slept so badly last night, Auntie,' she said abruptly. 'I feel washed out. Would you mind if I went back to bed for a while? A good rest should pull me round. The atmosphere feels so heavy today – I'm sure there's a storm brewing. And what with everything this morning ...'

'That's all right, dear, you go on up ... and thank you for everything you've done this morning. You've been wonderful. I really don't know how I would have managed on my own.'

*

After August had despatched the package to Ann the previous day, he had fallen asleep in his chair, dead to the world through sheer fatigue. At around ten o'clock that evening, he had awoken to find himself unable to move. He couldn't open his eyes or cry out. But he could hear grief-stricken voices calling to him:

> Black Wand! Black Wand!
> Where are you, Wizard Wand?
> Gone is our ecstasy
> Anguish is on us

> Woe's in our hearts, Wand!
> Dread's in the depths of us
> Sped is our happiness
> Joy is gone from us

> Come with your wealing, Wand!
> Dragga bewrays us
> Come with your healing, Wand
> Weal us, O Wand

Then a confusion of more prosaic appeals mixed with the laments:

'Where is Black Wand? Why doesn't he come?' That was Baddy.

'Can't say, old man,' answered Loy. 'Expect he's busy somewhere.'

> Save us from Sickness, O Wychy!
> Our Wands have let us stray
> Your beloved White One is stricken
> Her Wand has cast her away!

'This place is getting me down,' said Edmund's voice. 'Why the devil couldn't he have left us in peace at *Mens Sana*? We were happy there, weren't we, Barney?'

'Were we? Suppose we were. All I know is I've got toothache in my guts and I want a doctor –'

> The Weal is flowing with sadness
> Our hearts are in disarray
> Our Wych hath suffered the Sickness
> Her Wand has cast her away

'Gwen, I'm scared stiff. I want to throw up, but I can't.'

'I know, Hetty, darling, but you must try not to give way to it. Try and think of something else.'

'I can't! Is it just me, or is everyone making this banshee noise? You know, Gwen, Black Wand promised to kiss me before he went away.'

'Then you hold on to that, Hetty. He'll be back soon.'

> We are lone, we are lost
> Our weirds are in dread
> Our ways are all wiled
> For the Wands may not wed!

Smye's voice now: 'Black Wand! Dear, kind, beloved Black Wand. The fault is all mine, I know, because I shouldn't have told. You are angry with me because I pried your high secrets. I told the forest you had quarrelled with the Wych over the little fat one. But please soften your heart towards me, Black Wand … I meant no mischief. If it would assuage your wrath, I would willingly ask for the Bane, but the White One is gone from us too.'

'There's a thick mist of misery all over the Weal, Loy,' came Fizzy's voice. 'Our friends are sickening by the dozen. They lie in holes and clefts shivering in mortal terror. What is to become of us? How are we to live without the Wands?'

'I don't know, Fizzy … I don't understand what's

happening. I've just been to Wandleside and called Black Wand. But the island's dead and the Weirds are terrible. There's a horrible green fog rolling down on them …'

With a huge effort of will, August managed to struggle properly awake and groped his way upstairs. He swallowed the contents of the tiny phial and returned to his study.

Two hours later, freed from his mortal body, he clung to Ann's windowsill, listening in bewilderment to her hysterical weeping. He heard her wish that he should vanish out of her life altogether.

'Done!' he cried, leaping to the ground and racing into the forest – a fierce, determined little elf who vowed he would never, ever return.

*

The moon was on the point of setting when he came away from the Wealspring, properly attired once more. To his horror, instead of finding the fae safely hidden away for the time between moonset and sunrise, he came upon them sprawled heedlessly in the open without shelter or covering. He swept as many as he found into his arms and bundled them into the nearest hiding places; below tangled roots, between clefts and under leaves – anywhere that would preserve them from the seeking fingers of the hungry Dragga that were already creeping across the Weal.

When he arrived at *Woe Begone!* he found a dozing fay leaning against the door. She started awake as he bent down to pick her up.

'Black Wand!' she whimpered like a tired child. 'Gwen said you'd be back because you never kissed me.'

He made good the promise before she sank into oblivion, then opened the door and placed her gently inside. Half a dozen more were quickly gathered and placed in safety with her before he became aware that another was awake and active in the Weal. He sped off in the direction of Great Oak.

A resplendent figure in gold and silver was performing the same work of mercy. It turned and smiled on him as he entered the clearing.

August felt shamed. 'My Liege,' he said humbly.

'Hael and wyn, Wychy! Our people are sadly careless. I have covered many. Another still lies at the foot of yonder monster.'

August looked and recognised Smye kneeling at the feet of the floral Dragon Dreadful, still drowsily murmuring his petition.

'Your Majesty will forgive me ...?' August begged. He placed his arm around the drooping wicca and laid him tenderly on the grass. Then, removing his Weird, he laid it carefully over the unconscious fay, completely covering him.

The King smiled his approval before his face saddened again. 'The Woe lies upon our Weal, Wychy. Your absence has filled all with alarm. They believe there will be none to wed the Wands this High Moon.'

August bowed his head at the implied rebuke. 'My Weird is not of my weaving, my Liege,' he answered. 'He who went before me so wiled my ways that I feel I have been made the sorry subject of some joke – one that I have failed to understand.'

'I have no art to read the mystery of any Wand but my own, Black One. In mine resides the tradition and destiny of our race; in yours the welfare and protection of its individuals. But without the Black and White to draw their virtue from my gold, they remain unblessed. Without their wedding the ancient power will not be renewed.'

'She who is gone wove a new Weird, my Liege. Its wearer must exist somewhere among us.'

'Weird and Wand lie waiting at the foot of Great Oak,' said the King solemnly.

August turned and stared. Draped over the seat he had used so many times lay the new Weird, dazzling white and brilliant with tiny flashing gems. And on it rested the White One's Wand and crown.

'It is my intention that before we gather on The Wandle tonight, a trial shall be made here,' said Alder. 'I shall summon our wiccies to this place before Sunné reaches his zenith, and bid each one to test the Wand. Mona grant there will be one who may succeed. There is no more that I can do now, Wychy. By good fortune, this interregnum is a short one. I will summon our Vintner at Sunné's rise to administer to all who have not succumbed to Dragga's Scathe. Hael and wyn, Black One!'

'Hael and wyn, my Liege!'

The King departed, and soon the sun rose and the forest returned to life.

*

Tears falling on his cheek woke Barnsley, and warm lips pressed trembling on his own. He was happily holding on to this unexpected surprise when he found himself pushed roughly away.

'Oh, it's you!' Hetty's voice cried indignantly. 'You beast! I thought you were Black Wand.'

'I wish I was,' he answered enviously. 'That fellow seems to have all the luck. Sorry to disappoint you, ducks – you must have been dreaming.'

'I wasn't!'

'Must have been,' said Barnsley. 'He's not here. There's only Fizzy, Jean, Loy, Gwen, Baddy and Pwyll, and me and you.'

'What's up, Het?' asked Loy.

'Black Wand's back.'

'Hooray! Where is he?'

'I don't know … but he was here. He kissed me.'

'You're wrong there, Hetty. You were kissing *me*!' said Barnsley.

'When you've all sorted yourselves out and decided who was kissing who,' said Gwen suddenly, 'will someone please tell me how it is that we're all inside *Woe Begone!*? I never went to sleep in here – I wouldn't know how to get in.'

'I remember!' Hetty cried triumphantly. 'I was half asleep outside the door and Black Wand picked me up and brought me in … and he kissed me!'

'Black Wand walks the Weal!'

The cry sped through the forest with the speed of light. Excited fae bounded from cover into the open with shouts of joy, embraced their friends, and everyone trooped off to Great Oak. Since the presence of their Wychies is known by their Weirds, there was bewilderment to see the Black One's mantle lying on the ground.

'Perhaps he's having a kip under it,' said Baddenham.

The mantle moved, and a sad looking Smye peered out from under it.

'Well, I'm a monkey's uncle –' began Loy.

'What on earth do you think you're doing under there, Smye?' interrupted Gwen.

'Hael and wyn,' Smye greeted them solemnly. 'What's the matter with you all?'

'What's the matter with *you*, you mean,' said Hetty tartly. 'What are you doing going to sleep under Black Wand's Weird?'

Smye sat up, looked down at the rippling mantle, and covered his bulging eyes from the awesome sight. 'Mona preserve me!' he howled. 'How shall I survive his blazing anger when he returns and finds me like this?'

'He *has* returned, Smye,' said Gwen. 'It seems he found you out in the open, like he did the rest of us.'

'I was,' Smye agreed. 'I was calling to him for forgiveness because of the terrible wrong I did him. I was confessing the whole thing to Dreadful. And then –'

'… And then Black Wand came and covered you up to save you from Dragga,' Gwen finished patiently.

'B-but, why me?' spluttered the fay.

'Because he's forgiven you!' Fizzy laughed. 'Oh, Smye, can't you see? He's honoured you above all of us.'

Wonder, joy and relief spread across Smye's face. 'Black Wand has forgiven me! O, wonderful Wychy. I swear I shall never tell another tale that isn't strictly true. In fact, I'll never tell tales about anyone ever again. I'll –'

'Come on, Smye,' Loy interrupted. 'What are you going to do about the Weird? You can't go on wearing it you know.'

'Oh dear, oh dear! What *can* I do? It's all over me. I daren't pick it up. I daren't even move from under it.'

Everyone looked at Gwen, since she had always seemed closest to Black Wand. She nodded, removed the resplendent garment from the cowering elf, folded it carefully, kissed it reverently, and faced the crowd with a serene smile. They parted before her and she bore it off to *Woe Begone!*

*

Knowing all that was going on in the Weal, August was thankful for Gwen's intervention. He was busy with the stricken fae that he had been unable to rescue. He kept finding them, lying in the open where they had slept, or wandering around in deep melancholy, hardly conscious of where they were. The moping figures of Simmons and Edmund, who had hardly looked up at his cheerful greeting, were not too serious a concern. The remains of their mortality would protect them, and they should respond well to the Vintner's ministration. While some sufferers brightened when they saw him, others needed to be reasoned with and cosseted, and here and there were those who pleaded piteously for the Bane that he could not give. It wrenched his heart that he could only exhort them to hold on and wait for their new Wych.

He made for The Wandle, hoping to find some help in his book of wisdom, and at the foot of Windaway came upon the most heart-rending of all the victims of the Scathe.

His urgent call: 'Gwen! Gwen! Bring me my Weird! Come quickly! I wait below Windaway,' reached Gwen as she neared *Woe Begone!*

She found him kneeling beside the narrows, supporting an unconscious fay.

'It is the White One,' he whispered. 'And I am powerless to save her.'

CHAPTER 25

LADY OF THE WEIRD

Moving closer, Gwen saw that the Wych had become almost unrecognisable – a tenuous, emaciated form covered by an evil green aura.

'Wh-what's happened to her?' she stammered.

'It's the Wanion,' August said. 'The fatal wasting of the wraith. And I have no knowledge of how to give her the Bane.'

'I don't understand,' said Gwen, fastening his Weird about his shoulders. 'I thought the Bane destroyed us.'

'The Bane is given in the final stages of the Sickness to *preserve* our departing wraiths from complete dissolution.'

'You mean she really *is* dying and will never come back to the little kingdom?'

'It is inevitable unless I can find the remedy, Gwen,' said August miserably. 'Now I must go away for a little while, but you must not see the way of my going.'

He placed the tip of his Wand on her shoulder and she sank to the ground, unconscious.

Very tenderly, he carried the Wych to her home on The Wandle, trusting that she would have a store of the Bane somewhere within it. But despite his desperate searching, he could find nothing that looked anything like the plant. So where else might it be?

He remembered the Wych's secret conversations with the dreamer. It had been too painful to think about Ann since listening to her rejection of him. But now he realised that the Wych could have been instructing her with the secret of the Bane, knowing that her end was near. He could only hope that Ann could be persuaded to come – for the sake of the Wych, if not for himself.

Still carrying her, he quickly returned to Gwen and woke her. 'Bear my Weird once more into the Weal, dear sister. Go heedlessly and openly by many ways, for none must know my true direction.'

Gwen rose, folding the Weird over her arm, and noticed with horror that the lovely Wych she had known was now only half her former size. The writhing coils of phosphorescence seemed to be consuming the silent fay.

'Go now!' August ordered firmly. His voice dispelled the hypnotic effect that the Wanion had begun to have on her, and Gwen fled.

August took the opposite direction. Common sense told him that if Wisher's Barn was a corruption of Wych's Bane, then that was where he must take the dying Wych. Carefully, he laid the tiny form by the side of the stunted spruces. Then he stood in silence and visualised Ann; not as he had last seen her but as the dreamer he had met at High Moon. Concentrating on that memory and their recognition of each other, he sent the two words she had to hear to know where she was needed:

'Wisher's Barn!'

It was painful to have to leave his Wych where he laid her, but he was trespassing beyond his domain. He might never know if Ann came in time to save her – or if she would even come at all after what he had heard her say.

*

Gwen was blazing a maze-like trail of his whereabouts that had the whole Weal perplexed. Possession of the

Weird had given her the ability to know where her fellows were, and since she had to avoid meeting anyone who would expose the Wychy's absence, she had to run away from any she would encounter. Since Wychies do not normally play hide-and-seek with their charges, the whole thing was turning into a wonderful new game of Hunt-the-Wychy, to which everyone was attracted.

'He's north of Woe Begone!'

'He's turning south –'

'… Making for the Wynn –'

'… Circling east – back to Wandleside!'

'He's outside Honeyball's hideout!'

When August told her that he was beyond the point where anyone was likely to find him, she stopped trying to hide and walked into a glade where Rozyn was distributing his pick-me-ups.

He greeted her with a cheerful 'Hael and wyn, Lady of the Weird!' and leapt from his dray to embrace her.

The sight of his merry face affected her so strangely that she broke down and wept with relief in his arms.

Barnsley gaped. 'Well, strangle me with sock-suspenders …!'

'Stew yourself with dewberry punch, you wit-loose sot!' said Rozyn gruffly. He turned to Simmonds. 'Draw me a goblet from that silver-bound barrel at your side, friend Simmo. There's little that a noggin of Rozyn's Rapture won't cure.' He turned to Gwen and began kissing away her tears. 'But should the Rapture fail, dear lady, you shall have a cup of the royal ambrosia!'

*

August waited until the Royal Herald had arrived before making his return, so he went unnoticed by everyone except Gwen who was ensconced up on the dray overlooking the crowd. Kye announced Alder's decree with a fanfare:

'Hear the words of Alder the King, O little people! "O my people ancient from of eld, heed this edict that none may disregard! Let every wiccy come at once to Great Oak at the meeting of all ways, and there test the Wand that lies at its foot. Hear and obey, beloved people! Hael and wyn!"'

Everyone immediately looked at Gwen. She was the Lady of the Weird, who for some reason had been deputising for Black Wand. Surely the White One's Wand needed only her hand to be poised above it for all their woes to be at an end? When they saw the direction of her gaze, they turned and ran with shouts of excited joy to welcome back their Wychy, and for a moment, their exuberance and spontaneity eased his concern for the ailing Wych.

Rozyn helped Gwen down from the dray and escorted her to Black Wand. She showed no sign of embarrassment but sank in a graceful curtsey before the Wand, who bowed just as gracefully in response. Then she fastened the Weird around his shoulders once more.

'And so to Great Oak, fair ones!' called Rozyn, mounting his dray and urging everyone forward.

*

They found Alder standing to one side of the trysting tree, with the Chamberlain, the Herald and Black Wand, whom no one was surprised to see had somehow arrived before them. The Herald sounded his fanfare and the Chamberlain stepped out and invited the wiccies to come forward one by one.

Pwyll and Baddenham clutched each other with almost uncontrollable anxiety as their favourite fay drew nearer and nearer to the brilliant Weird, diadem and Wand.

When Gwen's turn came, every breath was suspended. A moment's hesitation, then her hand went out, palm down.

Did the Wand start to rise? No one ever knew. A fireball struck the huge oak, followed instantly by an air-splitting crack. The great tree rent in two and burst into flames, and Gwen was hurled away to lie motionless on the ground.

*

The flash of lightning and instantaneous crash of thunder brought Ann wide awake, sitting bolt upright and clutching fearfully at her bed coverings. The whole house trembled with the violence of the crash, and then a sudden solid downpour of rain hammered on the roof and against the windows.

Footsteps hurried up the stairs and her aunt opened the door.

'Are you all right, Ann, dear? You must have been fast asleep. It's only a passing storm. Mrs Mye has just come back; I'll get her to bring you up a pot of tea.'

Left to herself once more, Ann buried her head in her hands. She felt sick, dizzy and distinctly feverish.

She had fallen asleep almost immediately when she had returned to bed. If it had been August summoning her, she assured herself, he would enable her to reach Wisher's Barn. And sure enough, she had found herself by the railings, clothed in the same dream robe that she had worn before. Above her, a heavy pall of clouds swept across the forest, promising a storm at any moment. She ducked through the rails to shelter beneath the spruce trees, and stopped. At her feet, a strange little patch of green phosphorescence was writhing like a tight mass of green worms. Terror rooted her to the spot, but she found it impossible to look away. She felt as if she had seen something like it before somewhere, yet she knew that she hadn't. Then she remembered August's description of the Wreak, and realised that she could be looking at a manifestation of the same thing. But why, of all places, should she find it here and at this hour?

Curiosity helped her overcome her repugnance, and she looked more closely. Then she started back in horror as she noticed the pathetic outlines of a tiny fay; a withered miniature of one of the joyous beings she had laughed and danced with on The Wandle.

Immediately, the memory of a sweet, clear voice came to her:

'The trees you know as Wisher's Barn are the guardians of the secret growth we call the Wych's Bane. This tiny plant thrives beneath their bark, stunting their growth. Break off a small segment of the bark and you will find the tiny berries. Just one of these eaten by any of our people will dissolve – but not destroy – the wraith …'

Ann ran to the nearest tree and tore at its bark. A small piece came away with difficulty, and within it lay the promised cluster of berries, like tiny purple grapes. She plucked off a whole bunch and returned to the tormented fay. With no fear now of the writhing ferment, she put her hand beneath the shrivelled head, raised it, and squeezed every berry she could between the half-opened lips, feeling that nothing less would do. To her joy, the mouth closed about them. The sickening green stuff heaved violently as if it was alive and been dealt a mortal blow. It gathered itself, reared up, and lashed out at her. But Ann instinctively dodged it, then watched as, coil by coil, the mist wreathed away like smoke and disappeared into nothingness, leaving the ghostly outline of a dissolving elemental.

Two faint but still starry eyes opened and weak little arms rose towards her. Ann, at last recognising the Wych with her lips curved in a phantom smile, knelt and kissed her, weeping with relief that she had been just in time, and in sorrow at the once beautiful Wych's doom.

Then there had been a brilliant flash of light behind her, and the sharp, ear-splitting crack of thunder that had woken her.

Mrs Mye arrived with a tray of tea and placed it on the small cupboard beside the bed. She looked at Ann with concern.

'You look really poorly, Miss Ann,' she said. 'Are you all right?'

Ann changed the subject. 'Have they finished next door?' she asked, as her mind searched frantically for some reason to account for her flu-like symptoms.

The housekeeper nodded. 'Dr Winter says there'll be an inquest. He's sent for an ambulance to take him away.'

'What about his relatives?' she asked, trying to stop her teeth from chattering. 'Have they been told?'

'No one knows anything about them, Miss. But the doctor says he'll telephone Mr Gus's solicitors. They'll know who to send for.'

Ann hardly heard her. She was wondering if she could have been exposed to the cause of August's death – Wizard's Woe. But how?

Never mind *how*, she suddenly thought in panic. It could be more a case of *how long* did she have left to live! 'I must write to Sir Edward,' she said aloud, more to herself than Mrs Mye. She asked the housekeeper to pass her the leather-bound writing case, then began writing quickly:

> Dear Sir Edward,
>   This will only come to you in the event of my death. August wrote the enclosed to me before he died, and I know it will be safe in

your hands, for you are its proper and natural guardian.

As far as my aunt and anyone else here is aware, this manuscript is simply the latest – and now the last – of the many stories he wanted me to read and discuss with him. Because that was not to be, I hope it will appear natural that I should request it to be forwarded to you for your opinion if I am not in a position to do so myself.

In the manuscript you will find that August writes of making sure of his death by taking enough Wizard's Woe to kill him a hundred times over. It never occurred to me when I kissed him that I might be in contact with it myself. If I have been, then I am thankful – at least I shall be where he is, and that will be heaven for me.

I shall look forward to seeing you too, dear friend. Although we both know that you will be unable to see us, I hope you will hear our voices on your morning and evening walks.

Hael and wyn, Lord of the Weirs! Long may your loving heart protect us all.

In haste

Ann Singlewood

She nearly tore it up when she read it through, for it seemed so melodramatic. Then she relaxed with the thought that the Weir Ward would not be seeing it while she still lived. But if she did die then she would be grateful that she had written it.

Quickly retrieving the manuscript from her suitcase, she wrote on the envelope:

'*Private and Personal. To Sir Edward We'ard, Bart., Weir Court, Three Weirs, Sussex.*' And added the word '*From*' beside her own name.

It was such a weight off her mind that after resealing the package with the letter inside, she sank back on her pillows with a sigh of relief.

Thank God, she thought. If I really *am* going, then I am ready. She tried to put aside how ill she felt, and concentrated instead on the song of longing she had learned from August's writing. She made herself sing it softly into her pillow until she lost consciousness.

*

She knew exactly what had happened the moment she opened her eyes and found herself sitting on her bed in moonlight beside the huge form of her human body. Blissfully happy and unafraid, she bounded to the open window and looked out on a moonlit wonderland that was just as August had described. She felt none of the fears and doubts that had assailed him, however; only the elemental joy of her freedom to join him at last.

Light as a feather, she dropped to the ground and sped away to the forest.

CHAPTER 26

*IN THE EYE
OF THE MOON*

The deluge that fell on the forest quenched the fire in the oak. But the crowd, including the Chamberlain, Herald and Vintner, had already run from the glade shrieking in terror and scattering blindly in all directions for any shelter they could find. Only Alder, August and the unconscious Gwen remained.

The King and August were too shaken to move for a moment. Then the Wychy made for the fallen fay, only to be restrained by Alder who pointed sadly at the oak.

'Our tree of meeting is riven, Black One … and see!'

August looked and gasped. The Weird and crown shone in the blaze without harm, but the Wand of Power had disappeared. August met the King's gaze with consternation, then hurried to the oak and retrieved the remaining symbols of office.

'It will be unwise to leave these here, my liege,' he told the grief-stricken King. 'If I place them in the Circle of Rejoicing on The Wandle, then our people will at least be protected from knowing the full extent of this calamity.'

Alder inclined his head. 'You are right, my Wychy; this please do.' He looked at Gwen's still huddled figure. 'I do not know how we might allay our people's wretchedness, but here is one that my wisdom tells me only I can help.' He raised the fay tenderly from the saturated ground and bore her off in his arms.

August hurried through the cascading rain to The Wandle with the white regalia, which he laid reverently on the White One's seat. He then went and stood before the throne. After taking a few moments to compose himself for what he had to do, he drew away the gold and scarlet covering and stared into the crystal depths. His Wych had once warned him not to gaze on it for too long, and from his book of wisdom he had learned why: Mona's Eye would connect him to the creative power of his office. He knew it would be disastrous if he failed to understand the extent of that power, or be unable to control the direction of its influence. But equally, it was difficult to think that there could be anything more catastrophic than the way things already were.

When the eye became visible, he allowed himself to enter – and time vanished …

When he recovered, it was as if there had been no interval at all, but now he knew what had happened to the Wand, and why. It would have been so wrong if the Wand had risen to Gwen's hand, as it surely would have done. So he had used his own powers to prevent the Wand from rising – and that had caused the fireball. And now, flowing towards him from the Weal, he could feel the plight of the little people as they wept in abject fear and cowered in their hiding places from the great storm that had followed. Things would have been much worse, though, if Gwen had taken the Wand. And that still might be the case if the rightful person failed to appear. But would his new Wych come? He knew who she was now, but Wychy law forbad him to wile her. It had to be of her own free will, or not at all.

*

Loy, who was with Jean and Hetty in the cavity of another oak, also began to recover his presence of mind, and suddenly surprised them with an unfae-like oath. The two fae instantly grabbed onto him as he tried to jump up to the opening.

'Don't go away, Loy!'

'You can't leave us!'

'I must,' he said, struggling to free himself. 'We left Gwen out there!'

'But Black Wand will have seen to her,' Hetty insisted. 'He isn't afraid of fire or lightning. Which reminds me, Jean ... I never had a go at the Wand! We were all supposed to try it, weren't we? But I was in such a blue funk that I ran away with the rest of you.' Her tone became eager. 'I'll come with you, Loy. We'll look for Gwen ... and then I'll –'

'Don't leave me!' Jean wailed. 'I'll take the Sickness if you leave me here alone.'

'Then come with us!' they cried, picking her up and going out into the storm.

Great Oak was now a sizzling, smoking black ruin, with a gaping hole where the White One's regalia had lain. Jean sobbed in terror.

'They have been destroyed!' she gasped. 'Now woe will be everywhere! No more Wych, no wedding of the Wands, no rejoicing in the King. All our weirds shall be worn and we shall wither and be wannioned, for there will be none to give us the blessing of the Bane ...'

Before Hetty could stop her, the words had rung through the telepathic currents of the Weal, deepening the universal despair.

'Weird and Wand are destroyed, and Gwen has been taken away ...'

'Oh, for heaven's sake, Jean!' said Hetty crossly. 'Talk about "woe is me for I am undone!". For a moaning

Minnie, you really do take the biscuit. You don't *know* any such thing. None of us know what's happened.'

Rozyn, who had ventured out to find his dray, felt doubly harrowed. The fauns had stampeded and raced back to the Wynn, the dray had overturned, and his beloved barrels were spilling their precious contents on the rain-soaked ground. The once merry little fay succumbed to the general misery, crawled into a rabbit hole, and sobbed inconsolably.

*

Replacing the cover over the great throne, August was about to return to his charges when he stopped. In the midst of all the misery and anguish, he could hear a voice singing the song of longing. His heart leapt. She was coming! His new Wych was coming!

> Black Wand! Black Wand!
> Be thou my Wychy, Wand
> Be thou my lover, Wand
> Anguish is upon me
>
> Give me thy wealing, Wand
> Love now bewrays me
> Bless with your healing, Wand
> Wyn me my Wand

He knew it was no one in the Weal, where everyone was far too busy being miserable to be singing in the throes of unrequited love. It was his new Wych!

For now, all he could do was wait for her … but he could at least take the promise of her coming to the little people.

*

The moon shone in a cloudless sky as Ann reached the path into the forest. She knew exactly where she was going. She would make her way to Wandleside and down the elfin track to the meeting of the Weirds, and there, once again, sing her song of longing to August.

As she passed Wisher's Barn, however, she stopped and looked back, sure that she had seen something shining palely under the trees. Retracing her steps, she saw that she had not been mistaken. On the same spot where the Wych had lain were the gold-chased white Wand and a new robe of silver and white with a pearl encrusted girdle. She realised then that she was naked – although her hair was far longer than it had been when she was alive, and now covered her to her knees.

Gratefully, she clothed herself, and then stood looking at the Wand, wondering how it came to be there when it had already cast the White Wych away. And where were the Weird and diadem? Obviously the lovely Wand couldn't be left where it was.

'I know,' she murmured. 'I'll take it to Black Wand. He'll know what to do with it.'

She picked it up but nearly dropped it again when it tingled in her hand. Grasping it more firmly, she began to run. As she ran, she became aware of the silence that should have been alive with greetings and curiosity at her arrival. But there was not a whisper or response of any kind; only heaviness. No one was curious. No one wanted to know. Something must be seriously wrong. It spurred her on to greater effort, knowing that she held in her hand the means by which Black Wand could restore their happiness. Joy surged through her – she was taking her beloved August the heartsease that he needed.

Reaching the head of Windaway, she leaped down onto its tiny path and began to sing the song of longing:

> Black Wand! Black Wand!
> Be thou my Wychy, Wand …

But the song was too mournful and she was so happy. So she sang of her joy instead:

> Be thou my Lover, Wand
> Gladness is on me
>
> Joy's in my heart, Wand
> Bliss in the depths of me
> Gone is my loneliness
> Rapture is on me
>
> Come with thy wealing Wand
> Love now surrounds me
> Bless with thy healing, Wand
> Wyn me my Wand

At the water's edge she peered across the narrows. It was difficult to see against the darkness of the firs, but she gradually made out the glittering Weird drawn closely around a tall, silent, unmoving figure.

'Black Wand!' she cried. 'It's the Wand!' She waved it over her head. 'I've found it! I've found the White One's Wand! It was lying around in Wisher's Barn.'

Yet he neither moved nor answered.

'Don't you want it?' she called.

She saw him shake his head.

'Then what am I to do with it?' she asked in bewilderment. 'I gave White Wand the Bane and she is gone; the Wand will need to choose a wiccy to replace her. How will anyone be able to try it, though, if it's not on The Wandle at High Moon?'

At last he spoke, the amusement in his voice carrying clearly across to her. 'The Law is adamant. I may not wile the Wand of my Wych.'

Tormented by his apparent slowness in understanding her difficulty, she shouted, 'Well, how am *I* going to bring it across then? There's no bridge.'

'Upon your own two feet, my love,' he answered with a gentle laugh.

But still she didn't understand, and began to stammer that only Wychies could walk on water.

Again he laughed, his tone alive with joy. 'If you fear for yourself, my love, then throw it to me. *If* it will come …!'

That seemed sensible, she thought. But how on earth was she going to manage to throw it that far?

The Wand flashed away a few feet … and returned to her hand. She stared at it in amazement, and then stared across at the Wychy in awe as the significance finally dawned on her. Love, joy and wonderful buoyancy overwhelmed her, and she found herself floating across to him. Throwing back his Weird, he met her with open arms.

'Oh, my Wychy, my dearest August,' she sighed, 'I do so love you.'

'My Wych, my dearest Ann,' he said, 'I have not changed. You are all I desire. But am I not the same "witless wizard" you *never ever* wanted to see in your life again?'

'In my *human* life, August,' she corrected him. 'How could I have borne it, knowing I had separated you from all this?'

'It *was* unfair of me,' he acknowledged. 'Am I forgiven?'

'With all my heart, dearest August.'

But their kiss could not last long.

'Come,' he said. 'There is one above all who should know of this.' And he led her into the Circle of Rejoicing where they stood before the throne.

'*A White One is with us once more, O King!*' he cried. '*The Wand has elected its own, and our Wych awaits her investment.*'

'*Praise be to Mona! Let our Wych be robed immediately, O Wychy! Only by your united magic may the bridge of crystal reappear and bring our people to The Wandle. Hasten to it and delay not, my faithful Wychies!*'

August raised an eyebrow in invitation to his new Wych. She smiled and responded shyly, 'We hear and will attend, O King!'

'Bless you, my love,' August whispered, and led her to her station where she knelt. Fastening her Weird around her shoulders and placing the brilliant diadem upon her head, he helped her to her feet with a kiss.

CHAPTER 27

'WEALED ARE OUR WEIRDS, O WYCH!'

The ethereal telegraph sprang to life once more, and from end to end the golden message ran that set the Weal alive with joy:

> Raise up your heads, my sorrowing people!
> The Darkness and Dread are done
> Your Weal is renewed and a new Wych is won!
> Waned is the Woe! Let grieving be gone!
> The Wych wears her Weird and the Wands are as one!

Rozyn, always ready to bound into a celebration, sprang into the air in consternation.

'My dray!' he cried. 'My fauns! My supernal specifics! How shall I face my Liege and my Wychies? I have *nothing.*'

'What, no beer?' cried Barnsley.

'Oh, come on, Rosy!' said Loy. 'You must have a reserve stashed away somewhere?'

'Gallons!' he was assured. 'But how am I to transport it? My fauns are back in the royal stables … it's much too far to fetch them here in time for the opening of the bridge.'

'Hold it!' Loy interrupted, with an air of unfae-like competence. 'Rosy, you cut along to your cellars and start rolling out the barrels. We'll have them up to the foot of Windaway in two shakes of a wiccy's leg. Come on – look lively, now!'

'But what about my fauns?'

'Who's talking about fauns? I said *we'll* do it. You leave it to us.' He turned to the others. 'Simmo?' he called. There was no response. 'Pass the word for Simmo, someone! And I want Edmund, Baddy, Apples, Fizzy, Winzey and Pwyll as well. The rest of you follow me.'

With whoops of joy, a dozen wiccas ran with him in the direction of the overturned dray. Simmonds came racing up shortly after they reached it. The look on his leader's face revived an ancient memory.

'Permission to come aboard, sir?'

'Ah, there you are Simmo. I want this wagon righted and limbered up. It's got to be shipshape in less than two minutes dead. Get to work on these traces and splice 'em into a couple of drag ropes!'

'Aye, aye, sir!' The ex-Chief Petty Officer pounced on the traces. Loy turned his attention to reorientating the dray.

'Belay there, you flat-footed imps!' he yelled at two wiccas who were playing at leaping over it. Then he plunged into a circle of half a dozen others who were gleefully spinning one of the upturned wheels – to the delighted squeals of Jean who was sitting on the hub.

Never had fae worked so well – or at all – as the swelling crowd who now clamoured to lend a hand. As the vehicle rose, canted and landed gently upright upon its four wheels, great applause went up.

But Loy had scarcely turned his back to examine the barrels already being rolled to him, than a host of gnomic hands pushed aside his assistants and rolled the dray back on its side again, with the intention of repeating the whole activity for their own enjoyment. It was soon tossing and rolling like a lugger in a stormy sea.

Simmonds found himself hanging on to one end of a half-completed trace while bawling gnomes hauled at the other. Barnsley, Edmund and Pwyll ran happily to help him, and it became a great game of tug of war.

Loy did his best, but the shouts and roars of laughter drowned him out. The Weal had gone mad and everyone was drunk with joy. His newly remembered authority evaporated, and he dissolved in tears of frustration.

'Loy, darling!' Jean flew to him. 'Surely you can't be woeful *now*? See how happy everyone is. Watch how merrily they roll the wheels. Look, Whitegold and Feldspar are going to race against Dig-me-down and Iron-Wright.'

Two great arms suddenly enfolded them both and the Master of Gnomes's deep voice sounded over their shoulders.

'What? Tears of anguish on this day of all days, O winsome wicca? Fie on you for a dismal drag-me-down!'

'It's those infernal fellows of yours,' said Loy. 'All our work is twice undone.'

'*Work?*' The Master spun him round and stared at him in astonishment. 'Since when have wiccas *worked*, my brother? Only we gnomes know the meaning of the word.'

'They were working all right until your jolly pirates arrived,' said Loy, and he explained how the Vintner's need had inspired the little people to help. 'We might have been at the Brook of Wynn by now if they hadn't stolen our wheels and played tug of war with the traces.'

The Master regarded him with respect. 'You intended to make them draw the dray all the way there and back again?' he asked. 'It cannot be allowed! My brothers would never hold their heads up again.'

He at once commanded silence and began bellowing orders. Within moments the dray was put back together, replenished with unbroken casks, and propelled off at tremendous speed by the gnomes, all yelling like demons.

'Now that's what I call magic!' said Barnsley in admiration.

'Lousy baskets,' growled Simmonds. 'They might have waited 'til I'd finished splicing the blasted harness.'

*

From within the trees, Ann and August watched the crystal bridge take shape across the Weirds. Colourful streams of little people began pouring down Windaway and clustered on its ledges to await the arrival of the royal barge. There was intense speculation about the identity of the new Wych. As Gwen was the only wiccy unaccounted for, many thought it possible that the Wand had elected *her* after everyone else had run away from the blast.

As the royal barge came into view, the fae danced in delight on the perilous edges of the steep track, waving their caps and shouting ecstatically to each other.

'A Queen! A Queen! King Alder has won him a Queen!'

Then Pwyll's voice came clearly through the din. He had climbed onto Baddenham's shoulders for a better view. To Ann it seemed as if he was about to lose his balance, and she raised her Wand instinctively to save him. His astonished expression as he felt himself pressed gently upright was a joy to her.

''Tis Gwen! 'Tis Gwen!' he yelled, waving his arms as tears of joy ran down his cheeks. ''Tis the Lady of the Weird!'

The shout was echoed all along Wandleside in huge delight and applause.

'Gwen Cwen! Gwen Cwen! Gwen Cwen!'

'Queen Gwen?' Ann shot an astonished look at August, and he smiled. He had learnt a lot in the eye of the moon that he had not yet had time to tell her.

'Come, Sister Wand,' he said. 'We must greet our Liege and his Lady.'

They moved together out of the shadow of the trees and took their stand beside the near end of the bridge.

Ann knew that she would never forget the gasp of awe and wonder as their presence registered, or the wave of love that rolled down to her from the adoring fae.

'A Wych! A Wych! A Wych!' they greeted, before breaking into an elemental expression of their joy as everyone sang:

> Hael and Wyn! Hael and Wyn
> White Wand is with us!
> Wealed are our Weirds, O Wych
> Joy is within us!
>
> Splendour and beauty!
> Wonder and wynningness!
> Spread far your Weird, Dear Wych
> Always about us!
>
> Banish with wave of Wand
> Sorrow and sighing!
> Wandle our loving hearts
> When woe is nighing!

She longed to give some sign to assure them of her love for them also, but August's warning pressure on her hand told her that the barge was almost upon them.

The two Wychies sank before the King as Alder handed his Queen ashore. Ann noticed that Gwen looked bewildered at not recognising her. But when she came to kiss the Queen's hand, she found it clasped warmly, and her equally warm smile told her that she was content that Black Wand had found his true companion.

The royal party vanished into The Wandle and the long line of fae came streaming across the bridge. Ann recognised them all from August's description. Her wyché vision took in the coquettishness of Hetty's curtsey to Black Wand, while Dina and Sylvie followed with wondering looks in her direction. When all were across, the Wychies followed to witness the presentation of Barnsley, Edmund, Hetty, Apples, and the other newcomers.

Gwen held everyone's attention. She sat beside the King in a silver robe embroidered with emerald oak leaves and jade acorns. On her head was a crown of faerie platinum, its tall points tipped with beryls, emeralds and diamonds that flashed in the moonlight.

The Wychies went to kneel and cross their Wands before the King, which Alder touched with his own, evoking the sign of power, and the two glided to their stations.

'Wed the Wands, O Wychies! Wed the Wands!'

Ann watched August's eyes and on his signal hurled her Wand. The two Wands met, performed their whirling pattern of light, and returned to their waiting hands. The throng went wild. It was their final assurance that all was well upon The Wandle. Now nothing could mar their enjoyment of the most wonderful of all revels.

While the King partnered White Wand in a dance, the Queen accepted Black Wand's hand to do likewise.

'Dear Black Wand,' she sighed as he took her in his arms. 'What a miraculous day this has been.'

'A wyché one indeed, my Queen.'

'You know, I really believe I would have been accepted by the Wand if that terrible thunderbolt hadn't blasted everything.'

'Indeed. But now you wear a worthier Weird, my Lady.'

'Yes, I see that,' she agreed, though with the faintest suggestion of doubt in her voice. 'Tell me, who is your lovely Wych? Where did she come from? Our people seem to think she is come from Mona herself.'

'Our people are very wise, my Queen. I would not question their belief.'

She completed the dance in silence, her eyes trying to search his for answers, but August kept them veiled.

*

The dancing, the pageants, the solos, the stories, parades and pranks went on in unbroken and unflagging succession. At first, Ann felt quite embarrassed by all the attention she received from the wiccas. While the wiccies showered the Wychy with caresses, her wiccas approached with the deepest respect and courtesy. Loy and Fizzy were falling over each other to bring her the choicest wines. Feldspar and Whitegold followed her around forlornly, gazing on her with disconcerting reverence. Baddenham daringly asked her if she would be coming to Great Oak when Black Wand continued his story.

'You are an ass, Baddy!' said Fizzy before Ann could reply. 'Great Oak is riven – and Dreadful and Fizzlebane and Fumingwort aren't there any more.'

'I will consult with Black Wand,' the Wych promised.

'He's dancing with the Queen again …' Smye began, then remembered his vow never to tell stories again.

'Then *you* shall dance with *me*, Smye,' she said, taking compassion on him.

In the middle of this ecstatic partnership, Smye relapsed into his habit of gossiping.

'Isn't it a wonderful secret, White Wand?'

'All secrets are wonderful, dear Smye.'

'But even more so when they are royal ones, White Wand!'

'Then is it wise to speak of them?' she asked gently.

*

At last the two Wychies stood watching the vanishing wisps of the phantom bridge quiver into nothingness in the rays of the rising sun, and the fading sound of tinkling laughter merged into the crest of Windaway above the opposite shore. Ann's curiosity could wait no longer.

'Dear lover, what *is* this tremendous royal secret?'

'A barge that the gnomes are determined to make for the Queen's personal use, my sweet. And a glorious wrangle it's causing. Gnomes might know about things under the earth, but precious little about what will float on the Weirds! The kind of thing they are proposing will sink under the weight of gems as soon as it hits the water.'

'So what's to be done?' she asked.

He laughed happily, sliding his arm around her. 'Oh, my dear Wych, have I not told you that your Wychy is incomparable?'

'Have I ever been allowed to forget it?' she murmured contentedly, pressing the arm encircling her. 'And what, O incomparable Wychy, was your wisdom in the matter of the Queen's new barge?'

'Just a little courtly intrigue, my love. The King has been pleased to appoint Loy as master of the Queen's barge, and Simmo as her pilot, before whose combined authority even the gnomes must bow!'

'Ah, then not so incomparable after all …' she said with a smile '… just artful!'

His tone suddenly changed. 'For Mona's sake, Ann, my darling. If you don't learn to veil your eyes when you look at me in that manner, you will involve us both in the direst calamity. Will you never learn that even a Wychy may not love a mortal and live?'

'But didn't you know, my dearest, blackest Wychy? I am *not* mortal. I really have died and come to heaven!'

'What? But how?' he asked incredulously.

'I kissed you, August. It was the death sweat on your forehead. You said yourself that you had taken enough Wizard's Woe to kill a hundred times over. I'm sorry it will be such a shock for Aunt Alicia, but I've seen to it that the Weir Lord gets your manuscript.'

'Then Wealed are our Weirds indeed, my Wych,' he said, drawing her to him and pressing his lips to hers.

NOT THE END

THE SONG OF ROZYN-WHO-KNOWS

For brightening eyes that are dreamy or dull
A minim of sloe is specific
For sighing and yearning, what better than Mull?
But Juniper jolts are terrific!

Strawberry Dew and Rose-petal kiss
And Philtre of Cran melt the eye,
And a sip of the Rowan one never should miss;
But Honeysuck Rum hits the sky!

Oh, possets and potions are marvellous brews,
And Fix-me-up-Foxglove's tremendous;
Cranberry Wine wambles lover-like stew,
And essence of Quince is stupendous!

Blackberry Dew bringeth love to the lips,
On Dewberry punch you will wandle!
But there's nothing like Tincture of Jasamin Tips
If a gossamer waist you would fondle!

A draught from the Vine bringeth light to the eye
And spasms of joy to the middle;
But what essence of Nectar does to the shy,
I leave you, my darlings, to riddle!